I0755866

Devi for Millennials

Also by the author

Inked in India: Fountain Pens and a Story of Make and Unmake
(co-authored by Sovan Roy)

Navaratri: When Devi Comes Home
(co-edited by Anuradha Goyal)

The Bhagavad Gita for Millennials

Manmatha Nath Dutt: Translator Extraordinaire

On the Trail of the Black: Tracking Corruption
(co-edited by Kishore Arun Desai)

Devi for Millennials

Bibek Debroy

RUPA

Published by
Rupa Publications India Pvt. Ltd 2022
7/16, Ansari Road, Daryaganj
New Delhi 110002

Sales centres:
Allahabad Bengaluru Chennai
Hyderabad Jaipur Kathmandu
Kolkata Mumbai

ISBN: 978-93-5520-785-2

First impression 2022

10 9 8 7 6 5 4 3 2 1

Printed in India

For Nirmala Sitharaman and Vangmayi

CONTENTS

NOTE ON THE TEXT

If one writes Sanskrit words in English and does not use diacritical marks for transliteration, like the International Alphabet of Sanskrit Transliteration (IAST), there is always a problem, since pronunciation is not that easy. But unless people are familiar with diacritical marks, they may put them off. For Indians, I think the Devanagari script is easier. Therefore, when necessary, I have used Devanagari, not diacritical marks.

What does 'devi' (देवी), the feminine of 'deva' (देव), mean? The immediate answer would be—devi means 'goddess' and deva means 'god'. This answer isn't wrong, provided we are clear about what we mean by goddess or god. The etymological root of the word 'deva' is 'to shine'. Therefore, deva simply means 'the shining one', 'the resplendent one', 'the radiant one' or 'the one who is worthy of being worshipped and respected'. Deva is used as an address to show respect. Devi is no different. A respected male, like a king, is addressed as deva and a respected female, like a queen, is addressed as devi. In this book, we, of course, use the word 'Devi' in the sense of a feminine divinity, as in Durgaa, Lakshmi or Sarasvati.

Since I haven't used diacritical marks, there is a need to differentiate Durga (दुर्ग) from Durgaa (दुर्गा). The masculine form of दुर्गा, which is दुर्ग, has been spelt as 'Durga' in the text.

Depending on what we have in mind, we find information about Devi in the Vedas and the texts allied to them, which we can call the Nigama strand. There is information in the Agama texts, of which the tantra texts are a subset. Naturally, there are stories and rituals in major and minor Puranas. More on this later. This book is based on textual sources. However, we must remember that there are archaeological sources too.

Throughout the text, I will state a mantra in Sanskrit, followed by a simple verbatim translation. All the translations in this book are mine. Therefore, in choice of words, they may differ a bit from other translations. But these are minor differences. If you are interested in interpretations, there are more scholarly books. For all the mantras, since these are simple translations without interpretations, I deliberately have not drawn out many allusions to the inner meanings. That's not the intention of this book.

PREFACE

I was introduced to Devi without being completely conscious of it. When I was young, around seven years old, I spent a great deal of time with my maternal grandparents. Every day, both of them did a pujaa, separately, and read Chandi, which is how Bengalis refer to the Devi Mahatmya. I was too young to appreciate this. However, I did appreciate the daily prasad of a banana and milk, with me getting the banana and the pet cat getting the milk. I remember flipping through the pages of their copies of Chandi (each possessed one) and the image of Raktabija, in particular, leaving a deep impression—it scared me. Perched on my maternal grandfather's shoulders, I remember going to a community pujaa, where the Dasha Mahavidyaas used to be worshipped. The image of Dhumavati also left a mark and still remains with me.

Eventually, my grandparents died. Life moved on. My parents were professed atheists. Nevertheless, we used to observe an annual ritual, driven by my father's enthusiasm. As with generations of Bengalis from that era, on the day of Mahalaya, which signifies the onset of Durgaa Pujaa, my father would wake us up in the morning to listen to the remarkable voice of Birendra Krishna Bhadra reciting 'Mahisasura Mardini' (these were songs in addition to the stotram) on the radio. Depending on where we were geographically based, there was the subsequent annual ritual of either visiting the local pandal for Durgaa Pujaa or pandal hopping across the city. For the three days of saptami, ashtami and navami, my father actually kept a tally of how many pandals we visited. Furthermore, in the Ramakrishna Mission School, Narendrapur, where I studied, Devi used to be annually worshipped in the form of Sarasvati. Until I left my parents' domestic nest, these rituals continued. Devi was constantly around me. When I married and we had sons, I tried to emulate my father by listening to Birendra Krishna Bhadra and going pandal hopping. However, things weren't quite the same. Our sons were more interested in the food, and television had taken over. But Devi remained with me.

Devi appeared to me clearly when I embarked on the Itihasa-Purana translations. She had remained in the background as long as it was pure *itihasa* (Mahabharata and Valmiki Ramayana). With Markandeya Purana, how could one avoid Devi? It brought back memories from my childhood. My dear friend, Anuradha Goyal, triggered matters by requesting me to edit a book with her: *Navaratri: When Devi Comes Home*. I have also been engaged in translating the corpus of the 18 Mahapuranas, and there is a long way to go.

Unless you are a Devi devotee, Devi Bhagavata Purana is not classified as a Mahapurana. There are also Upapuranas, like Kalikaa Purana, and tantra texts, where Devi features prominently. However, in the process of writing my essay for *Navaratri: When Devi Comes Home*, I reread these. A thought gnawed at me: when would my present Purana project be over? When would I translate Devi Bhagavata Purana? Since I had translated the Bhagavad Gita and was translating Ashtavakra Gita, would I ever translate the Devi Gita? Meanwhile, at home, in our pujaas, there was Devi, along with Shiva. Chanting those mantras brought bliss. Shouldn't those mantras be communicated to a wider audience?

A few months ago, Rajya Sabha TV was unified with Lok Sabha TV, and the newly formed Sansad TV requested me to anchor a fortnightly programme titled *Itihasa*. This isn't an entirely studio-based programme, and the field-based elements, along with episodes on tantra and temples, took me to places of Devi worship, like Kamakhya and Birbhum.

Having translated the Bhagavad Gita, I wrote a book titled *The Bhagavad Gita for Millennials*. This wasn't a translation or a commentary but was meant to introduce and popularize the Bhagavad Gita among younger readers. The book was well-received by readers, suggesting that it had served its purpose. Subsequently, I thought: how about writing *Devi for Millennials*, along similar lines? Rupa liked the idea and the present volume is the result.

When does a book get written? An egoistical author would suggest a conscious decision is taken to write a book, perhaps even by surveying the market. To me, that *ahamkara* is completely illusory. Something gnaws at you from the inside and a book is the result. I think I have only been the instrument, *nimitta matram*. Devi's constant presence motivated the book. She is the one who made me write it. She is the one who will make you read it or ignore it. *Ya Devi sarvagrantheshu*. Nothing more remains to be said.

Nirmala Sitharaman is Union Minister, finance and corporate affairs. Before that, she has been the defence minister. These roles, in finance, defence and commerce and industry, are important, but they come and go. Inevitably, I have interacted with her, especially since 2014, on issues concerning the economy, but they come and go too. There are topics more permanent—those concerning *adhyatma*, dharma and Devi. Down the years, my conversations with her on such topics, including the Puranic text—Lalitaa Sahasranama—and Devi, have enriched me. This book is dedicated to her as a token of gratitude. Since this book is targeted at millennials, it is also dedicated to Vangmayi. Perhaps Vangmayi and her friends will learn a little bit more about Devi from this book.

Bibek Debroy
Delhi, July 2022

one

A FEW SUKTAMS

Sanskrit is a language that flows freely—it does not lend itself to stops and pauses. When you speak Sanskrit quickly, adjacent words are usually combined. For example, the last letter of a word is combined with the first letter of the next word. Sanskrit grammar has rules for such unions to take place, called *sandhi*, which means 'union' or 'joining'. Sandhi also means 'a pact not to fight', to become allies. In exactly the same way, the word *suktam* (सूक्तम्) has more than one meaning. The most common meaning is based on this division of the word: सु+उक्तम् = सूक्तम—meaning, 'good saying', 'well-spoken', 'well-said'. A bit more specifically, a suktam is a chant that has been recited properly—a hymn to a divinity. For the purpose of this book, the divinity is Devi.

A similar word is *stotram* (स्तोत्रम्). The words suktam and stotram are often used synonymously. A suktam doesn't always have to be a hymn or a chant of praise—it can also be a popular aphorism. In contrast, a stotram always has to be a hymn of praise because of the root meaning.

In this chapter, I have discussed five such Devi suktams/ stotrams.[1] We hear many of them chanted often. Therefore, it

[1]'sUkta', Sanskrit Documents, https://bit.ly/3z28Xkc. Accessed on 14 July 2022; 'Stotras - Sanskrit Mantras & Slokas-Divine Space of Bhakti & Bhava', Green Message: The Evergreen Messages of Spirituality, Sanskrit and Nature, https://bit.ly/3RysxLX. Accessed on 14 July 2022.

is good to know what they mean. These are mantras (मन्त्र). A mantra is anything that delivers or restrains and controls the mind. In the same vein, tantra (तन्त्र) is anything that delivers the body or restrains and controls the body, while yantra (यन्त्र) is anything that restrains and controls in general. Mantra, tantra and yantra are used for worship. Therefore, they are also used for worshipping Devi, and all three have been discussed in this book. The purist may argue that mantra, tantra and yantra don't exactly mean what I have said they do. Words have multiple usages, and what I have said isn't wrong either. The usage depends partly on the context. These suktams/stotrams are also mantras.

There are different types of mantras. Some are used to praise, like suktams or stotrams; others are used for dhyana or meditation; still others are used for *japa* or silent chanting; and some are also used in the rituals of worship or pujaa. However, mantras are not divided into neat silos. The same mantra can be used for more than one purpose. Why am I starting a book on Devi with mantras? This is because the sound of a mantra is a deity's true form. A deity's image is secondary and their sound is primary. This is true of Devi as well. These mantras are Devi herself.

Perhaps, I should say that we are more familiar with suktams/stotrams composed relatively recently. We may be less familiar with the sentence structures and grammar of hymns that go back to the time of the Rig Veda or Aranyakas. Nevertheless, the translations should make the meanings clear.

These are good and reliable sources for many suktams/stotrams. Otherwise, the suktams/stotrams that float around are prone to grammatical errors and typos. Therefore, it is always better to refer to reliable sources.

The Devi Suktam from Rig Veda

The Devi Suktam[2] from Rig Veda is one of the earliest suktams/stotrams to Devi. While dating this suktam precisely may be difficult, I have chosen it because it is one of the earliest Devi suktams. We tend to be more familiar with later suktams, but this one deserves to be known much more. It is the 125th suktam in the 10th *mandala* or collection of the Rig Veda, which is divided into 10 mandalas. It is also known as Ambhrini Suktam. Ambhrini was a *rishikaa,* the feminine form of rishi. Contrary to popular belief, several hymns in the Rig Veda have been composed by rishikaas. The name of the rishikaa who composed this suktam was Vak, and since she was the daughter of the Sage Ambhrina, she was known as Ambhrini. In this suktam, she praises herself, since she has completely identified herself with Devi.

> ॐ अहं रुद्रेभिर्वसुभिश्चराम्यहमादित्यैरुत विश्वदेवैः ।
> अहं मित्रावरुणोभा बिभर्म्यहमिन्द्राग्नी अहमश्विनोभा ।। (1)

> OUM! I move with Rudras, Vasus, Adityas and Vishvadevas.[3] I support Mitra, Varuna, Indra and Agni. I do that for the two Ashvins too.

> अहं सोममाहनसं बिभर्म्यहं त्वष्टारमुत पूषणं भगम् ।
> अहं दधामि द्रविणं हविष्मते सुप्राव्ये ए यजमानाय सुन्वते ।। (2)

> I support the pressed soma, Tvashta, Pushan and Bhaga.[4] I bestow wealth on the one who is offering oblations,

---

[2]'devIsukta (Rigveda)', Sanskrit Documents, https://bit.ly/3A4gMXx. Accessed on 24 June 2022.

[3]In the list of 33 devas, there are 11 Rudras, 12 Adityas, 8 Vasus and 2 Ashvins. The Vishvadevas, typically 10 in number, are not normally part of the 33 devas.

[4]Tvashta is the architect of the gods. For our purposes, stated simply, Pushan and Bhaga are aspects of Aditya, the sun.

the attentive performer of the sacrifice, the one doing the pressing.

अहं राष्ट्री संगमनी वसूनां चिकितुषी प्रथमा यज्ञियानाम् ।
तां मा देवा व्यदधुः पुरुत्रा भूरिस्थात्रां भूर्या वेशयन्तीम् ।। (3)

I am the queen, the one who gathers wealth, the one who knows, foremost among those who deserve a sacrifice. Devas have established me, with abodes to enter and reside in.

मया सोऽअन्नमत्ति यो विपश्यति यः प्राणिति य ईं शृणोत्युक्तम् ।
अमन्तवोमान्त उपक्षियन्ति श्रुधिश्रुत श्रद्धिवं ते वदामि ।। (4)

It is through me that he[5] eats food, sees, breathes and hears what is said. Those who do not know, also reside near me. O one willing to listen! I will tell you what can be trusted.

अहमेव स्वयमिदं वदामि जुष्टं देवेभिरुत मानुषेभिः ।
यं कामये तं तमुग्रं कृणोमि तं ब्रह्माणं तमृषिं तं सुमेधाम् ।। (5)

I am stating this myself and it will be cheered by devas and men. I make whoever I wish powerful, a Brahmana or a rishi, or make him extremely wise.

अहं रुद्राय धनुरातनोमि ब्रह्मद्विषे शरवेहन्त वा उ ।
अहं जनाय समदं कृणोम्यहं द्यावापृथिवी आविवेश ।। (6)

I bend Rudra's bow so that his arrow can kill one who hates a Brahmana. For people, I excite battles. I enter heaven and earth.

अहं सुवे पितरमस्य मूर्धन् मम योनिरप्स्व अन्तः समुद्रे ।
ततो वितिष्ठे भुवनानु विश्वो तामूं द्यां वर्ष्मणोपस्पृशामि ।। (7)

---

[5]'He' refers to the living entity, the person.

I bring forth the Father[6] on the summit of the world. My womb is in the water and inside the ocean. Established there, I enter the worlds. I touch heaven with the top of my head.

अहमेव वातऽइव प्रवाम्यारभमाणा भुवनानि विश्वा ।
परो दिवा परएना पृथिव्यै तावती महिना सम्बभूव ॥ (8)

I am the one who blows like a storm, holding together the worlds and the universe. I am beyond heaven. I am beyond earth. Such is the greatness that originates in me.

Shri Suktam from Rig Veda

The second suktam[7] is Shri Suktam from the appendices of the Rig Veda, known as the Khila portions, which have clearly been composed later than the main text of the Rig Veda. There is more than one Shri Suktam, and this one is a hymn to Shri or Lakshmi, the goddess of wealth and prosperity. The Shri Suktam is often sung and recited. I have chosen this suktam not only because it is old but also because it is about Shri or Lakshmi, one of Devi's manifestations.

ॐ ॥ हिरण्यवर्णां हरिणीं सुवर्णरजतस्रजाम् ।
चन्द्रां हिरण्मयीं लक्ष्मीं जातवेदो म आवह ॥ (1)

OUM! Her complexion is golden. Her image is golden. She wears gold and silver garlands. She is like a golden moon. O Jataveda![8] Invoke that Lakshmi for me.

तां म आवह जातवेदो लक्ष्मीमनपगामिनीम् ।
यस्यां हिरण्यं विन्देयं गामश्वं पुरुषानहम् ॥ (2)

---

[6]The creator

[7]'shrI sUkta (Rigveda)', Sanskrit Documents, https://bit.ly/3xYZFUo. Accessed on 24 June 2022.

[8]Jataveda refers to Agni.

O Jataveda! Invoke for me that Lakshmi, whose arrival is not futile. Through her, I will obtain gold, cattle, horses and men.

अश्वपूर्वां रथमध्यां हस्तिनादप्रबोधिनीम् ।
श्रियं देवीमुपह्वये श्रीर्मादेवीर्जुषताम् ॥ (3)

Horses precede her, and she is seated in a chariot in the middle. She is woken up by the trumpeting of elephants. I invoke Devi Shri. May Devi Shri be pleased with me.

कां सोस्मितां हिरण्यप्राकारामार्द्रां ज्वलन्तीं तृप्तां तर्पयन्तीम् ।
पद्मे स्थितां पद्मवर्णां तामिहोपह्वये श्रियम् ॥ (4)

Who is she, the smiling one? There is a tender golden glow around her. She blazes. She is satisfied, and she is the one who satisfies. She is seated on a lotus. Her complexion is like that of a lotus. I invoke that Shri here.

चन्द्रां प्रभासां यशसा ज्वलन्तीं श्रियं लोके देवजुष्टामुदाराम् ।
तां पद्मिनीमीं शरणमहं प्रपद्येऽलक्ष्मीर्मे नश्यतां त्वां वृणे ॥ (5)

Her radiance is like that of the moon. Her blazing glory is radiant in the world. Devas worship the generous one. I seek refuge with her who resides in a lotus. Through her favours, let the Alakshmi[9] in me be destroyed.

आदित्यवर्णे तपसोऽधिजातो वनस्पतिस्तव वृक्षोऽथ बिल्वः ।
तस्य फलानि तपसा नुदन्तु मायान्तरायाश्च बाह्या अलक्ष्मीः ॥ (6)

O one with a complexion like that of the sun! Your austerities are like a large tree, and through them, a tree, like *bilva* (wood-apple), has originated. May the fruits of these austerities drive away the internal mayaa and the external Alakshmi.

---

[9]This refers to adversity—the antithesis of Lakshmi.

उपैतु मां देवसखः कीर्तिश्च मणिना सह ।
प्रादुर्भूतोऽस्मि राष्ट्रेऽस्मिन् कीर्तिमृद्धिं ददातु मे ॥ (7)

Let the friend of devas approach me with deeds and jewels. I will originate in this kingdom, which will bestow deeds and prosperity on me.

क्षुत्पिपासामलां ज्येष्ठामलक्ष्मीं नाशयाम्यहम् ।
अभूतिमसमृद्धिं च सर्वां निर्णुद मे गृहात् ॥ (8)

I will destroy the older sister, Alakshmi, associated with hunger, thirst and impurities. Drive away from my house every kind of misfortune and adversity.

गंधद्वारां दुराधर्षां नित्यपुष्टां करीषिणीम् ।
ईश्वरींग् सर्वभूतानां तामिहोपह्वये श्रियम् ॥ (9)

She is like the portal to all fragrances. She is difficult to approach. She is always nourished. She is a region full of dung.[10] She is the power in all beings. Invoke that Shri for me.

मनसः काममाकूतिं वाचः सत्यमशीमहि ।
पशूनां रूपमन्नस्य मयि श्रीः श्रयतां यशः ॥ (10)

In thoughts, wishes, intentions and words, I truly try to reach. Shri will abide with me in the form of animals, beauty, food and prosperity.

कर्दमेन प्रजाभूता मयि सम्भव कर्दम ।
श्रियं वासय मे कुले मातरं पद्ममालिनीम् ॥ (11)

Prajas[11] resulted from Kardama. O Kardama! Remain in me. Make Shri, the mother, reside in my lineage.[12]

---

[10]This phrase is symbolically indicative of Devi's abundance.

[11]This refers to offspring, descendants, progeny or subjects.

[12]There are several allusions here that may not be obvious. Kardama was a Prajapati and all creation and living beings originate in Prajapatis. According

आप: सृजन्तु स्निग्धानि चिक्लीत वस मे गृहे ।
नि च देवीं मातरं श्रियं वासय मे कुले ॥ (12)

The waters create pleasantness. O moisture (of the waters)! Reside in my house. May you thus ensure that Devi, the mother and Shri reside in my lineage.

आर्द्रां पुष्करिणीं पुष्टिं पिङ्गलां पद्ममालिनीम् ।
चन्द्रां हिरण्मयीं लक्ष्मीं जातवेदो म आवह ॥ (13)

She is like the moisture from a pond of lotuses. She is garlanded with yellow lotuses. She is like the moon. She is golden. O Jataveda! Invoke that Lakshmi for me.

आर्द्रां य: करिणीं यष्टिं सुवर्णां हेममालिनीम् ।
सूर्यां हिरण्मयीं लक्ष्मीं जातवेदो म आवह ॥ (14)

She is the moisture. She is the staff that supports all acts. She is golden and wears a golden garland. She is like the golden sun. O Jataveda! Invoke that Lakshmi for me.

तां म आवह जातवेदो लक्ष्मीमनपगामिनीम् ।
यस्यां हिरण्यं प्रभूतं गावो दास्योऽश्वान्विन्देयं पुरुषानहम् ॥ (15)

O Jataveda! Invoke her, the Lakshmi whose arrival is not futile. Through her, I will obtain a lot of gold, cattle, servants, horses and men.

य: शुचि: प्रयतो भूत्वा जुहुयादाज्य मन्वहम् ।
श्रिय: पञ्चदशर्चं च श्रीकाम: सततं जपेत् ॥ (16)

If a person is pure and controlled and offers oblations of ghee every day, constantly performing japa with these 15 verses of Shri Suktam, he obtains Shri and his desires.

---

to some accounts, Brahmaa meditated on Shiva and Parvati before creating Kardama through the power of his mind. Therefore, Kardama's mother is Devi/Parvati. Kardama also means mud/filth, and all of us originate from it.

Devi Suktam from Tantra Texts

The third suktam is a prayer to Devi that features in tantra texts.[13] In one form or another, all of us have heard this suktam being sung or chanted, though we probably know it through what is known as Chandi, Durgaa Saptashati or Devi Mahatmya from the Markandeya Purana. The text is about Devi's greatness. As the name Durgaa Saptashati suggests, the text should have seven hundred verses (*saptashata* means seven hundred). However, the 13 chapters of Devi Mahatmya don't quite add up to seven hundred verses. The difference is made up by some additional introductory verses. In the Markandeya Purana, two *asuras*, known as Shumbha and Nishumbha, caused depredations. That is when the devas prayed to Devi for deliverance through this suktam. Each one of Devi's names invoked in this suktam means something. But we will skip the individual meanings for the moment and come back to them in a later chapter.

नमो देव्यै महादेव्यै शिवायै सततं नमः ।
नमः प्रकृत्यै भद्रायै नियताः प्रणताः स्म ताम् ।। (1)

We bow down before Devi, before Mahadevi. We always bow down before Shivaa.[14] We bow down before Prakriti, before Bhadraa. We control ourselves and prostrate ourselves before her.

रौद्रायै नमो नित्यायै गौर्यै धात्र्यै नमो नमः ।
ज्योत्स्नायै चेन्दुरूपिण्यै सुखायै सततं नमः ।। (2)

We bow down before Raudraa, before Nityaa. We bow down before Gouri, before Dhatri. We prostrate ourselves

[13] 'atha tantroktaM devIsUktam,' Sanskrit Documents, https://bit.ly/3xYZRmA. Accessed on 24 June 2022.

[14] शिवा, spelt as 'Shivaa,' means Devi, while शिव, spelt as 'Shiva,' means Mahadeva.

before her. We bow down before the one whose form is moonlight, the one whose form is the moon. We always prostrate ourselves before the one who is happiness.

कल्याण्यै प्रणतां वृद्ध्यै सिद्ध्यै कुर्मो नमो नमः ।
नैरृत्यै भूभृतां लक्ष्म्यै शर्वाण्यै ते नमो नमः ॥ (3)

We prostrate ourselves before the one who grants good fortune, prosperity and success. We bow down before the one whose form is a tortoise.[15] We prostrate ourselves. We bow down before Nairriti, before the one who holds up the earth. We bow down before Lakshmi, before Sharvani. We prostrate ourselves.

दुर्गायै दुर्गपारायै सारायै सर्वकारिण्यै ।
ख्यात्यै तथैव कृष्णायै धूम्रायै सततं नमः ॥ (4)

We always bow down before Durgaa, the one who enables us to cross the impassable, the essence, the cause behind all action, the famous one, the dark one, the one with a smoky complexion.

अतिसौम्यातिरौद्रायै नतास्तस्यै नमो नमः ।
नमो जगत्प्रतिष्ठायै देव्यै कृत्यै नमो नमः ॥ (5)

We bow down before the one who is extremely gentle and exceedingly terrible. We bend down. We prostrate ourselves. We bow down before the one in whom the universe is established. We bow down before Devi Krityaa. We prostrate ourselves.

या देवी सर्वभूतेषु विष्णुमायेति शब्दिता ।
नमस्तस्यै नमस्तस्यै नमस्तस्यै नमो नमः ॥ (6)

We bow down before Devi, who is in all beings and is

---

[15]This is an allusion to a tortoise holding up the world—Vishnu's Kurma avatara.

spoken of as Vishnumayaa. We bow down before her. We prostrate ourselves before her. We bow down before her. We prostrate ourselves. Namah.

या देवी सर्वभूतेषु चेतनेत्यभिधीयते ।
नमस्तस्यै नमस्तस्यै नमस्तस्यै नमो नमः ॥ (7)

We bow down before Devi, who is in all beings and is spoken of as consciousness. We bow down before her. We prostrate ourselves before her. We bow down before her. We prostrate ourselves. Namah.

या देवी सर्वभूतेषु बुद्धिरूपेण संस्थिता ।
नमस्तस्यै नमस्तस्यै नमस्तस्यै नमो नमः ॥ (8)

We bow down before Devi, who is established in all beings in the form of intellect. We bow down before her. We prostrate ourselves before her. We bow down before her. We prostrate ourselves. Namah.

या देवी सर्वभूतेषु निद्रारूपेण संस्थिता ।
नमस्तस्यै नमस्तस्यै नमस्तस्यै नमो नमः ॥ (9)

We bow down before Devi, who is established in all beings in the form of sleep. We bow down before her. We prostrate ourselves before her. We bow down before her. We prostrate ourselves. Namah.

या देवी सर्वभूतेषु क्षुधारूपेण संस्थिता ।
नमस्तस्यै नमस्तस्यै नमस्तस्यै नमो नमः ॥ (10)

We bow down before Devi, who is established in all beings in the form of hunger. We bow down before her. We prostrate ourselves before her. We bow down before her. We prostrate ourselves. Namah.

या देवी सर्वभूतेषु छायारूपेण संस्थिता ।
नमस्तस्यै नमस्तस्यै नमस्तस्यै नमो नमः ॥ (11)

We bow down before Devi, who is established in all beings in the form of a shadow. We bow down before her. We prostrate ourselves before her. We bow down before her. We prostrate ourselves. Namah.

या देवी सर्वभूतेषु शक्तिरूपेण संस्थिता ।
नमस्तस्यै नमस्तस्यै नमस्तस्यै नमो नमः ॥ (12)

We bow down before Devi, who is established in all beings in the form of power. We bow down before her. We prostrate ourselves before her. We bow down before her. We prostrate ourselves. Namah.

या देवी सर्वभूतेषु तृष्णारूपेण संस्थिता ।
नमस्तस्यै नमस्तस्यै नमस्तस्यै नमो नमः ॥ (13)

We bow down before Devi, who is established in all beings in the form of thirst. We bow down before her. We prostrate ourselves before her. We bow down before her. We prostrate ourselves. Namah.

या देवी सर्वभूतेषु क्षान्तिरूपेण संस्थिता ।
नमस्तस्यै नमस्तस्यै नमस्तस्यै नमो नमः ॥ (14)

We bow down before Devi, who is established in all beings in the form of forbearance. We bow down before her. We prostrate ourselves before her. We bow down before her. We prostrate ourselves. Namah.

या देवी सर्वभूतेषु जातिरूपेण संस्थिता ।
नमस्तस्यै नमस्तस्यै नमस्तस्यै नमो नमः ॥ (15)

We bow down before Devi, who is established in all beings in the form of existence.[16] We bow down before her. We prostrate ourselves before her. We bow down before her. We prostrate ourselves. Namah.

---

[16]Jati should not be confused with varna. Jati is the category that one is born into. Hence, the word 'existence' has been used here.

या देवी सर्वभूतेषु लज्जारूपेण संस्थिता ।
नमस्तस्यै नमस्तस्यै नमस्तस्यै नमो नमः ॥ (16)

We bow down before Devi, who is established in all beings in the form of modesty. We bow down before her. We prostrate ourselves before her. We bow down before her. We prostrate ourselves. Namah.

या देवी सर्वभूतेषु शान्तिरूपेण संस्थिता ।
नमस्तस्यै नमस्तस्यै नमस्तस्यै नमो नमः ॥ (17)

We bow down before Devi, who is established in all beings in the form of peace. We bow down before her. We prostrate ourselves before her. We bow down before her. We prostrate ourselves. Namah.

या देवी सर्वभूतेषु श्रद्धारूपेण संस्थिता ।
नमस्तस्यै नमस्तस्यै नमस्तस्यै नमो नमः ॥ (18)

We bow down before Devi, who is established in all beings in the form of faith. We bow down before her. We prostrate ourselves before her. We bow down before her. We prostrate ourselves. Namah.

या देवी सर्वभूतेषु कान्तिरूपेण संस्थिता ।
नमस्तस्यै नमस्तस्यै नमस्तस्यै नमो नमः ॥ (19)

We bow down before Devi, who is established in all beings in the form of beauty. We bow down before her. We prostrate ourselves before her. We bow down before her. We prostrate ourselves. Namah.

या देवी सर्वभूतेषु लक्ष्मीरूपेण संस्थिता ।
नमस्तस्यै नमस्तस्यै नमस्तस्यै नमो नमः ॥ (20)

We bow down before Devi, who is established in all beings in the form of prosperity. We bow down before her. We prostrate ourselves before her. We bow down before her. We prostrate ourselves. Namah.

या देवी सर्वभूतेषु वृत्तिरूपेण संस्थिता ।
नमस्तस्यै नमस्तस्यै नमस्तस्यै नमो नमः ॥ (21)

We bow down before Devi, who is established in all beings in the form of subsistence. We bow down before her. We prostrate ourselves before her. We bow down before her. We prostrate ourselves. Namah.

या देवी सर्वभूतेषु स्मृतिरूपेण संस्थिता ।
नमस्तस्यै नमस्तस्यै नमस्तस्यै नमो नमः ॥ (22)

We bow down before Devi, who is established in all beings in the form of memory. We bow down before her. We prostrate ourselves before her. We bow down before her. We prostrate ourselves. Namah.

या देवी सर्वभूतेषु दयारूपेण संस्थिता ।
नमस्तस्यै नमस्तस्यै नमस्तस्यै नमो नमः ॥ (23)

We bow down before Devi, who is established in all beings in the form of compassion. We bow down before her. We prostrate ourselves before her. We bow down before her. We prostrate ourselves. Namah.

या देवी सर्वभूतेषु तुष्टिरूपेण संस्थिता ।
नमस्तस्यै नमस्तस्यै नमस्तस्यै नमो नमः ॥ (24)

We bow down before Devi, who is established in all beings in the form of contentment. We bow down before her. We prostrate ourselves before her. We bow down before her. We prostrate ourselves. Namah.

या देवी सर्वभूतेषु मातृरूपेण संस्थिता ।
नमस्तस्यै नमस्तस्यै नमस्तस्यै नमो नमः ॥ (25)

We bow down before Devi, who is established in all beings in the form of a mother. We bow down before her. We prostrate ourselves before her. We bow down before her. We prostrate ourselves. Namah.

या देवी सर्वभूतेषु भ्रान्तिरूपेण संस्थिता ।
नमस्तस्यै नमस्तस्यै नमस्तस्यै नमो नमः ॥ (26)

We bow down before Devi, who is established in all beings in the form of confusion. We bow down before her. We prostrate ourselves before her. We bow down before her. We prostrate ourselves. Namah.

इन्द्रियाणामधिष्ठात्री भूतानां चाखिलेषु या ।
भूतेषु सततं तस्यै व्याप्त्यै दैव्यै नमो नमः ॥ (27)

We bow down before Devi, who presides over the senses of all beings and is always established in all beings and pervades them. Namah.

चित्तिरूपेण या कृत्स्नमेतद्व्याप्य स्थितां जगत् ।
नमस्तस्यै नमस्तस्यै नमस्तस्यै नमो नमः ॥ (28)

She is established in the form of consciousness and pervades this entire universe. We bow down before her. We prostrate ourselves before her. We bow down before her. We prostrate ourselves. Namah.

Ratri Suktam from Tantra Texts

Although this suktam[17] to *ratri* (night) features in tantra texts, it also finds a place in the Devi Mahatmya, which narrates the following story.

After a deluge, everything was submerged in water, and Vishnu was fast asleep in his yoga nidraa.[18] Desiring to create the worlds, Brahmaa manifested himself from a lotus in Vishnu's navel. However, two asuras, known as Madhu and

---

[17]'Tantroktam rAtrisUktam,' Sanskrit Documents, https://bit.ly/3SoZE5t Accessed on 24 June 2022.

[18]This is a state of sleep (nidraa) where one is deeply immersed in yoga. This is often associated with Vishnu but Devi also has her own yoga nidraa.

Kaitabha, manifested themselves from the wax in Vishnu's ears and were about to kill Brahmaa. Therefore, using this suktam, Brahmaa prayed to Devi so that she could wake Vishnu up.

I have quoted the main Ratri Suktam. The source cited has an additional sloka at the beginning, laying the ground for Brahmaa's prayer, and a few (five) additional slokas at the end, essentially saying that no one is capable of praising Devi. Since these aren't part of the main suktam, I have omitted them. In the slokas, the word *svahaa* is the exclamation made when oblations are offered to devas; and the word *svadhaa* is the exclamation made when oblations are offered to ancestors/manes. The word *vashat* is a general exclamation used when offering oblations, and the term *vashatkara* means the act of making that exclamation. *Matraa* (मात्रा) is the length of time that is taken to pronounce a short vowel sound. So, a long-drawn-out (*pluta*) *akshara*, like OUM, has three matraas. These explanations will make the meaning of the first verse clear.

त्वं स्वाहा त्वं स्वधात्वं हि वषट्कारः स्वरात्मिका ।
सुधा त्वमक्षरे नित्ये त्रिधा मात्रात्मिका स्थिता ॥ (1)

You are svahaa. You are svadhaa. You are vashatkara. Sound is your *atman*. Your sweet form exists eternally in aksharas. Your atman is established in the three matraas.

अर्धमात्रा स्थिता नित्या यानुच्चार्या विशेषतः ।
त्वमेव सन्ध्या सावित्री त्वं देवी जननी परा ॥ (2)

In particular, you are always established in the half a matraa that cannot be pronounced.[19] Indeed, you are Sandhyaa and Savitri. You are Devi, the Supreme Mother.

---

[19]This refers to the nasal sound in OUM.

त्वयैतद्धार्यते विश्वं त्वयैतत्सृज्यते जगत् ।
त्वयैतत्पाल्यते देवि त्वमत्स्यन्ते च सर्वदा ॥ (3)

You are the one who sustains the universe. You are the one who creates the universe. You are the one who preserves. O Devi! In the end, you are the one who always devours.

विसृष्टौ सृष्टिरूपात्वम् स्थितिरूपा च पालने ।
तथा संहृतिरूपान्ते जगतोऽस्य जगन्मये ॥ (4)

At the time of creation, you assume the form of creation. At the time of protection, you assume the form of preservation. Like that, when it is time for the universe to end, you assume the form of destruction. You pervade the universe.

महाविद्या महामाया महामेधा महास्मृतिः ।
महामोहा च भवती महादेवी महासुरी ॥ (5)

You are Mahavidyaa. You are Mahamayaa. You are Mahamedhaa. You are Mahasmriti. You are Mahamohaa. You are Mahadevi. You are Mahasuri.[20]

प्रकृतिस्त्वं च सर्वस्य गुणत्रयविभाविनी ।
कालरात्रिर्महारात्रिर्मोहरात्रिश्च दारुणा ॥ (6)

You are everything in Prakriti. You are the one who creates the three *gunas*.[21] You are Kalaratri, Maharatri and the terrible Moharatri.[22]

---

[20]In these lines, *maha* (great) prefixes knowledge, illusion, intellect, memory and delusion, respectively. Both Mahadevi and Mahasuri mean the great goddess.

[21]The three gunas include *sattva* (purity), *rajas* (passion) and *tamas* (darkness/ignorance).

[22]Kalaratri refers to the night of destruction; Maharatri, to the great night; and Moharatri, to the terrible night of delusion.

त्वं श्रीस्त्वमीश्वरी त्वं ह्रीस्त्वं बुद्धिर्बोधलक्षणा ।
लज्जा पुष्टिस्तथा तुष्टिस्त्वं शान्तिः क्षान्तिरेव च ॥ (7)

You are Shri. You are Ishvari. You are modesty. You are intelligence. You are characterized by intelligence. You are shame and nourishment. You are contentment, tranquillity and forbearance.

खड्गिनी शूलिनी घोरा गदिनी चक्रिणी तथा ।
शङ्खिनी चापिनी बाणभुशुण्डीपरिघायुधा ॥ (8)

You wield a sword and trident. You are terrible and wield a club and a chakra. You hold a conch shell and bow and arrows. Your weapons are a *bhushundi*[23] and a bludgeon.

सौम्या सौम्यतराशेषसौम्येभ्यस्त्वतिसुन्दरी ।
परापराणां परमा त्वमेव परमेश्वरी ॥ (9)

You are gentle. You are gentler than that. Your gentleness is unlimited. You are exceedingly beautiful. You are the best. You are superior to the best. Indeed, you are Parameshvari.

यच्च किञ्चित् क्वचिद्वस्तु सदसद्वाखिलात्मिके ।
तस्य सर्वस्य या शक्तिः सात्वं किं स्तूयसे तदा ॥ (10)

You are everything that exists and you are everything that does not exist. Your atman is in everything. The power in everything is yours. Since you are all this, how can I possibly extol you?

यया त्वया जगत्स्रष्टा जगत्पात्यत्ति यो जगत् ।
सोऽपि निद्रावशं नीतः कस्त्वां स्तोतुमिहेश्वरः ॥ (11)

You are the one who creates the universe. You are the one who destroys the universe. You are the universe. Since

[23]This refers to some kind of catapult or sling.

you have brought the Great Lord under the subjugation of sleep, who can possibly extol you?

Durgaa Suktam from Taittiriya Aranyaka

In this suktam,[24] Devi Durgaa (दुर्गा) is identified with Agni. Who is Durgaa? It is simply one of Devi's names, and there is no difference between them. Alternatively, Durgaa is one of Devi's manifestations. Both assertions are true. Etymologically, the word Durgaa means 'difficult to reach.' Indeed, it is not very easy to reach Devi or Durgaa. But if you fix your mind on them, these mantras help. I have chosen this suktam because it is specifically meant for Durgaa, not Devi in general. It is one of the earliest-known suktams of its kind that takes note of the identification of Durgaa with Agni.

जातवेदसे सुनवाम सोम मरातीयतो निदहाति वेदः ।
स नः पर्षदति दुर्गाणि विश्वा नावेव सिन्धुं दुरिताऽत्यग्निः ॥ (1)

We press soma for Jataveda. This knowledge burns down enemies. This world is full of great hardships and is difficult to cross. Like a boat on the ocean, may Agni carry us across.

तामग्निवर्णां तपसा ज्वलन्तीं वैरोचनीं कर्मफलेषु जुष्टाम् ।
दुर्गां देवीँ शरणमहं प्रपद्ये सुतरसि तरसे नमः ॥ (2)

Her complexion is like that of Agni. She blazes in her austerities. She was born from the fire. We worship her because of the fruits of karma. I prostrate myself and seek refuge with that Devi Durgaa. May the most excellent among those who convey carry me across. Namah.

[24]'durgAsUktam,' Sanskrit Documents, https://bit.ly/3No1BeK. Accessed on 24 June 2022.

अग्ने त्वं पारया नव्यो अस्मान् स्वस्तिभिरति दुर्गाणि विश्वा ।
पूश्च पृथ्वी बहुला न उर्वी भवा तोकाय तनयाय शंयोः ॥ (3)

O Agni! You are praised as the one who carries across.[25] Please use your auspicious nature to carry us across this universe, which is so difficult to traverse.

विश्वानि नो दुर्गहा जातवेदः सिन्धुन्न नावा दुरिताऽतिपर्षि ।
अग्ने अत्रिवन्मनसा गृणानोऽस्माकं बोध्यविता तनूनाम् ॥ (4)

O Jataveda! You are the remover of difficulties. You are like a boat in the ocean. This is very difficult to cross. Please save us. O Agni! Like Atri, our minds are praising you.[26] Help bring understanding to our bodies.

पृतनाजितँ सहमानमुग्रमग्निँ हुवेम परमाथ्सधस्थात् ।
स नः पर्षदति दुर्गाणि विश्वा क्षामद्देवो अति दुरितात्यग्निः ॥ (5)

He is unvanquished in battles. He is the fierce and victorious Agni. We invoke the one who is supreme in an assembly. He will carry us across the universe, which is very difficult to cross. Deva Agni pacifies extreme difficulties.

प्रत्नोषि कमीड्यो अध्वरेषु सनाच्च होता नव्यश्च सथ्सि ।
स्वां चाग्ने तनुवं पिप्रयस्वास्मभ्यं च सौभगमायजस्व ॥ (6)

You are invoked as the one who spreads bliss through sacrifices. You are the eternal one who offers oblations but you also exist as new. O Agni! Your own form is also a source of bliss for us. Please bring good fortune on our sacrifice.

गोभिर्जुष्टमयुजो निषिक्तन्तवेन्द्र विष्णोरनुसंचरेम ।
नाकस्य पृष्ठमभि संवसानो वैष्णवीं लोक इह मादयन्ताम् ॥ (7)

---

[25]To the other side of samsara.

[26]Sage Atri composed several hymns to Agni.

Our senses are pleased and not attached. O Indra! You have sprinkled us. O Vishnu! We will follow you. Now that we have been delighted here, we will reside in Vishnu's world, in the vault of heaven.

two

MARKANDEYA PURANA

While mantras are fine for meditation, most of us prefer stories about Devi and Durgaa. These stories that we have heard feature in the Puranas, which are ancient accounts. According to belief, after classifying the Vedas and composing the Mahabharata, Krishna Dvaipayana Vedavyasa composed the Puranas. Of these, 18 are major and are known as Mahapuranas, though sometimes, there is a little bit of disagreement about which text should be included in these 18. However, there is agreement on the fact that one of these Mahapuranas is the Markandeya Purana. Mahapuranas vary enormously in size, and the Markandeya Purana is relatively short, with 9,000 verses or slokas.

It is impossible to determine when these Puranas were composed in their present form. After all, they were passed down orally, with continuous additions. In any event, the Markandeya Purana is one of the earlier Puranas, probably composed between 250 CE and 700 CE. Its name comes from its contents—Sage Markandeya answering questions asked by Sage Jaimini. As I have said before, tucked into the Markandeya Purana is the section known as Devi Mahatmya, which is the only part of the Markandeya Purana with which we are concerned.[1] It is not my intention to suggest that stories

[1]There is a translation of the complete text in English. *The Markandeya Purana*, translated by Bibek Debroy, Penguin, 2019.

about Devi only occur in the Markandeya Purana. However, this chapter recounts Devi's story (Devi Mahatmya) from it.[2]

Once upon a time, there was a king named Suratha. Enemies had defeated him and driven him away from his kingdom. Desperate and despondent, he wandered off to a forest. There, he arrived at the hermitage of a Brahmana named Sumedha. He met a Vaishya named Samadhi at the hermitage. Samadhi, too, had been robbed and driven out by his wicked wife and sons. Suratha and Samadhi went and asked Sumedha about the reasons for their misfortunes. Sumedha told them that this was happening to them because of the delusion caused by Mahamayaa.

But who is Mahamayaa? The text explains that she is in everything. She is present everywhere. However, to accomplish tasks, she appears. We think she has originated. That's not true. She is eternal and always present. It is just that she manifests herself occasionally. It is these manifestations that give us the many stories of Devi and how she saves the world time and again.

Mahishasuramardini

For the asuras, Madhu and Kaitabha, Devi intervened indirectly, through Vishnu, whom she awoke after Brahmaa's prayer—the Ratri Suktam (see, pp. 15–19). For Mahishasura, with whom we associate Devi much more, her intervention was direct. At that point in time, the leader of the asuras was Mahishasura. The word *mahisha* means 'buffalo,' and Mahishasura is described as a buffalo-demon. In texts other than the Markandeya Purana, we are told that Mahishasura's

---

[2]When the great scholar Hara Prasad Shastri (1853–1931) went to Nepal to collect manuscripts from the Royal Library there, he found a copy of Devi Mahatmya, written in the old Newari script and dated 998 CE.

father, Rambhasura, had intercourse with a female buffalo, and Mahishasura was born from this union. Asuras used to perform austerities and obtain boons, typically from Brahmaa, making it impossible for them to be killed. In some texts, we are told that Mahishasura obtained a boon from Brahmaa that he could only be killed by a woman. Other texts also tell us that a beautiful Devi, named Trikalaa (त्रिकाला), emerged from the combined beauty of Brahmaa, Vishnu and Shiva, and that Mahishasura fought the devas because he coveted her.

Regardless, the devas and asuras were always fighting, and, more often than not, the devas used to be ousted from heaven by a powerful asura. This is precisely what happened with Mahishasura too. The ruling Indra of the time—Indra is a title, not a name—was named Purandara. Mahishasura drove Purandara out and became Indra himself. He usurped the positions of the other devas too. With Brahmaa leading the way, all the devas went to see Vishnu. Shiva was already there. A mass of energy emerged from the bodies of the devas and united, manifesting in the form of Devi.

Table 1:
The components of energy from the devas that formed various parts of Devi

Name of deva whose energy was used	*Part of Devi's body that was formed using that energy*
Shiva	Face
Yama	Hair
Vishnu	Arms
Moon (Soma)	Breasts
Purandara	Waist
Varuna	Shanks
The earth	Hips

Brahmaa	Feet
Sun (Surya)	Toes
Vasu	Fingers
Kubera	Nose
Prajapati[3]	Teeth
Agni	Three eyes
Sandhyaa[4]	Two eyebrows
Vayu	Ears

After this, all the deities gave Devi her weapons and ornaments.

Table 2:
Major weapons and ornaments bestowed upon Devi

Name of deva or divine entity	*Name of the weapon bestowed upon Devi*
Shiva	Trident
Krishna[5]	Chakra
Varuna	Conch shell
Agni	Spear
Vayu	Bow and a quiver filled with arrows
Indra	Vajra and a bell from his elephant, Airavata

---

[3]Who is Prajapati? The word, meaning 'lord of beings,' is applied to many. Usually, though not always, it is Brahmaa's name. Here, Brahmaa has already been mentioned separately. Therefore, we can only speculate about Prajapati. In all probability, it means Vishvakarmaa.

[4]The word *sandhyaa* means 'the meeting point between day and night,' i.e., dawn and dusk. Sometimes, the word is also applied to midday. Here, Sandhyaa refers to the deity who presides over sandhyaas.

[5]The text says Krishna, not Vishnu.

Yama	Staff
Varuna	Noose
Brahmaa	String of aksha beads and a water-pot
Surya	Filled the pores of her body with his rays
Kala (Time/The Destroyer)	A sword and a shield
Ocean of Milk	A sparkling necklace and garments that do not decay
Vishvakarmaa	Assorted ornaments, a battleaxe, weapons and an impenetrable armour
The Ocean	A lotus and a garland made out of lotuses
Himalaya	A lion as a mount and jewels
Kubera	A drinking vessel, never emptied of liquor
Shesha Naga	A garland made out of serpents

When this was done, Devi started roaring. The sound of her roar attracted Mahishasura, and he came to see what was going on. When he saw Devi, a great battle started between her and Mahishasura's soldiers. There were many great asura generals, and to fight against them, Devi also created many *gana*s or attendants. After the soldiers and generals had been killed, Mahishasura himself came to fight. He could assume whatever form he willed and not only fought in the form of a buffalo but also as an elephant and a lion, not to mention, as a man. Eventually, Devi pressed down on the throat of the buffalo with her foot and struck him with her trident. When Mahishasura attempted to fight back, emerging from his buffalo form, she slit his throat with a large sword, and Mahishasura died. This is the picture we are familiar with, from images and paintings—Mahishasura killed while he has only partially emerged from his form as a buffalo. Once he was killed, the gods prayed to Devi and eulogized her. Everyone rejoiced. Blessing the devas, Devi vanished, promising to appear again whenever there was a calamity.

Devi Mahatmya gives us three main stories about Devi's manifestations, which were results of the depredations caused by Madhu/Kaitabha, Mahishasura and Shumbha/Nishumbha. Of the three, somehow, the Mahishasura account resonates most with us, probably because it was a one-on-one fight. In the other two accounts, Devi was confronted with two opponents.

Shumbha and Nishumbha

Sure enough, two more great asuras, the brothers Shumbha and Nishumbha, caused a calamity again, driving the gods away from their positions. The gods prayed to Devi again. In all such prayers, Devi is addressed by different names. Different explanations are given for these names, and what has been discussed in this subsection may be in apparent conflict with what you have heard. But do remember that, at the moment, we are sticking to the Markandeya Purana and not referring to other texts. This prayer is a long and beautiful one. The verses included as the Devi Suktam from tantra texts in Chapter 1 (see, pp. 9–15) is part of this prayer.

At the time when the gods were praying, Parvati (पार्वती), who is named after the Himalaya mountain (पर्वत) because she is his daughter, was bathing in the waters of Gangaa. Hearing the devas' prayer, she asked them, 'Who are you praying to?' As soon as she said this, Shivaa (शिवा), also known as Ambikaa (अम्बिका), manifested herself from the sheath on

Parvati's body. Having originated this way, Shivaa or Ambikaa came to be known as Koushiki (कौशकी), originating from कोश, also spelt as कोष, which means 'sheath'. Once Ambikaa had emerged, Parvati grew dark and came to be known as Kalikaa (कालिका)—the dark one. She continued to live in the Himalayas. Meanwhile, Ambikaa assumed a beautiful form. 'They are praying to me,' Ambikaa responded. 'They have been defeated by Shumbha and Nishumbha.'

Chanda and Munda, the servants of Shumbha and Nishumbha, saw Ambikaa and thought this beautiful woman should belong to Shumbha, the elder of the two brothers, and no one else. Messengers were sent to her, but Ambikaa told them that she had pledged to only marry someone who defeated her in battle. So, Dhumralochana, a general in the asura army, was sent to her with a huge army. Ambikaa killed him. Next, it was the turn of Chanda and Munda, and their armies. During that battle, Ambikaa's face turned dark with rage and Kali (काली), terrible to behold, emerged from her forehead. It was Kali who killed Chanda and Munda. Having killed them, she brought the heads to Chandikaa (चण्डिका)[6] and told her that Shumbha and Nishumba would have to be killed by Chandikaa.

Shumbha and Nishumbha came to fight, accompanied by their large armies. But Chandikaa and Kali, too, had the support of the energies of different gods, which assumed the forms of goddesses and fought against the asuras—Brahmaa's energy as Brahmani, Maheshvara's (Shiva's) energy as Maheshvari, Kumara's (Skanda's) energy as Koumari, Vishnu's energy as Vaishnavi, Nrisimha's (Narasimha) energy as Narasimhi, Indra's energy as Aindri and so on. Chandikaa sent Shiva as a messenger to Shumbha and Nishumbha, asking them to

---

[6]Chandikaa is also one of Ambikaa's names. All these different names need not confuse us. All of them are Devi's manifestations.

run away to the nether regions so that their lives would be spared. That is the reason Devi is also known as Shivaduti, the one who sent Shiva as a messenger.

Shumbha and Nishumbha refused. They sent their terrible general named Raktabija to fight her. When a drop of his blood (*rakta*) fell to the ground, it acted as a seed (*bija*), and another asura, who was just like him, appeared wherever the seed fell. It was very difficult to fight Raktabija. Eventually, as Chandikaa struck him, Kali licked up his blood before it fell to the ground. This is how Raktabija was killed. Nishumbha was killed next, followed by Shumbha.

After this victory, the devas prayed to Devi again. This prayer has been discussed below.

Narayani Suktam from Devi Mahatmya

The Narayani Suktam[7] is a famous, oft-recited prayer. Therefore, I have stated it, or at least parts of it, as a mantra. The parts I have not quoted are also extremely beautiful.

> देवि प्रपन्नार्तिहरे प्रसीद प्रसीद मातर्जगतोऽखिलस्य ।
> प्रसीद विश्वेश्वरि पाहि विश्वं त्वमीश्वरी देवि चराचरस्य ॥ (1)

> O Devi! Grant us your favours. You are the one who removes the afflictions of those who seek refuge. Show us your favours. You are the mother of the entire universe. O Vishveshvari! Show us your favours. Save the universe. O Devi! You are the Ishvari of everything that is mobile and immobile.

> आधारभूता जगतस्त्वमेका महीस्वरूपेण यतः स्थितासि ।
> अपां स्वरूपस्थितया त्वयैतदाप्यायते कृत्स्नमलङ्घ्यवीर्ये ॥ (2)

---

[7]'nArAyaNi suktam,' Sanskrit Documents, https://bit.ly/3cqb8oY. Accessed on 17 July 2022.

You alone support the entire universe. In your own form, you are established in the earth. In your own form, you are the one who is established in water. You are the one who pervades all this. Your valour cannot be transgressed.

त्वं वैष्णवीशक्तिरनन्तवीर्या विश्वस्य बीजं परमासि माया ।
सम्मोहितं देवि समस्तमेतत्त्वं वै प्रसन्ना भुवि मुक्तिहेतुः ।। (3)

You are the Vaishnavi power. You are infinite in valour. You are the seed of the universe. You are supreme mayaa. O Devi! All this is confounded by you. When you are pleased, you are the cause for liberation from this earth.

विद्याः समस्तास्तव देवि भेदाः स्त्रियः समस्ताः सकला जगत्सु ।
त्वयैकया पूरितमम्बयैतत् का ते स्तुतिः स्तव्यपरापरोक्तिः ।। (4)

You are all the different kinds of knowledge. O Devi! All the different kinds of women in the entire universe are your forms. O Mother! You alone fill everything up. How can one praise you? You are beyond praise. You are superior than the best of words.

सर्वभूता यदा देवी भुक्तिमुक्तिप्रदायिनी ।
त्वं स्तुता स्तुतये का वा भवन्तु परमोक्तयः ।। (5)

You exist in everything. O Devi! You bestow enjoyment and emancipation. You are the one who should be praised. But what supreme words can be used to praise you?

सर्वस्य बुद्धिरूपेण जनस्य हृदि संस्थिते ।
स्वर्गापवर्गदे देवि नारायणि नमोऽस्तु ते ।। (6)

You are the one who exists in the hearts of all beings in the form of intelligence. You are the one who bestows heaven and emancipation. O Devi! O Narayani! I prostrate myself before you.

कलाकाष्ठादिरूपेण परिणामप्रदायिनि ।
विश्वस्योपरतौ शक्ते नारायणि नमोऽस्तु ते ॥ (7)

You exist in the form of *kalaa, kashthaa* and the others.[8] You are the one who bestows the consequences. You are the power that leads to the destruction of the universe. O Narayani! I prostrate myself before you.

सर्वमङ्गलमाङ्गल्ये शिवे सर्वार्थसाधिके ।
शरण्ये त्र्यम्बके गौरि नारायणि नमोऽस्तु ते ॥ (8)

O beneficial one! O one who brings about every kind of auspiciousness! O Shivaa! O one who ensures every kind of success! O refuge! O three-eyed one! O Gouri! O Narayani! I prostrate myself before you.

सृष्टिस्थितिविनाशानां शक्तिभूते सनातनि ।
गुणाश्रये गुणमये नारायणि नमोऽस्तु ते ॥ (9)

O eternal power who is behind creation, preservation and destruction! O refuge of all the gunas! O one who is full of gunas! O Narayani! I prostrate myself before you.

शरणागतदीनार्तपरित्राणपरायणे ।
सर्वस्यार्तिहरे देवि नारायणि नमोऽस्तु ते ॥ (10)

O one who is devoted to saving the distressed and afflicted who seek refuge with you! O one who removes the afflictions of everyone! O Devi! O Narayani! I prostrate myself before you.

Devi was pleased when she was prayed to this way by the devas. She bestowed a boon upon them, saying that she would appear and save them whenever there was a calamity. She would reside on the slopes of the Vindhya mountains and be known as Vindhyavasini.

---

[8]Kalaa and kashthaa are different units for measuring time.

Manifesting through the Ages

There is a double yardstick used to measure time—*manvantaras* and *mahayugas*. Creation lasts for a *kalpa* (कल्प), which is the equivalent of one of Brahmaa's days. Subsequently, during Brahmaa's night, there is a temporary period of destruction and deluge, before creation starts afresh. A kalpa is divided into 14 manvantaras, each being a period during which a Manu presides and rules over creation. There are 71.4 mahayugas in a manvantara. A mahayuga is a cycle of Satya Yuga (also known as Krita Yuga), Treta Yuga, Dvapara Yuga and Kali Yuga. Our present kalpa is known as the Shveta Varaha Kalpa. Within it, six Manus have come and gone. The present Manu is known as Vaivasvata Manu. In this, the seventh manvantara, known as Vaivasvata manvantara, there will be 71.4 mahayugas, of which we are in the 28th.

Devi promised the devas that in the 28th Dvapara Yuga, she would be born through Yashoda's womb, in Nanda's lineage. This was, of course, Devi as Yogamayaa, connected to Kamsa's story. Later, she also said that she would devour demons and her teeth would turn as red as the flower of a pomegranate. Therefore, she would be known as Raktadantikaa, the one with red teeth. When there was a drought in the future, she would glance favourably with a hundred eyes and be known as Shatakshi (the one with one hundred eyes) for it. She would sustain the worlds with vegetables that grew from her body and would be known as Shakambhari (the one who bears vegetables). At the time, she would kill a giant asura named Durgama and be known as Durgaa. Another enormous asura, named Arunaksha, would cause depredations. Taking the form of a bee, she would kill him and be known as Bhramari (a bee). But all this would happen in the future, for whenever the universe suffered, she would manifest herself.

The Markandeya Purana tells us that we should especially recite and read Devi Mahatmya on the eighth, ninth and fourteenth lunar *tithi*s of ashtami, navami and chaturdashi. This should particularly be done during autumn.

Hearing this account from Rishi Sumedha, King Suratha and the Vaishya Samadhi worshipped Devi and obtained all that they desired. While the rest of Markandeya Purana goes on, this is where the Devi Mahatmya section ends.

Ayi Giri-Nandini and Beautiful Poetry

This chapter is only about the Markandeya Purana. However, the background provided so far is enough to make us understand the many allusions to stories about Devi, referred to in many stotrams, like the Argalaa (अर्गला) Stotram.[9] The word अर्गल means 'a bolt on a door'. Therefore, Argalaa Stotram is recited before Devi Mahatmya. This stotram is like a prelude, representing the opening of a door before we recite Devi Mahatmya. Most of us have heard it being recited. It begins:

> जय त्वं देवि चामुण्डे जय भूतापहारिणि ।
> जय सर्वगते देवि कालरात्रि नमोऽस्तु ते ।।

> O Devi! Victory to you. O Chamundaa! O destroyer of bhutas! Victory to you. O Devi! O one who goes everywhere! Victory to you. O Kalaratri! I prostrate myself before you.

The next sloka may be more familiar.

> जयन्ती मङ्गला काली भद्रकाली कपालिनी ।
> दुर्गा शिवा क्षमा धात्री स्वाहा स्वधा नमोऽस्तु ते ।।

[9]'argalAstotram', Sanskrit Documents, https://bit.ly/3yDzPqv. Accessed on 5 July 2022.

> Jayanti, Mangalaa, Kali, Bhadrakali, Kapalini, Durgaa, Shivaa, Kshamaa, Dhatri, Svahaa, Svadhaa—I prostrate myself before you.

I only wish to highlight the allusions made to the texts and stories in the Argalaa Stotram. For example, it refers to Devi as the destroyer of Madhu and Kaitabha and as the one who granted a boon to Vidhatri (Brahmaa). She is called the destroyer of Dhumranetra (the same as Dhumralochana), Raktabija, Chanda and Munda. She is also referred to as the one who brought welfare to the three worlds by killing Shumbha and Nishumbha. She is also mentioned as the daughter of Mount Himalaya (the same as Himachala).

Another beautiful stotram, like the Argalaa Stotram, also contains such allusions. Strictly speaking, this stotram is known as the Mahishasura-Mardini Stotram.[10] The word *mardana* (मर्दन) means to crush. Therefore, Devi is Mahishasura-Mardini, the one who crushed Mahishasura. We don't quite know who composed this stotram. Some speculate that it may have been Adi Shankaracharya. Others say that it could have been the sixteenth-century poet and scholar Ramakrishna Kavi, whom we also known as Tenali Ramakrishna.[11] Irrespective of whether it was Adi Shankaracharya or Ramakrishna Kavi, it is a beautiful stotram.

Because of its first few words, most people know it as the Ayi Giri-Nandini (अयिगिरिनन्दिनि) Stotram and it is often set to a melody. The word 'Ayi' is used to address someone—in this case, Devi. I could have translated 'Ayi' as 'Oh' or 'Hey,'

---

[10]'Part of bhagavatIpadyapuShpAnjalIstotra as Mahishasuramardini Stotra,' Sanskrit Documents, https://bit.ly/3IKRgc4. Accessed on 17 July 2022.

[11]When we hear of Tenali Ramakrishna, we should remember that he worshipped Devi, particularly in her form as Kali. We read and watch stories about Tenali Rama, but he wasn't only what those stories portray. He was also a great devotee of Devi.

but that does not convey the sense of entreaty and respect. Why is Devi referred to as Giri-Nandini? Because she is the daughter (*nandini*) of a mountain (*giri*). Again, I am not going to reproduce this stotram as a mantra. I only wish to indicate how some of Devi's accounts get woven into such compositions.

The entire composition is addressed to Devi. The first verse is indicative. It begins: गिरिवरविन्ध्यशिरोऽधिनिवासिनि—'O one who resides on the summit of Vindhya, the supreme mountain.' शितिकण्ठकुटुम्बिनि—'O one who is the wife of the one with the dark throat (Shiva)'. महिषासुरमर्दिनि—'O Mahishasura-Mardini'. शैलसुते—'O daughter of a mountain'. मधुकैटभगञ्जिनि—'O one who shamed (defeated) Madhu and Kaitabha'. धुरीणमहाशिव दूतकृत—'You sent the distinguished and great Shiva as a messenger', to ask Shumbha and Nishumbha to retreat. धूम्रविलोचन धूम्रशते—'O one who reduced Dhumravilochana (the same as Dhumralochana) into one hundred particles of smoke'. सुरथसमाधि समाधिसमाधि समाधिसमाधि—This phrase seems to be very complex, but it is not. We already know the reference to King Suratha and the Vaishya Samadhi. The word *samadhi* (समाधि) means to be immersed in intense meditation. Hence, Suratha-samadhi (सुरथसमाधि) simply means Suratha, who was immersed in this intense meditation. Samadhi-samadhi (समाधिसमाधि) simply means Samadhi, who was also immersed in intense meditation, and his meditation was equal to that of Suratha's (समाधिसमाधि). For the sake of beautiful poetry, this is nothing but a play on words.

Do read the complete stotram. It has superlative poetry. I particularly love the last line, which occurs as a refrain at the end of every verse: जय जय हे महिषासुरमर्दिनि रम्यकपर्दिनि शैलसुते—'Victory to you, O Mahishasura-Mardini! Victory to you. O one with beautiful hair! O daughter of a mountain!'

From Markandeya Purana, we will now move on to other stories about Devi from other texts.

three

DAKSHA'S YAJNA, SATI, SHAKTI PEETHAS AND PARVATI

As I said earlier, Devi's story doesn't feature only in the Markandeya Purana. One of her most familiar stories is probably about Daksha's yajna or sacrifice.[1] Just as the major Puranas are the Mahapuranas, there are also Upapuranas, which are minor Puranas. The story of Daksha's sacrifice and how Sati gave up her body has been recounted in many Mahapuranas and Upapuranas, with minor variations in details. I will narrate the version from Shiva Purana, which is a Mahapurana, since it has an interesting twist. The story comes from a section in the Shiva Purana called Sati Khanda, the section about Sati.

In the cycle of creation and destruction, everything was destroyed. When it was Brahmaa's day again, and a new kalpa began, he wished to create the various worlds again. Initially, Brahmaa begot sons through his mental powers. These were the Prajapatis, who were known as such because they were engaged in the task of creation. Daksha was a Prajapati who had several daughters. According to the Shiva Purana, Daksha prayed to Devi, who blessed him with another daughter—Sati. Since she was Daksha's daughter, she was also known as Dakshayani.

---

[1]Yajna (यज्ञ) is indeed a sacrifice, but the word 'yajna' carries a nuance of worship that the word 'sacrifice' doesn't necessarily convey.

Sati was married to Shiva. However, going back to the twist I had mentioned at the beginning of the chapter, before their marriage, Shiva told Brahmaa and Vishnu that he had taken a pledge: if his wife ever distrusted him, he would desert her. With this pledge, Shiva married Sati. On one occasion, Shiva and Sati saw Rama wandering around in the forest, along with Lakshmana, searching for Sitaa, who had been abducted by Ravana. Seeing them, Sati asked Shiva, 'Who is this person?' When Shiva said that this was Rama, Vishnu's avatara, Sati refused to believe him. She put Rama through a test, and Rama passed. But since Sati had distrusted her husband's words, her separation from Shiva was inevitable.

The Great Yajna

Daksha did not like his son-in-law, Shiva. According to him, neither did Shiva possess any of the desirable attributes a son-in-law should, nor was Shiva sufficiently deferential towards him. For example, Shiva did not bow down before Daksha. Hence, when Daksha performed a yajna (sacrifice), he didn't invite Shiva. All the other devas were invited, and Sati's sisters also turned up. From Mount Gandhamadana, Sati saw everyone travelling through the sky, going to Daksha's yajna. Despite Shiva wishing to restrain her, Sati decided to go, even though they had not been invited. 'Since when does one need an invitation to go to a father's house?' she argued. However, Daksha abused her and her husband. This was impossible for Sati to tolerate. She immersed herself in yoga and gave up her life. The fire that emerged from within her body burnt her down. Hearing that Sati had died, Shiva was enraged. From a strand of his matted hair, he created Virabhadra and Mahakali, and sent them to the sacrificial area. These two destroyed Daksha's sacrifice.

The Four Shakti Peethas

Most people know the even more popular story of the Shakti Peethas. *Peetha* (पीठ) means seat or pedestal, and a Shakti Peetha is a spot that is sacred to Devi or Shakti. The story of the Shakti Peetha is connected to Sati's death at the time of Daksha's sacrifice, and is recounted in the Kalikaa Purana, which is an Upapurana. In this version of the story, when Sati died, the dead body was not reduced to ashes. Grief-stricken, Shiva picked it up and carried it on his shoulders, rushing helter-skelter. Seeing this, Brahmaa and the other devas were devastated and worried about what would happen. Since Sati's dead body was on Shiva's shoulders, there was no question of it decaying or falling off. Brahmaa, Vishnu and Shanaishcara (Shani or Saturn) used the powers of yoga and entered Sati's dead body. Subsequently, they cut it into many parts and scattered them around the earth. According to the Kalikaa Purana, this wasn't done by Vishnu alone.

Because of his love for Sati, in the form of a lingam, Shiva remained at the spots where parts of Sati's body fell. Which were these places? The Kalikaa Purana mentions four. One should remember that each Mahapurana or Upapurana was composed in a certain part of the country, and, therefore, favours that part of the country over others. The Kalikaa Purana favours the eastern parts, such as the Kamarupa-Kamakhya region, especially associated with Devi worship. These are the three relevant slokas from the Kalikaa Purana in the context of this story. These texts have different manuscripts and versions that don't necessarily agree. I have quoted from my text of the Kalikaa Purana.[2]

देवीकूटे पादयुग्मं प्रथमं न्यपतत् क्षितौ ।
उड्डीयाने चोरूयुग्मं हिताय जगतां ततः ॥ (1)

---

[2] *The Kalikaa Purana*, B.N. Shastri (trans.), Nag Prakashan, New Delhi, 1992.

कामरूपे कामगिरौ न्यपतद्योनिमण्डलम् ।
तत्रैव न्यपतद् भूमौ पर्वते नाभिमण्डलम् ॥ (2)

जालन्धरे स्तनयुगं स्वर्णहारविभूषितम् ।
अंशग्रीवं पूर्णगिरौ कामरूपात्ततः शिरः ॥ (3)

> First, the two feet fell down on earth in Devikuta. Thereafter, for the welfare of the worlds, the two thighs fell down in Uddiyana. The part around the vagina fell to the earth in Kamarupa, on the mountain Kamagiri. The region around the navel also fell there. The two breasts, adorned with a golden necklace, fell in Jalandhara. Beyond the region of Kamarupa, the shoulders and neck fell in Purnagiri.

Where are these geographical places? This question will be addressed in a more comprehensive listing that comes later. For now, it is sufficient to note that traditionally, there are four peethas, known as Vidya Peetha, Mantra Peetha, Mudraa Peetha and Mandala Peetha. Vidya Peetha, as the name suggests, is a peetha associated with knowledge and learning. In particular, these were places where Agama texts were studied. Agamas are texts other than the Vedas, such as the tantra texts. Vidya Peetha has been identified in Kamarupa, that is, Kamakhya, which is, of course, in the Nilachal hills in Guwahati. Mantra Peetha is a peetha associated with mantras and is said to be located in Purnagiri, which is the Devi temple in Tanakpur in Uttarakhand. A place where Devi is particularly worshipped for the use of mudraas—symbolic and mystical positionings of the fingers and the thumb—is known as Mudraa Peetha. It is said to be located in Uddiyana, which is also known as Oddiyana. This place has been impossible to precisely locate. It might be in Odisha or in what is now Pakistan. That leaves Mandala Peetha, a place where Devi is especially worshipped through the use of mandalas—mystical diagrams. Mandala Peetha is said to be located in Jalandhara.

The Devi Purana and More Peethas

Besides these four Shakti Peethas, there are many more. Where do those names and those lists come from? To understand that, I have to say a few things about the Mahapuranas.

The 18 Mahapuranas have been mentioned in many texts, though their names sometimes vary. A standard list of the 18 includes: (1) Agni; (2) Bhagavata; (3) Brahma; (4) Brahmanda; (5) Brahmavaivarta; (6) Garuda; (7) Kurma; (8) Linga; (9) Markandeya; (10) Matsya; (11) Narada; (12) Padma; (13) Shiva; (14) Skanda; (15) Vamana; (16) Varaha; (17) Vayu; and (18) Vishnu. The Markandeya Purana is, of course, a part of the list. The second Purana, the Bhagavata Purana, has been the subject of some contention. But what does Bhagavata Purana mean? There is no qualifying adjective attached to the name. The devotees of Vishnu argue that Bhagavata Purana means the Purana that expounds Vaishnava dharma and has stories about Vishnu, also known simply as Bhagavatam. However, Devi's devotees say that Bhagavata Purana means Devi Bhagavata Purana. Indeed, if one wishes to understand Devi and her worship, in addition to the Markandeya Purana and Kalikaa Purana, one must read the Devi Bhagavata Purana.[3]

The Devi Bhagavata Purana is divided into sections, known as skandhas. Depending on the version of the text you are reading, the 30th chapter of the seventh skandha discusses Sati's birth as Daksha's daughter and Daksha's yajna. In the

---

[3]Many years ago, in 1890, Swami Vijnanananda translated the Devi Bhagavata Purana to English: *Srimad Devi Bhagavatam*, Swami Vijnanananda (trans.), Allahabad Panini Office, 1890. As far as I know, this is the only available translation of the text in English. It is quite a good translation. However, people were not always very careful while translating in that day and age. So, this is not really a verbatim translation and liberties have been taken.

version of the story in this text, Sati gave up her body at the time of the yajna. Miserable, Shiva wandered around, carrying her dead body on his shoulders, which agitated Brahmaa and the other devas. The Devi Bhagavata Purana tells us that Vishnu (there is no mention of Brahmaa or Shani) cut the body into pieces. It is believed that Vishnu did this with his chakra. According to the Devi Bhagavata Purana, however, Vishnu did this with his bow and arrows. Shiva, of course, stayed in the spots where Sati's body parts were scattered, in the form of a lingam.

The Devi Bhagavata Purana gives us a list of these places and describes them as Siddha Peethas. Sometimes, the expressions Siddha Peetha and Shakti Peetha are used synonymously, as with the Devi Bhagavata Purana. Other times, a distinction is drawn between the two. A Siddha Peetha is a place where one or more *sadhaka*s have obtained *siddhi* in their *sadhana*. It may or may not be a Shakti Peetha. In contrast, a Shakti Peetha is a place where a part of Sati's body fell. The Devi Bhagavata Purana, along with each location, mentions a name or form of Devi associated with it. Except for Varanasi, where Devi's face is said to have fallen, other locations do not mention a specific body part of Devi falling there. The number 108 is, of course, sacred and it is natural for such a list to have 108 Shakti Peethas. The Padma Purana has a similar list. We are also told that, under the name of Brahmakalaa, Shakti exists in the consciousness of all those with bodies. In the text, this entire account is recited by Vedavyasa to King Janamejaya. Vedavyasa concludes by saying, 'O Janamejaya! I have recounted the names of 108 peethas to you, the directions in which these exist and the names of Devi there. These Peethas are said to have originated because of Devi Sati's body parts. They exist on the surface of the earth and elsewhere too.'

The popular belief is that there are 51 Shakti Peethas. So,

you may be surprised to learn that a revered text like Devi Bhagavata Purana mentions 108 Shakti Peethas. When you read about Shakti Peethas and visit them, Table 3 is the list of 108 you should match them against.

Table 3:
List of Shakti Peethas and the form/name of Devi residing there

Location of the Shakti Peetha	*Devi's Name*
Varanasi	Vishalakshi
Naimisharanya	Lingadharini
Prayaga	Lalitaa
Gandhamadana	Kamuki
South of Lake Manasa	Kumudaa
North of Lake Manasa	Vishvakamaa
Gomanta	Gomati
Mount Mandara	Kamacharini
Chaitraratha	Madotkata
Hastinapura	Jayanti
Kanyakubja	Gouri
Mount Malaya	Rambhaa
Ekamrapeetha	Kirtimati
Vishva	Vishveshvari
Pushkara	Puruhutaa
Kedarapeetha	Sanmarga-dayini
Slopes of Himalaya	Mandaa
Gokarna	Bhadrakarnikaa
Sthaneshvara	Bhavani
Bilvaka	Bilvapatrikaa
Shrishaila	Madhavi
Bhadreshvara	Bhadraa

Mount Varaha	Jayaa
Kamalalaya	Kamalaa
Rudrakoti	Rudrani
Kalanjaara	Kali
Shalagrama	Mahadevi
Shivalinga	Jalapriyaa
Mahalinga	Kapilaa
Makota	Mukuteshvari
Mayapuri	Kumari
Santana	Lalitambikaa
Gayaa	Mangalaa
Purushottama	Vimalaa
Sahasraksha	Utpalakshi
Hiranyaksha	Mahtopalaa
Vipasha	Amogakshi
Pundravardhana	Padalaa
Suparsha	Narayani
Trikuta	Rudrasundari
Vipula	Vipulaa
Mount Malaya	Kalyani
Sahyadri	Ekaviraa
Harishchandra	Chandrikaa
Ramatirtha	Ramanaa
Yamunaa	Mrigavati
Kotatirtha	Kotavi
Madhava-vana	Sugandhaa
Godavari	Trisandhyaa
Gangadvara	Ratipriyaa
Shivakunda	Shubhanandaa
Devikatata	Nandini

Dvaravati	Rukmini
Vrindavana	Radhaa
Mathuraa	Devaki
Patala	Parameshvari
Chitrakuta	Sita
Vindhya	Vindhyadhivasini
Karavira	Mahalakshmi
Vinayaka	Uma Devi
Vaidyanatha	Arogyaa
Mahakala	Maheshvari
Ushnatirtha	Abhayaa
Mount Vindhya	Nitambaa
Mandavya	Mandavi
Maheshvari-pura	Svahaa
Chhaglanda	Prachandaa
Amarakantaka	Chandikaa
Someshvara	Vararohaa
Prabhasa	Pushkaravati
Sarasvati	Devamataa
Along the shore	Paravaraa
Mahalaya	Mahabhagaa
Payoshni	Pingaleshvari
Simhika	Kritashauchaa
Kartika	Atishankari
Utpalavartaka	Lolaa
Confluence of Shona	Subhadraa
Siddhavana	Lakshmi Mataa
Bharatashrama	Anangaa
Jalandhara	Vishvamukhi
Mount Kishkindhaa	Taraa

Devadaru-vana	Pushti
The circle of Kashmira	Medhaa
Himadri	Bhimaa Devi
Vishveshvara	Tushti
Kapalamochana	Shuddhi
Kayavarohana	Mataa
Shankhaddhara	Dharaa
Pindaraka	Dhriti
Chandrabhaga	Kalaa
Acchoda	Shivadharini
Vena	Amritaa
Badari	Urvashi
Uttarakuru	Aushadhi
Kushadvipa	Kushodakaa
Hemakuta	Manmathaa
Kumuda	Satyavadini
Ashvattha	Vandaniyaa
Vaishravanalaya	Nidhi
Vedavadana	Gayatri
In Shiva's presence	Parvati
In the world of devas	Indrani
In Brahmaa's mouth	Sarasvati
In the solar disc	Prabhaa
Among *matrikaas*[4]	Vaishnavi
Among *sati*s	Arundhati
Among *ramaas*[5]	Tilottamaa

I can imagine the surprise at this list. All of us have heard of Shakti Peethas and are familiar with some, if not all of

[4]Matrikaas are divine mothers.

[5]Ramaas are beautiful women.

the names. Where are those names in this list? Most of them don't feature in it at all. For example, where are Kamakhya and Kalighat? As I have said, there are different lists of Shakti Peethas in different texts.

For instance, there is a stotram about 18 Shakti Peethas, attributed to Adi Shankaracharya.[6] It mentions (1) Shankari Devi in Lanka; (2) Kamakshi in the city of Kanchika (Kanchipuram); (3) Shrinkhala Devi in Pradyumna; (4) Chamundi in Krounchapattana; (5) Jogalambaa in Alampura; (6) Bhramarambikaa in Shrishaila; (7) Mahalakshmi in Kolhapura; (8) Ekavirikaa in Mahurya; (9) Mahakali in Ujjayini; (10) Puruhutikaa in Pithika; (11) Girija Devi in Audhya; (12) Manikya in Dakshavataka; (13) Kamarupaa in Harikshetra; (14) Madhaveshvari in Prayaga; (15) Vaishnavi Devi in Jvalamukhi; (16) Mangalya-Gourika in Gaya; (17) Vishalakshmi in Varanasi; and (18) Sarasvati in Kashmira. The last line says that even yogis find it very difficult to access these peethas. Contrary to what you might read, this stotram doesn't mention the parts of Devi's body that are preset in these locations either.

लङ्कायां शाङ्करी देवी कामाक्षी काञ्चिकापुरे ।
प्रद्युम्ने शृङ्खलादेवी चामुण्डी क्रौञ्चपट्टणे ॥ (1)

अलम्पुरे जोगुलाम्बा श्रीशैले भ्रमराम्बिका ।
कोल्हापुरे महालक्ष्मी माहूर्ये एकवीरिका ॥ (2)

उज्जयिन्यां महाकाली पीठिक्यां पुरुहूतिका ।
ओढ्यायां गिरिजादेवी माणिक्या दक्षवाटके ॥ (3)

हरिक्षेत्रे कामरूपा प्रयागे माधवेश्वरी ।
ज्वालायां वैष्णवी देवी गया माङ्गल्यगौरिका ॥ (4)

---

[6]'aShTAdashashaktipITha stotram,' Sanskrit Documents, https://bit.ly/3bP314G. Accessed on 5 July 2022.
[7]Ibid.

वारणस्यां विशालाक्षी काश्मीरेषु सरस्वती ।
अष्टादश सुपीठानि योगिनामपि दुर्लभम् ।। (5)[7]

For some of the names in this list, the geographical identification is easy, such as Varanasi or Mathura. But something like Devadaru-vana could mean any forest that has *devadaru* trees.[8] Similarly, the following names may sound familiar: Lanka, Kanchi, Shrishaila, Kolhapura, Ujjayini, Kamarupa, Prayaga, Jvalamukhi, Gaya, Varanasi and Kashmira. It is plausible that Pradyumna indicates some place in Gujarat, just as Krounchapattana must be in Karnataka, since it means a habitation near Mount Krouncha. After all, in Krouncha Giri, in the Bellary district of Karnataka, there is a Parvati temple. The gap in this mountain might well have been the famous Mount Krouncha, which was shattered by Skanda's spear. Alampura is presumably in Andhra Pradesh and Audhya must mean Odisha. But what do Mahurya, Pithika and Dakshavataka mean?

There are two other lists too. For example, many people quote the Brahmanda Purana and say that it mentions 64 Shakti Peethas. My edition of the Brahmanda Purana[9] does not say anything about 64 Peethas, but this varies between different editions. However, right towards the end of this Purana, there is a section known as Lalitaa (ललिता) Mahatmya, the greatness of Lalitaa, who is one of Devi's manifestations. This section has a subsection on *nyasa,* which means the mental appropriation of different divinities to different parts of the devotee's body. When it is only done on parts of the

---

[8]Devadaru is a kind of pine, also known as deodar.

[9]*Brahmanda Mahapuran,* Krishnadas Academy, Varanasi, 1983.

[10]This clearly indicates what was Bengal then and includes present-day Bangladesh. Anything beyond that, such as the identification with Pandua in West Bengal, is speculative. However, evidently, there used to be a Shrinkhala Devi temple in Pandua once, which has since been destroyed.

hand, it is called *kara nyasa*. When it is done on the entire body, it is called *anga nyasa*. This part of the text states that this nyasa should be done with 51 peethas and lists them:

> (1) Varanasi; (2) Kamarupa; (3) Nepala; (4) Poundravardhana;[10] (5) Varasthira; (6) Kanyakubja; (7) Purnashaila: (8) Arbuda;[11] (9) Amratakeshvara; (10) Ekamra;[12] (11) Trisrota;[13] (12) Kamkoshtakam; (13) Kailasa; (14) Bhrigunagara; (15) Kedara; (16) Chandrapushkara;[14] (17) Shripeetha; (18) Ekavira; (19) Jalandhra;[15] (20) Malava; (21) Kulanna; (22) Devikota; (23) Gokarna; (24) Maruteshvara; (25) Attahasa; (26) Viraja; (27) Rajaveshma; (28) Mahapatha; (29) Kolapura;[16] (30) Kailapura; (31) Kaleshvara; (32) Jayantika;[17] (33) Ujjayini; (34) Chitra; (35) Kshiraka;[18] (36) Hastinapura; (37) Udira; (38) Prayaga; (39) Shashti-mayapura; (40) Gourisha; (41) Salaya; (42) Shrishaila; (43) Maru; (44) Girivara; (45) Mahendra; (46) Vamana Giri; (47) Hiranyapura; (48) Mahalakshmipura; (49) Purodyana; and (50) Chhayakshetra.

Though the text states that there are 51 peethas, only 50 peethas are listed in it. It then says that the nyasa must be

---

[11]This refers to Mount Abu.

[12]This is in Bhuvaneshvara.

[13]Since Trisrota means one with three flows, this indicates some place along the Gangaa.

[14]This refers to Pushkara.

[15]This refers to Jalandhara.

[16]This refers to Kolhapura.

[17]This is located in the Jaintia Hills of Meghalaya, but the original temple is across the border now, in Bangladesh.

[18]This refers to Kshiragrama, West Bengal.

performed according to the order of the letters of the Sanskrit alphabet. The Sanskrit alphabet has 25 consonants, four semi-vowels and three sibilants. There are 14 vowels and *anusvara* and *visarga*. So, in contempary times, Sanskrit has 48 letters. However, Sanskrit used to have *pluta* (long-drawn-out) sounds that are no longer used now. With those added, there are 51 letters. Hence, there is a connection between 51 letters and 51 as the number of Shakti Peethas. I hope you have noted that the Brahmanda Purana also does not mention parts of Sati's body.

The notion of Shakti Peethas evolved over time, and the numbers changed from four to 18 to 51. Tantra texts of much later vintage, say written 500 years ago, also discuss the Shakti Peethas. The Tantrachudamani, for example, has a section on the determination of peethas. It has a section where Devi herself speaks about 51 Shakti Peethas, the parts of her body that fell down after being severed by Vishnu's chakra, and the Bhairava (Shiva) who has, since, established himself in these places. However, this is merely one list according to one text. Our perceptions about Shakti Peethas, including the belief that Sati's body was severed by Vishnu's chakra, come from this text. Note that tantra texts, like this one, are the first time we find a specific mention of a part of Sati's body associated with a place. Note also that while Devi has a name associated with each location from this text, it also mentions an associated name of Bhairava.

While most Shakti Peethas are located in present-day India, some are in Bangladesh, Nepal, Pakistan and perhaps even Sri Lanka. They naturally tended to be concentrated in places known for Shakti worship, such as Birbhum and Bardhaman districts of West Bengal, parts of Bangladesh and Nepal. I am not going to quote the Sanskrit text. That's unnecessary. The table below compiles this information. You may come across other lists and be surprised that a Shakti

Table 4: List of Shakti Peethas as per the tantra text, Tantrachudamani

Part of body	*Place*	*Geographical identification*	*Devi's name*	*Bhairava's name*
Brahmarandhra[19]	Hingula	Now in Pakistan	Kottari	Bhimalochana
Three eyes	Karavira	Kolhapur	Mahishamardini	Krodhisha
Nose	Sugandha	Now in Bangladesh	Sunandaa	Tryambaka
Throat	Kashmira	Amarnath	Mahamayaa	Trisandhyeshvara
Tongue	Jvalamukhi	Kangra, Himachal	Siddhidaa	Unmatta
Breasts	Jalandhara	Jalandhar	Tripuramalini	Bhishana
Heart	Vaidyanatha	Deogarh	Jaya Durgaa	Vaidyanatha
Knee	Nepala	Kathmandu, Nepal	Mahamayaa	Kapali
Right hand	Manasa	Tibet	Dakshayani	Amara Bhairava
Navel	Viraja in Utakala	Puri	Vimalaa	Jagannatha
Cheek	Gandaki	Mustang, Nepal	Gandaki Chandi	Chakrapani
Left arm	Bahula	Bardhaman	Bahulaa	Bhiruka
Elbow	Ujjayini	Ujjain	Mangalachandikaa	Kapilambara
Right arm	Chattala	Chittagong, Bangladesh	Bhavani	Chandrashekhara
Right foot	Tripura	Tripura	Tripurasundari	Tripuresha
Left foot	Trisrota	Jalpaiguri	Bhramari	Ishvara

[19]There are 12 centres in the body, six below the brain and six in the brain, with Brahmarandhra as the 12th.

Vagina	Kamagiri	Kamakhya	Kamakhyaa[20]	Umananda
Big right toe	Kshiragrama	Bardhaman	Yugadyaa	Kshirakhandaka
Other toes of the right foot	Kalipitha	Kalighat	Kalikaa	Nakulisha
Fingers	Prayaga	Prayagraj	Lalitaa	Bhava
Left shank	Jayanti	Meghalaya/ Bangladesh	Jayanti	Kramadishvara
Diadem	Kirita	Murshidabad	Vimalaa	Samvarta
Earring	Manikarnika, Varanasi	Varanasi	Vishalakshi	Kalabhairava
Back	Kanyashrama	Kanyakumari	Sarvani	Nimisha
Ankle	Kurukshetra	Kurukshetra	Savitri	Sthanu
Bracelet	Manivedaka	Ajmer	Gayatri	Sarvananda
Neck	Shrishaila	Andhra Pradesh	Mahalakshmi	Sambarananda
Skeleton	Kanchi	Kanchipuram	Devagarbha	Ruru
Buttocks	Kalamadhava	Not identified	Kali	Asitanga
Buttocks	Narmada	Madhya Pradesh	Shonaa	Bhadrasena

In this stotram, Kamakhyaa is singled out for special mention. We are told that Devi is the presiding deity of this sacred spot. Hence, she is also present there as Shri Bhairavi, Prachanda Chandikaa, Matangi, Tripurambikaa, Vagalaa, Kamalaa, Bhuvaneshi and Dhumini. In addition to the form as Kamakhyaa, she is present in 10 different forms. Therefore, Bhairava is also present in ten different forms.

Breasts	Ramagiri	Chitrakoot	Shivani	Chanda
Tresses of hair	Vrindavana	Vrindavan	Umaa	Bhutesha
Upper row of teeth	Anala	Kanyakumari	Narayani	Samhara
Lower row of teeth	Panchasagara	Not identified	Varahi	Maharudra
Left ear	Banks of Karotaya	Bogra, Bangladesh	Aparnaa	Vamana
Right ankle	Shri Parvata	Leh	Shri Sundari	Sundarananda
Left ankle	Vibhashaka	Medinipur	Kapalini	Mahadeva
Stomach	Prabhasa	Prabhas	Chandrabhagaa	Vakratunda
Upper lip	Mount Bhairava	Ujjain	Avanti	Lambakarna
Chin	Janasthana	Nashik	Bhramari	Vikritaksha
Cheek	Banks of Godavari	East Godavari	Vishveshi	Dandapani
Right shoulder	Ratnavali	Not identified	Kumari	Shiva
Left shoulder	Mithila	Mustang, Nepal	Umaa	Mahodara
Hollow bone	Nalahati	Birbhum	Kalikaa	Yogisha
Head	Kalighata	Nadia	Jaya Durgaa	Krodhisha
Mind	Vakreshvara	Birbhum	Mahishamardini	Vakranatha
Hand	Yashora	Satkhira, Bangladesh	Yashoreshvari	Chanda
Lips	Attahasa	Birbhum	Phullara	Vishvesha
Necklace	Nandipura	Birbhum	Nandini	Nandikeshvara
Anklet	Lanka	Unidentified place in Sri Lanka	Indrakshi	Rakshaseshvara
Toes	Virata	Jaipur	Ambikaa	Amrita

Peetha mentioned in your list doesn't figure in this table. This is not worth arguing over. Lists vary according to texts. Any place mentioned was, and probably still is associated with Devi's worship. That is all that matters.

The Number 64

The number 64, which is the number of peethas named in the Brahmanda Purana, is associated with yoginis (योगिनी). Who is a yogini? She is simply the feminine form of a yogi. Therefore, a woman who takes to the path of yoga is a yogini. But there is a higher meaning of the word 'yogini.' Divine yoginis are Devi's manifestations. For example, Virabhadra and Mahakali arrived to destroy Daksha's sacrifice. There were 64 yoginis who supported Mahakali in her fight. Yoginis were sometimes identified with matrikaas and sometimes named separately. Different names are available for them, which change with different lists. The yoginis also have connections with tantra.

While that is not the subject matter of this book, there often were eight matrikaas or yoginis. Each yogini was, in turn, divided into eight yoginis; that is how we came to have 64 of them. One possible list of the original eight yoginis is Brahmani, Maheshvari, Vaishnavi, Koumari, Varahi, Narasimhi, Indrani and Chamundaa. If you are interested in *jyotisha* or astrology you will be familiar with the list of eight yoginis as Mangalaa, Pingalaa, Dhanyaa, Bhramari, Bhadrikaa, Ulkaa, Siddhaa and Sankataa. This is how the eight matrikaas are named in jyotisha texts. There are famous 64 Yogini temples in Odisha, Madhya Pradesh and Uttar Pradesh.

Many such older temples, which may not always have the 64 Yoginis, are lost, much like the many sites of Devi's worship. After all, if temples were made of wood, and not stone, they were unlikely to have survived over time, with plundering invaders making things worse. But there is plenty of information available through archaeological records and excavations of the Indus-Sarasvati civilization sites, which have revealed traces of Devi worship.

Before concluding the chapter, the story of Sati and Shiva cannot remain incomplete. We must mention Parvati. Sati died, and Shiva lived the life of a *brahmachari*. Meanwhile, Tarakasura caused depredations and drove the devas out of heaven. He could only be killed by Shiva's son. But since Shiva was living the life of a brahmachari, this seemed impossible. Meanwhile, Sati wanted to be reborn to marry Shiva again. She manifested as Parvati, the daughter of Himalaya and his wife, Menaa. Subsequently, Parvati began her *tapasya*—she fasted, not even eating a leaf (पर्ण). Thus, she is known as Aparnaa (अपर्णा). Her mother tried to restrain her from performing this terrible tapasya. Based on the Sanskrit word for 'don't', she came to be known as Umaa (उमा). After performing tapasya, Parvati got married to Shiva. Then, their son Skanda or Kumara was born, and he killed Tarakasura.

If you want to read a beautiful rendering of the entire story, you can find no better source than Kalidasa's *Kumarasambhavam*, based on the birth of Kumara.

four

NAVARATRI

'Navaratri' simply means 'nine nights.' Sometimes, people use the term 'Navaratra.' But since the word ratri (रात्रि) is feminine in Sanskrit, I prefer Navaratri.

A lunar fortnight is known as *paksha* and auspicious days are reckoned in accordance with the lunar day, tithi, which does not necessarily correspond to a solar day. When the moon waxes and increases every day, it is the bright lunar fortnight, known as *shukla paksha.* This ends in *purnimaa* or *pournamasi,* the night of the full moon. After that, when the moon wanes and diminishes every day, it is the dark lunar fortnight, known as *krishna paksha,* culminating in *amavasyaa,* the night of the new moon. Therefore, every month, there is a shukla paksha and a krishna paksha. In general, shukla paksha is propitious for worshipping devas and the krishna paksha for ancestors.

The nine nights of Navaratri are spread across the first lunar tithi to the ninth—pratipada, dvitiya, tritiya, chaturthi, panchami, shashthi, saptami, ashtami and navami. Often, the festivities end on dashami, the tenth lunar day. There is also a Navaratri every month, but out of those 12 Navaratris, four are special. These are Ashada Navaratri (in June/July), Sharada or Ashvina Navaratri (in September/October), Magha Navaratri (in January/February) and Vasanta or Chaitra Navaratri (in March/April).

Devi's worship happens every day, but these Navaratris are occasions when Devi's worship is given special importance. Our rites are divided into three types—*nitya, naimittika* and *kamya*. Nitya rites are those that are undertaken every day. Naimittika rites are those that are undertaken on special auspicious occasions. So, the four auspicious Navaratris are Devi's naimittika worship. Kamya rites are undertaken with a specific desire in mind. So, if Devi is worshipped to accomplish a particular wish, it is kamya worship. Most people have probably heard of Sharada Navaratri and Chaitra Navaratri. However, many people may not have heard of Devi being worshipped during Magha Navaratri or Ashada Navaratri. On these two occasions, Devi's worship is *gupta* or hidden. The priest undertakes the rituals in secret, and it is private worship. In contrast, the worship at the time of Sharada Navaratri or Chaitra Navaratri is public worship.

Means of Worship

In the third skandha of the Devi Bhagavata Purana, King Janamejaya asks Vedavyasa, 'When Navaratri arrives, please tell me what is to be done? What are the norms for the rites? What are the fruits? Please tell me, with a focus on Sharada Navaratri.'

Vedavyasa responds that the *vrata*s (vows) must be especially observed in autumn, during Sharada Navaratri. But they must also be lovingly observed in spring, during Chaitra Navaratri. This is because these two seasons are like the jaws of Yama for people. These two seasons are the times when people confront many kinds of diseases. Hence, in Ashvina and Chaitra, a learned person will devotedly worship Chandikaa. The preparations start on amavasyaa and involve restraint in diet. A pavilion and a platform must be properly constructed. The actual worship starts on pratipada. On this occasion, Devi's image should show her astride a lion. The image can be four-armed, holding a conch shell, a chakra, a mace and a lotus. She can also have 18 arms, holding different kinds of weapons.

If there is no image, a *kalasha* (कलश)—that is, a pot or a pitcher—can be used instead. A kalasha is important in all our pujaas and is often worshipped before all other rites. There are mantras for worshipping a kalasha. You will notice kalashas on tops of some temples. Indeed, kalasha is also the name of a particular type of temple. The word 'कला' means 'part' or 'portion' and a kalasha is formed by bringing together parts of everything that is good. It is said that Vishnu resides in the mouth of a kalasha, Rudra in its neck and Brahmaa in its base. All the matrikaas assemble in the middle of a kalasha. The sacred waters from all the rivers and all the *tirtha*s gather in it. A kalasha alludes to the pot of *amrita*, which was produced when the ocean was churned. The motif of a kalasha is explained in terms of the five elements (*pancha bhuta*) too. It is made from earth (*prithvi*) or metal that comes from the earth. The wide centre is water (*ap*) and is filled with water. The neck stands for fire (*agni*). The opening at the top represents wind (*vayu*). There is space (*akasha*) outside, which is covered with a coconut or mango leaves. When a kalasha is made out of earth, it is useless until it is baked because the water seeps out of it. When it is scorched by the fire and baked, it is made usable, perfected in the course of purification. Similarly, our pujaa is meant to purify us and bring us closer to perfection. In the end, a kalasha breaks and shatters, reduced to the earth it was made of. Therefore, it also reminds us that our physical bodies are temporary and transient. They, too, will be reduced to earth and dust one day. Hence, when Devi's image is not available, she is worshipped in the form of a kalasha. She is Chinmayi (चिन्मयी)—eternal and full of pure consciousness. She is also worshipped as Mrinmayi (मृण्मयी) —an image or a pot made out of earth.

According to the Devi Bhagavata Purana, when a kalasha is used for worship instead of an image, it must be sanctified with mantras. A yantra, marked with a navarna mantra (नवार्णमन्त्र), is also used in worship. A yantra is a mystical geometric diagram, used extensively in tantra. It is similar to a mandala but tends to be smaller in size. In the Shiva Purana, Shiva tells us about yantra, mantra and tantra. He tells Sati about the five parts of a yantra, which are bija mantras, associated with the five elements of space, air, fire, water and earth. A bija mantra is a mystic akshara or syllable from a mantra. Yantras are often used in conjunction with bija mantras. As mentioned earlier, yantra means something that restrains, and a yantra focuses and restrains the mind, facilitating worship and meditation. Indeed, the Sanskrit word for a machine or implement is also yantra. In excavations in Baghor, Madhya Pradesh, a triangular object was found, dated to between 9000 BCE and 8000 BCE. It is thought that this triangular object was a yantra.[1] Hence, the use of yantras in connection with Devi's worship can be dated back to ancient times.

In a typical yantra, geometrical shapes radiate outwards—shapes that have triangles and circles, with lotuses. Usually, everything is enclosed inside a square, which signifies the four directions. The centre is called a *bindu*. Not every yantra is two-dimensional—it can be three-dimensional too. Every yantra is associated with a specific deity, and if it is Devi's yantra, it has a triangle pointing downwards. Accordingly, you will find Shri yantra, Kali yantra, Lakshmi yantra and so on. Sometimes, a mantra or a bija mantra is inscribed inside a

---

[1]Chamunda Swami Ji, 'Baghor Stone: 11000-Year-Old Shakti', SpeakingTree, 1 December 2021, https://bit.ly/3QcnTSy. Accessed on 27 June 2022; Kalbag, Chaitanya, 'Indo-US Archaeology Team Stumbles upon Evidence of Prehistoric Shakti Worship in MP', IndiaToday, 12 October 2013, https://bit.ly/3NoSgTK. Accessed on 27 June 2022.

yantra, which captures the mystical essence of that mantra. Sometimes, it has numbers, too, which are often in the form of magic squares or triangles.

So far so good. But a yantra must also be marked with a navarna mantra (नवार्णमन्त्र). What is a navarna mantra? Strictly speaking, the Devi Bhagavata Purana doesn't tell us. But etymologically, *arna* means 'letter' and *nava* means 'nine'. Therefore, any mantra with nine letters is a navarna mantra. Some say that Devi's navarna mantra is: ऐं ह्रीं क्लीं चामुंडाये विच्चे. All such mantras are to be prefixed with OUM, which is itself a kind of bija mantra. If you count the number of letters in the mantra I have just stated, with *yuktaksharas*[2] being counted as a single letter, you will find it has nine letters. Thus, it is a navarna mantra. More pertinently, there are nine aksharas too. What does this navarna mantra mean? That's a bit more difficult to explain, since it has several bija mantras. चामुंडाये is simple. It means, 'To Chamundaa'. The ऐं stands for Maha Sarasvati, signifying creation. The ह्रीं stands for Maha Lakshmi, signifying preservation. The क्लीं stands for Maha Kali, signifying destruction. The विच्चे brings in knowledge and consciousness. Another version of the navarna mantra is: ह्रीं श्रीं चण्डिकाये नम. In this mantra, the term 'चण्डिकाये' means 'to Chandikaa', and there is no need to explain the namah part.

There can be more complicated explanations of bija mantras. For example, ह्रीं doesn't simply signify Maha Lakshmi. There are actually five components in it: ह, र, ई, the sound known as *nada* and bindu, which indicates the nasal sound

---

[2]Literally, *arna* means a letter. *Akshara* is the segment of a word with a single vowel sound. So, one or more *arna*s make up one *akshara*, if one is being finicky. If one is less pedantic, the terms *arna* and *akshara* are often used synonymously. In Sanskrit, because it is a spoken language, as all languages originally were, a preceding *akshara* tends to combine with a succeeding *akshara*. When that happens, it is called a *yuktakshara*. For example, क्ष, consisting of क् and ष्, is a *yuktakshara*.

that is never pronounced. In a relatively more complicated explanation, ह stands for Hara (Shiva), र stands for Prakriti, ई stands for Mahamayaa, nada stands for the mother of the universe and bindu for the removal of all afflictions. Similarly, श्रीं includes श, which signifies Maha Lakshmi; र, which signifies prosperity; ई, which signifies contentment; and an anusvara, which indicates the removal of afflictions. All bija mantras can be similarly broken down. They are typically used by those who practise some form of tantra. For most of us, when we worship Devi, any simple mantra suffices.

One such simple mantra is the familiar Gayatri Mantra: ऊँ भूर्भुवः स्वः तत्सवितुर्वरेण्यं भर्गो देवस्य धीमहि धियो यो नः प्रचोदयात्. This mantra is actually the Savitri Mantra, dedicated to the divinity Savitar. Gayatri is a meter (*chhanda*), with three lines and eight aksharas in each line. Since the Savitri Mantra has been composed in Gayatri chhanda, it has become much more familiar as Gayatri Mantra. It has been translated numerous times. So, the words used in my translation may not actually match with earlier translations. A loose translation of the Gayatri Mantra would be: 'That Savitar (the sun-god) is the glorious one. We meditate on the self-luminous deva. May he urge our intelligence.' Notice that ऊँ भूर्भुवः स्वः isn't actually part of the core Gayatri Mantra, as given in Rig Veda. This part is known as *vyahriti*, and it stands for *bhuloka* (earth), *bhuvaloka* (firmament) and *svarloka* (heaven).

What is not as well known is that there are other Gayatri Mantras too, addressed to specific deities. This includes forms of Devi as well. For example, one of Durgaa's Gayatri Mantras is: ऊँ कात्यायन्यै विद्महे कन्याकुमार्ये च धीमहि, तन्नो दुर्गा प्रचोदयात्. If you know that Katyayani and Kanyakumari are Durgaa's names, the meaning is clear. Similarly, Lakshmi's Gayatri Mantra reads: ऊँ महादेव्यै च विद्महे विष्णुपत्न्यै च धीमहि, तन्नो लक्ष्मी प्रचोदयात्. Annapurnaa's Gayatri Mantra is: ऊँ भगवत्यै च विद्महे महेश्वर्यै च धीमहि तन्नोन्नपूर्णा प्रचोदयात्. Kali's Gayatri Mantra reads: ऊँ कालिकायै

च विद्महे स्मशानवासिन्यै धीमहि, तन्नो घोरा प्रचोदयात्. For most of us, these mantras should suffice during pujaa, without getting into bija mantras. At least, that's what I think.

Celebrations and Stories

The Devi Bhagavata Purana tells us that Rama worshipped Devi at the time of Ashvina Navaratri. After Sita was abducted by Ravana, *Devarshi* (the divine sage) Narada asked Rama to worship Devi. Rama and Lakshmana fasted for nine days and worshipped her, starting on pratipada. At midnight on ashtami, Devi appeared and granted him his desired boon.

Worshipping Devi at the time of Navaratri has been a hallowed tradition. Rama was born on navami, right in the middle of Ashvina Navaratri. The Kalikaa Purana, another Upapurana, also has a story about Rama worshipping Devi, in a section on Mahishasura. This is not an account that occurs in the Valmiki Ramayana or any other Sanskrit version of the Ramayana. According to the Kalikaa Purana, on navami, in autumn, using mantras and tantras and offering *bali* (बलि), Durgaa must be worshipped. Bali doesn't necessarily mean an offering. Taxes paid to a king are also bali. When used in the sense of a sacrificial offering, it doesn't necessarily mean an animal sacrifice, though this is not precluded. The Kalikaa Purana tells us that Brahmaa woke Mahadevi up in the middle of the night to ensure that Rama might kill Ravana. Accordingly, Devi's *avahana*, the ritual invocation of a deity, occurred on pratipada during shukla paksha in the month of Ashvina. Once Rama had killed Ravana on navami, the *visarjana*—the ritual dismissal of the deity after the pujaa or worship is over—was performed on dashami. Note that in this version of the story, Brahmaa worshipped Devi on behalf of Rama. Rama didn't worship Devi himself. I guess you could say that Brahmaa was the priest who performed the pujaa, while Rama was the *yajamana* (यजमान), the person for whom the pujaa was being done.

In one form or another, Navaratri is celebrated throughout India and even abroad. In the book *Navaratri: When Devi Comes Home*, my co-author and I documented the varied forms in which Devi is worshipped throughout the country during Navaratri.[3] Devi's worship in Kashmir, including during Navaratri, is documented in Nilamata Purana (sixth to eighth century CE). The eastern parts of the country are known to celebrate Durgaa Pujaa during Navaratri. In Tamil Nadu, there are *kolu* dolls and there is Ayudha Pujaa. Although, today, the worship of weapons has been replaced with tools during this pujaa. There are Bathukamma festivities in Telangana. In Gujarat, Navaratri is associated with Dandiyaa and Garbaa.

In some parts of the country, Kumari Pujaa is practised during this period. The word *kumari* is usually translated as 'young girl' or 'maiden,' say a girl who is less than 12 years of age. Sometimes, this is taken to be as less than 16 years of age. These girls represent Devi and are, therefore, worshipped during Navaratri. The Devi Bhagavata Purana tells us that a girl below two years of age cannot be accepted as a kumari for the purposes of worship. According to this text, depending on the age, there are different names for such kumaris: 3-year-olds, Trimurti; 4-year-olds, Kalyani; 5-year-olds, Rohini; 6-year-olds, Kalikaa; 7-year-olds, Chandikaa; 8-year-olds, Shambhavi; 9-year-olds, Durgaa; and 10-year-olds, Subhadraa. The Devi Bhagavata Purana doesn't approve of the worship of girls who are older. Other texts have other stipulations, and the names of kumaris differ. After all, the modes of worshipping Devi differ. What is constant is Devi's worship.

---

[3]Debroy, Bibek and Anuradha Goyal (eds), *Navaratri: When Devi Comes Home*, Rupa, 2021.

Kumari is also one of the matrikaas. In Raktabija's case, she manifested to drink up the blood of the demon named Andhaka. Hence, in tantra, there is a tradition of worshipping Devi as Kumari, not in the form of young girls, on the nine days of Navaratri—Kumari on pratipada, Trimurti on dvitiya, Kalyani on tritiya, Rohini on chaturthi, Kalikaa on panchami, Chandikaa on shashthi, Sambhavi on saptami, Durgaa on ashtami and Bhadraa on navami. Yes, practices vary.

Durgaa Pujaa

As you probably know, the United Nations Educational, Scientific and Cultural Organization (UNESCO) has a system of inscribing tangible and intangible heritage, which are important enough to belong to the world's natural and cultural heritage. At the moment, India has 40 such UNESCO-inscribed world heritage sites. Examples of natural ones are Kaziranga and Manas wildlife sanctuaries. Out of the present list of 40, 32 have been labelled as cultural and 7 have been labelled as natural. A national park in Sikkim has been labelled as mixed heritage—it is part natural and part cultural heritage.

When we think of tangible cultural heritage sites, we tend to think of caves, forts, temples, monuments, heritage buildings, even the mountain railways. You may not know that all such heritage sites need not be tangible. Late in 2021, UNESCO added Kolkata's Durgaa Pujaa to the list of intangible heritage items,[4] making it one of the 40.

In the eastern parts of the country, there used to be three types of Durgaa Pujaa. The first category consisted of Durgaa Pujaa as hosted by noble and aristocratic families,

[4]'Durga Pujaa inscribed on the UNESCO Representative List of the Intangible Cultural Heritage of Humanity', UNESCO, 15 December 2021, https://bit.ly/3yn5NXZ. Accessed on 27 June 2022.

some of whom were historically zamindars. These go back to the seventeenth century, and some of these famous pujaas are now hosted in Bangladesh. The most famous of these is Tahirpur, associated with the name of Raja Kansa Narayan. As these noble and aristocratic families declined in importance, those pujaas also died out. The second type of Durgaa Pujaa was associated with a *math* or mandir. Monks reside in maths, and no specific deity is worshipped there. For example, a Durgaa Pujaa still takes place in Kolkata's Belur Math. In contrast, a mandir is a temple where a deity permanently resides. Traditionally, Durgaa Pujaa was hosted in such mandirs. The third type of Durgaa Pujaa is the one that has taken over now. Members of a community gather, contribute money and perform the pujaa. To the extent that the first and second types of Durgaa Pujaas still remain, they follow their own rules and methods of worship, with their own iconography about Durgaa's image. What is now considered the standard Durgaa Pujaa starts on saptami and ends on navami, and it uses a certain kind of Durgaa image. But that's because the third kind of Durgaa Pujaa has taken over the first two.

There are different kalpas or modes for Durgaa Pujaa and all of these are acceptable. Mahalaya falls on amavasyaa in the month of Bhadra. It is a day when oblations are offered to the ancestors and the Pitri Paksha (the fortnight associated with the ancestors) ends. From the pratipada in the ensuing shukla paksha, Devi Paksha (the fortnight associated with Devi) starts. All the following forms of Durgaa Pujaa perfectly conform to what all texts say:

1. commencing with krishna paksha navami in the fortnight preceding Mahalaya and ending with shukla paksha navami in Ashvina;
2. commencing with shukla paksha pratipada in Ashvina

and ending on navami;
3. commencing with shukla paksha shashti in Ashvina and ending on navami;
4. commencing with shukla paksha saptami in Ashvina and ending on navami; and
5. commencing on shukla paksha ashtami and ending on navami.

Durations of 15, 9, 4, 3 and 2 days are all possible for Durgaa Pujaa. One shouldn't presume point (4) as the only way of celebrating Durgaa Pujaa, with 3 days being the only type. Indeed, Durgaa Pujaa can also be done for a day, on shukla paksha ashtami or shukla paksha navami. You possibly haven't heard of these other kalpas because these practices have been standardized over time.

The pujaa starts with worshipping a bilva tree. Then, the nine plants (नवपत्रिका) are worshipped. Traditionally, these plants include plantain, turmeric, jayanti (sesbania), bilva, pomegranate, arum, paddy, colocasia and ashoka. A kalasha must be used, marked with the sign of a swastika. Invoking waters from all the rivers and tirthas in some Gangaa water, the priest purifies himself. In the due order, the standard Gayatri Mantra is recited and Ganesha, Vishnu, Surya, Shiva, among other deities, are worshipped. Using *upachara* (offerings), one can then commence the Durgaa Pujaa. The Sandhi Pujaa (in the intervening period between two tithis) and the Arddha-Ratri Pujaa (conducted at midnight) are of particular significance. Naturally, the actual process is much more complicated. These are just the bare minimum principles.

The Nine Durgaas

You may have heard of Nava Durgaa (the nine forms of Durgaa) and must also be familiar with their names. The navapatrikaa I mentioned are associated with nine forms of Durgaa—Brahmani, Raktadantikaa, Shakrohitaa, Kalikaa, Durgaa, Kartiki, Shivaa, Chamundaa and Lakshmi. You may have heard of another set of Nava Durgaa names—Shailaputri, Brahmacharini, Chandraghantaa, Kushmandaa, Skandamataa, Katyayani, Kalaratri, Mahagouri and Siddhidatri. This list is indeed more common and familiar. The names included here depend entirely on the kalpa being used for the pujaa. In the Shiva Purana, we have another list of nine Durgaas who joined Virabhadra when he went to destroy Daksha's sacrifice. As should be obvious, there is a correspondence between nine nights of Navaratri, nine forms of Nava Durgaa, Navapatrikaa and Navagraha (nine planets).

The Nava Durgaa Stotram[5] describes the forms of the Nava Durgaas. Let's take a look at the verses one by one. The chakras described in the verses are centres of meditation within the body, ascending upwards, though the 'body' needs to be understood in the sense of the subtle body, not the physical body. In yoga and tantra, six or seven chakras have been mentioned. More on this later.

> देवी शैलपुत्री ।
> वन्दे वाञ्छितलाभाय चन्द्रार्धकृतशेखराम् ।
> वृषारूढां शूलधरां शैलपुत्रीं यशस्विनीम् ॥
>
> To obtain what I desire, I worship Devi Shailaputri. The half-moon is on her crest, and she is astride a bull. The illustrious Shailaputri holds a trident.

Shailaputri means the daughter of a mountain (Himalaya). This is Devi in her childhood. In iconography, Shailaputri is shown with two hands. She is established in the Muladhara Chakra (more on chakras later) and is worshipped on pratipada.

---

[5]'Nava Durga Stotram,' Sanskrit Documents, https://bit.ly/3bQ6vUA. Accessed on 5 July 2022.

देवी ब्रह्मचारिणी ।
दधाना करपद्माभ्यामक्षमालाकमण्डलू ।
देवी प्रसीदतु मयि ब्रह्मचारिण्यनुत्तमा ॥

In her two lotus hands, she holds a string of *aksha* (*rudraksha*) beads and a *kamandalu* (water-pot). May the excellent Devi Brahmacharini be pleased with me.

Brahmacharini means someone who is observing *brahmacharya*. This represents Parvati during her tapasya. In iconography, she is shown as an ascetic, dressed in white, with two hands. She is established in the Svadhishthana Chakra and worshipped on dvitiya.

देवी चन्द्रघण्टेति ।
पिण्डजप्रवरारूढा चण्डकोपास्त्रकैर्युता ।
प्रसादं तनुते मह्यं चन्द्रघण्टेति विश्रुता ॥

O one who is astride the best of mammals! You are terrible in your rage and possess weapons. O famous Chandraghantaa! Please extend your blessings to me.

You will see all kinds of explanations for the name 'Chandraghantaa.' 'Chandra' means the moon and Chandraghantaa is identified with Shiva's Shakti, when Shiva is in the form of Chandrashekhara. Chandraghantaa is Devi's form as Chandikaa, when she rides into battle to slay asuras. 'Ghantaa' means a bell, and Chandraghantaa is the one who holds a bell. When she rides into battle to fight asuras, the sound of her bell stupefies them. Despite the many explanations for Chandraghantaa, I think the name is a reference to the moon and the bell. *Pindaja* means something born from a lump—it means a mammal, as opposed to something born from an egg, like a bird or a reptile. Despite being Chandikaa's terrible form, in iconography, Chandraghantaa's form is quite amiable. She possesses ten arms and rides a tiger or a lion.

However, iconography is not standardized. Typically, in her ten hands, she holds a trident, a mace, a bow, an arrow, a sword, a lotus, a string of beads, a bell and a water-pot. The last hand is in Abhaya Mudraa, which signifies freedom from fear. If the bow and arrow are held in the same hand, the additional hand is in Varada Mudraa, which signifies the granting of boons. She is established in the Manipura Chakra and is worshipped on tritiya.

देवी कूष्मांडा ।
सुरासम्पूर्णकलशं रुधिराप्लुतमेव च ।
दधाना हस्तपद्माभ्यां कूष्माण्डा शुभदास्तु मे ॥

In her two lotus hands, she holds a pitcher full of liquor and a pitcher overflowing with blood. May Kushmandaa bestow everything auspicious upon me.

Asked for the meaning of the word *kushmandaa*, most people will say pumpkin or ash-gourd. While that's not wrong, words have multiple meanings. Kushmandaa also means the foetus in a womb. Devi, as Kushmandaa, is the energy behind the creation of the cosmic egg, Brahmanda. Another explanation comes from breaking the word as such: कु+उष्म+अण्ड. So, Kushmandaa is the one who offered a little warmth to the egg. As the iconography for this form of Devi is not standardized, Kushmandaa is often shown with eight hands. Two hands hold the two pitchers. The others hold a lotus, a chakra, a bow, an arrow, a mace and a water-pot. If the image has ten hands, there usually is a string of rudraksha beads, and the last hand is in Abhaya Mudraa. She is established in the Anahata Chakra and is worshipped on chaturthi.

देवीस्कन्दमाता ।
सिंहासनगता नित्यं पद्माश्रितकरद्वया ।
शुभदास्तु सदा देवी स्कन्दमाता यशस्विनी ॥

She is always astride her seat on a lion. In two hands, she holds two lotuses. May the illustrious Devi Skandamataa always bestow what is auspicious on me.

Skandamataa is obvious enough. She is Skanda's mother. Seated atop a lion, she holds Skanda in her lap. In the usual iconography, she is depicted with four hands. Two of these hold lotuses. Of the other two hands, one holds Skanda, while the other is in Abhaya Mudraa. She is established in the Vishuddha (vishuddhi) Chakra and is worshipped on panchami.

देवीकात्यायनी ।
चन्द्रहासोज्ज्वलकरा शार्दूलवरवाहना ।
कात्यायनी शुभं दद्यादेवी दानवघातिनी ॥

The shining Chandrahasa is in her hand. Her mount is an excellent tiger. May Devi Katyayani, who slays *danava*s, bestow all that is auspicious on me.

You will recall that to destroy Mahishasura, the collective energies of devas were brought together to manifest Devi. Where did this happen? It happened in the hermitage of the Sage Katyayana. Therefore, Devi is Katyayani, Sage Katyayana's daughter. It is difficult to translate the word *chandrahasa* in English. 'Scimitar' is a bad attempt at finding an equavialent. It is a type of sword that rivals the moon in its resplendence. It is a sword that resembles a half-moon at the tip. It is a sword that Devi always wields. Apart from being seated on a tiger, Katyayani's iconography is standardized even less. For instance, the number of arms can be anything between two and 18. She is established in the Ajna Chakra and is worshipped on shashthi.

देवीकालरात्रि ।
एकवेणी जपाकर्णपूरा नग्ना खरास्थिता ।
लम्बोष्ठी कर्णिकाकर्णी तैलाभ्यक्तशरीरिणी ॥

वामपादोल्लसल्लोहलताकण्टकभूषणा ।
वर्धन्मूर्धध्वजा कृष्णा कालरात्रिर्भयङ्करी ॥

She has a single braid of hair. She wears *japa* (hibiscus) flowers in her ears. She is naked and astride a donkey. Her lips are elongated and hang down. She wears *karnika* ornaments in her ears.[6] Her body is smeared with oil. Her shining left foot is adorned with iron ornaments and thorny creepers. Her abundant and flowing hair is dark. Kalaratri is terrible.

We have already encountered the name Kalaratri earlier. She is the terrible dark night of destruction. She is Kali, the destroyer of demons. In the Mahabharata, when Ashvatthama kills many Pandavas in the middle of the night, it is Kalaratri who appears before him. This more or less describes Kalaratri's iconography, who is often equated with Kali's image. She is established in the Sahasrara Chakra and is worshipped on saptami.

देवीमहागौरी ।
श्वेते वृषे समारूढा श्वेताम्बरधरा शुचिः ।
महागौरी शुभं दद्यान्महादेवप्रमोददा ॥

She is astride a white bull. She is the pure one, attired in white garments. She is the one who causes delight to Mahadeva. May Mahagouri bestow all that is auspicious on me.

Gouri is the fair one, and Mahagouri is the great Gouri. These are Devi's forms when the demons have been destroyed, and Devi seems to be returning to Kailasa to meet Mahadeva, astride a white bull. For those into tantra, it is as if the ascent up the chakras is over. In standard iconography, Mahagouri

---

[6]While karnika is a kind of earring, it also means the pericarp of a lotus.

is depicted with four hands. Two of these hold a trident and a *damaru* (the hourglass-shaped drum that Shiva plays). The other two are in Abhaya and Varada mudraas. Mahagouri is worshipped on ashtami.

देवीसिद्धिदात्रि ।
सिद्धगन्धर्वयक्षाद्यैरसुरैरमरैरपि ।
सेव्यमाना सदा भूयात् सिद्धिदा सिद्धिदायिनी ॥

For the sake of obtaining siddhi, she is always served by *siddhas*, *gandharvas*, *yakshas*, asuras and immortals. May the bestower of siddhi bestow that on us too.

Siddhidatri is the one who bestows siddhi. Loosely, *siddhi* means success in the process of sadhana. Siddhis mean powers. Specifically, yoga leads to eight major siddhis or powers. These are *anima* (the ability to become as small as one desires), *mahima* (the ability to become as large as one desires), *laghima* (the ability to become as light as one wants), *garima* (the ability to become as heavy as one wants), *prapti* (the ability to obtain what one wants), *prakamya* (the ability to travel where one wants), *vashitvam* (the power to control creatures) and *ishitvam* (the ability to obtain divine powers). Siddhidhatri is Devi's ultimate form, and she is worshipped on navami. In common iconography, she is seated on a lotus or a lion. Her four hands hold a mace, a conch shell, a lotus and a chakra.

The Dasha Mahavidyaa

We must also mention Devi's ten forms as Dasha Mahavidyaa (दश महाविद्या). These forms are especially worshipped when one follows tantra. The names of the ten Mahavidyaas can vary. But they are usually mentioned as Kali, Taraa, Tripurasundari, Bhuvaneshvari, Chhinnamastaa, Bhairavi, Dhumavati,

Bagalamukhi, Matangi and Kamalaa (Shodhashi). There is an Upapurana, known as the Mahabhagavata Purana, which narrates a story about how the ten Mahavidyaas manifested themselves. It is connected to Daksha's yajna, which Sati wanted to go to. When Shiva tried to restrain her, Sati showed Shiva her ten terrible forms, in ten directions, scaring him in the process. Kali was in front of Shiva, Taraa was above, Chhinnamastaa was on his right, Bhuvaneshvari was on his left, Bagalamukhi was behind him, Dhumavati was towards the south-east, Tripurasundari was towards the south-west, Matangi was towards the north-west, Shodhashi was towards the north-east and Sati herself was Bhairavi. Convinced by Sati's terrible forms, Shiva let her go.

With a natural correspondence between the ten directions and ten Mahavidyaas, there is a Dasha Mahavidyaa kavacha mantra. The word *kavacha* means armour, and a kavacha mantra protects the devotee in ten directions—north, north-east, east, south-east, south, south-west, west, north-west, above and below. Each of these directions is associated with a Bhairava (Shiva's form). Sometimes, a natural correspondence is drawn between Vishnu's ten avataras and the ten Mahavidyaas. The ten Mahavidyaas reside in Manidvipa. This is Devi's abode, described in detail in the Devi Bhagavata Purana.

In tantra, the iconography of ten Mahadvidyaas has mystical significance. Let's look at a few examples. First, Kali has many different forms. Next time you see an image or picture of Kali, count the number of skulls in her garland of skulls. Is it 51 or 108—the two numbers we have come across earlier? When she is standing on Shiva, is her right foot slightly ahead or is her left foot slightly ahead? These details often indicate whether the right-handed or left-handed path of tantra is being followed by the devotee. When she is depicted with four hands, are the Abhaya and Varada mudraas on the right or the left hand? This book is not meant to answer these questions or get into all the mystical significance of the iconography, but I am only suggesting that you should notice these details and understand their significance.

Second, Taraa is Devi's form, which enables a person to cross over the ocean that is *samsara*. This is based on the etymology of the word for crossing over. Taraa, too, has many forms, but whatever the form, look at an image of Taraa in detail. It is very easy to confuse Kali with Taraa. But invariably, Taraa is blue, while Kali is dark. In all probability, Kali has her right foot slightly forward, while Taraa has her left foot slightly forward.

Third, Tripurasundari is also known as Shodhashi or Lalitaa. Although, as discussed in the reference to the Mahabhagavata Purana earlier, Shodhashi is equated with Kamalaa. 'Shodashi' means someone who is 16 years old, and that is the form Tripurasundari is usually depicted in, seated on a lotus.

Fourth, when you look at Bhuvaneshvari's image or picture, is her complexion red? It should be. Everything about her should be red—ornaments, garlands, garments. Fifth, unlike Bhuvaneshvari, Chhinnamastaa is meant to look terrible. She has severed her own head, symbolic of the destruction of mayaa, the transient universe and ego. Why do you think there are three flows of blood emerging from her severed head?

Sixth, Bhairavi is also meant to be terrible, but not as terrible as Chhinnamastaa. Typically, there aren't any weapons in her hands, but she wears a garland of skulls around her neck. Seventh, Dhumavati is depicted as an aged widow. Why a widow? Because Purusha has been destroyed, and she is the Shakti that is left. Eighth, in iconography, everything about Bagalamukhi is yellow. The name should actually be written as Vagalamukhi, but it is invariably written as Bagalamukhi. Since the word *bagala* (not *vagala*) means crane in some non-

Sanskrit languages (it doesn't have any specific meaning in Sanskrit), the word Bagalamukhi is interpreted as the goddess with the head of a crane, and she is often depicted accordingly. I prefer a derivation based on the etymology of her being the goddess who restrains and reins in. Ninth, Matangi is a manifestation of Sarasvati and, in all probability, her image holds a veena. This leaves the tenth example of Kamalaa, a manifestation of Lakshmi, seated atop a lotus. I realize I have only piqued your interest about the iconography of the ten Mahavidyaas and have not given detailed explanations. But, in this book, this has been my limited intention—to pique your attention and get you to probe into such topics.

Sapta-shloki Stotram from Devi Bhagavata Purana

Towards the end of the Devi Bhagavata Purana, there is a mention of a stotram dedicated to Devi through seven slokas. Devi told Shiva that in Kali Yuga, this is the best stotram to worship Devi. Out of the seven slokas, two are the same as the Narayani Suktam from Devi Mahatmya. Let us conclude this chapter with the Sapta-shloki Stotram from Devi Bhagavata Purana.

ॐ ज्ञानिनामपि चेतांसि देवि भगवती हि सा ।
बलादाकृष्य मोहाय महामाया प्रयच्छति ॥ (1)

OUM! Devi Bhagavati is the one who uses force to take away the consciousness of those who possess *jnana*. Mahamayaa is the one who bestows this delusion.

दुर्गे स्मृता हरसि भीतिमशेषजन्तोः
स्वस्थैः स्मृता मतिमतीव शुभां ददासि ।
दारिद्र्यदुःखभयहारिणि का त्वदन्या
सर्वोपकारकरणाय सदार्द्र चित्ता ॥ (2)

O Durgaa! You are the one who takes away every kind

of fear from creatures who remember you. When you are remembered, you ensure all is well. You bestow auspicious intelligence. Who other than you can take away poverty, misery and fear? Your mind is always wet with compassion to take away every kind of harm.

सर्वमङ्गलमाङ्गल्ये शिवे सर्वार्थसाधिके ।
शरण्ये त्र्यम्बके गौरि नारायणि नमोऽस्तु ते ॥ (3)

O beneficial one! O one who brings about every kind of auspiciousness! O Shivaa! O one who ensures every kind of success! O refuge! O three-eyed one! O Gouri! O Narayani! I prostrate myself before you.

शरणागतदीनार्तपरित्राणपरायणे ।
सर्वस्यार्तिहरे देवि नारायणि नमोऽस्तु ते ॥ (4)

O one who is devoted to saving the distressed and afflicted who seek refuge with you! O one who ends the afflictions of all! O Devi! O Narayani! I prostrate myself before you.

सर्वस्वरूपे सर्वेशे सर्वशक्तिसमन्विते ।
भयेभ्यस्त्राहि नो देवि दुर्गे देवी नमोऽस्तु ते ॥ (5)

O one who is in every kind of form and in all the lords! O one who possesses every kind of Shakti! Please save us from all fears. O Devi Durgaa! I prostrate myself before you.

रोगानशेषानपहंसि तुष्टा रुष्टा तु कामान् सकलानभीष्टान् ।
त्वामाश्रितानां न विपन्नराणां त्वामाश्रिता ह्याश्रयतां प्रयान्ति ॥ (6)

When you are pleased, you destroy all ailments. But when you are angry, you destroy everything desired. Men who seek refuge with you never suffer. Those who seek refuge with you give refuge to others.

सर्वाबाधाप्रशमनं त्रैलोक्यस्याखिलेश्वरि ।
एवमेव त्वया कार्यमस्मद्वैरि विनाशनम् ॥ (7)

You are the one who destroys all impediments. You are Ishvari over everything in the three worlds. This way, your task is to destroy our enemies.

five

DEVI'S ONE THOUSAND NAMES

We have already encountered several of Devi's names. I have mentioned that Tripurasundari is also known as Lalitaa (ललिता). One of the most famous lists of Devi's names is Lalitaa Sahasranama, the one thousand names of Lalitaa. Some people think that Lalitaa Sahasranama is part of the Brahmanda Purana.[1] That's not quite true. The Brahmanda Purana does tell us about Lalitaa and about her manifestation to kill an asura named Bhanda.

The Lalitaa Sahasranama

Most people know the story about Shiva burning down Kama or Madana, the god of love, in rage. Bhandasura was born from that rage. Because of his strength and prowess, Bhandasura became insolent and oppressive. In turn, Devi manifested as Lalitaa and killed him.

However, before this happened, the devas recited a beautiful eulogy to Lalitaa, entreating her to kill Bhandasura. I will quote it but without the Sanskrit. I will also focus on some of Devi's names, at least the shorter ones.

---

[1]'Lalitha Sahasranamam - Divine mother's 1000 names,' Abirami Ashram, https://bit.ly/3B8NpDT. Accessed on 22 July 2022.

O Devi! Victory to you. O mother of the universe! Victory to you. O Devi! You are greater than the greatest. O abode of auspiciousness! Victory to you. O one who knows about the arts of love! Victory to you. O Vamakshi (वामाक्षि)![2] You are the one who brings about victory. O beautiful Kamakshi (कामाक्षि)![3] Victory to you.

O one who deserves to be worshipped by all the gods! Victory to you. O Kameshi (कामेशि)![4] O one who bestows honours! O Brahmamayi (ब्रह्ममयि)! Victory to you. O Devi! O one who represents the essence of the Brahman! O Narayani (नारायणि)! Victory to you. O supreme one!

O one who bestows delight on the entire world! O one who is loved by Shrikantha![5] Victory to you. O illustrious Lalitaa![6] O Ambikaa (अम्बिका)![7] Victory to you. O one who conquers prosperity! Victory to you. O Devi!

O one who bestows victory, wealth and prosperity! You are the cause behind what has been born and will be born, the cause behind *ishta* and *purti*.[8] I prostrate myself before the one who preserves the three worlds. You are greater than the greatest. Your atman possesses kalaa, *muhurta*, kashthaa, days, months, seasons and years![9] I prostrate myself before the one with one thousand heads, one thousand faces and one thousand eyes. I prostrate

---

[2]Vamakshi is someone with beautiful eyes.

[3]Kamakshi is someone with desirable eyes.

[4]Kameshi can be translated in various ways. The desired Ishvari (Ishi) is one possibility.

[5]Shrikantha is the one with the beautiful throat—Shiva.

[6]Lalitaa can be translated in different ways. The beautiful one will do.

[7]Ambikaa can be translated as mother.

[8]Ishta can loosely be translated as sacrifices, while purti stands for civic works.

[9]All these are different units for measuring time.

myself before the one who is adorned with one thousand hands and feet that resemble lotuses.

You are smaller than the smallest. O Devi! You are greater than the greatest. You are beyond the supreme. O mother! You are more energetic than the most energetic. Your feet are Atala.[10] Your knees are Vitala. The area around your waist is Rasatala. The earth is your stomach. Bhuvarloka is your heart, and Svarloka is said to be your face. The sun, moon and fire are your eyes. O Ambikaa! The directions are your arms. The wind is your breath, and all the Shruti texts are your speech. The creation of the worlds is your sport. Shiva, full of consciousness, is your friend. Your foods are truth and bliss. You reside in the hearts of the virtuous. The worlds are your forms—visible and invisible. The clouds are your hair, and the stars are flowers in your hair. Dharma and the others are your arms. *Adharma* and the others are your weapons. *Yama* and *niyama* are the nails on your hands and feet.[11] Your breasts are utterances of svahaa and svadhaa, which bring life to the worlds. *Pranayama* is your nose. Your tongue is Sarasvati. Your senses are *pratyahara*.

O excellent one! Dhyana is your intelligence. *Dharanaa* is your mind, and *samadhi* is your heart. The large trees are the hair on your limbs. Dawn is your garment. The past, present and future are always your images. O Jagaddhatri (जगद्धातृ)![12] Sacrifice is your form. O Vishvarupaa (विश्वरूपा)![13] You are the one who sanctifies.

---

[10]There are seven nether worlds—Atala, Vitala, Sutala, Rasatala, Talatala, Mahatala and Patala.

[11]To understand the terms yama, niyama, pratyahara, dharanaa and samadhi, see p. 134.

[12]Jagaddhatri is the one who sustains the universe.

[13]Vishvarupaa is the one with the universe as a form.

In the beginning, out of compassion, it is she who created all beings. She is in in the hearts of everyone. However, because of delusion, she cannot be seen. In her own pastimes, she creates the divisions of her names and forms. She is established, and she presides. But she is not attached. She is the one who bestows *artha* and *kama*.

I prostrate myself before Mahadevi. I prostrate myself before the one who is every kind of Shakti. I bow down. It is because of her command that fire, the sun, the moon, the winds and earth and all the elements function. I prostrate myself before that Devi. I bow down. At the beginning of creation, she is the one who created Vidhatri. She is the one who bestowed the original prosperity. She alone is the one who sustains. I prostrate myself before that Devi. I bow down. She is the one who holds up earth and space. She is immeasurable. The sun rises because of her. I prostrate myself before that Devi. I bow down. The entire universe rises because of her and is established in her, is sustained. At the time of destruction, it is into her that it merges. I prostrate myself before that Devi. I bow down. I prostrate myself.

I bow down before the rajas that is the origin. I prostrate myself. I bow down before the sattva that preserves. I prostrate myself. I bow down before the tamas that destroys. I prostrate myself. I bow down before Shivaa (शिवा),[14] who is devoid of gunas. I prostrate myself. I bow down before the only Mother of the Universe. I prostrate myself. I bow down before the only Father of the Universe. I prostrate myself. I bow down before the one who assumes all the forms in tantra. I prostrate myself. I bow down before the one who assumes all the forms in yantra. I prostrate myself. I bow down before the one who

[14]Shivaa refers to the auspicious one.

is the Supreme Guru in the worlds. I prostrate myself. I bow down before the one who is every kind of splendour in speech. I prostrate myself before Lakshmi, the only one who brings satisfaction to the universe. I prostrate myself. I bow down before Shambhavi (शाम्भवी),[15] who possesses every kind of Shakti.

You do not have a beginning, a middle or an end. You are not made out of the five elements. You cannot be reached through words or thoughts. You are beyond debate. You are without form and devoid of the opposite pair of sentiments.[16] You cannot be perceived through sight. Your power is great. O Ambaa (अम्बा)![17] How can you be described? O Vishveshvari (विश्वेश्वरी)![18] Be pleased. O Vishvavanditaa (विश्ववंदिता)![19] Be pleased. O Vedarupini (वेदरूपिणी)![20] O Mayamayi (मायामयी)![21] Be pleased. O Mantravigrahaa (मन्त्रविग्रहा)![22] Be pleased. O Sarveshvari (सर्वेश्वरी)![23] O Sarvarupini (सर्वरूपिणी)![24]

Thus prayed to and eulogized by devas, Lalitaa killed Bhandasura.

---

[15]Shambhavi has several meanings. Naturally, Shambhu (Shiva) and Shambhavi go together. But Shambhavi also means possibility and is the hole in the crown of the head, through which emancipation is achieved. Thus, Shambhavi represents the possibility of liberation from this world. Shambhavi also means *sushumna nadi.*

[16]For instance, hot and cold, joy and misery, and so on.

[17]Ambaa means mother.

[18]Vishveshvari refers to the Ishvari of the universe.

[19]Vishvavanditaa is the one who is worshipped by the universe.

[20]Vedarupini is the one whose form is the Vedas.

[21]Mayamayi is the one who is full of mayaa.

[22]Mantravigrahaa is the one whose form is made out of mantras.

[23]Sarveshvari refers to the Ishvari of everyone/everything.

[24]Sarvarupini is the one who is in all forms.

Lalitaa's Names

The Brahmanda Purana tells us many other things about Lalitaa. The entire section about Lalitaa's names is spoken by Vishnu, as Hayagriva, to Sage Agastya. It describes Devi's abode of Shripura or Shrinagari. Lalitaa is associated with the number 16. The devas requested her to divide herself into 16 forms, since they planned to construct 16 cities for her. Nine of these are on earth, in the mountains—Meru, Nishadha, Hemakuta, Himalaya, Gandhamadana, Nila, Mesha, Shringara and Mahendra. The remaining seven are in the seven oceans. She is associated with 16 coverings. Her lotuses have 16 petals. Her chakras (as in wheels) have 16 spokes. She is worshipped with 16 offerings (upachara). Because of the number 16, Lalitaa gets identified with Shodashi. There are many other beautiful and mystical details we will skip.

If you read that the Brahmanda Purana has sections on Lalitaa Mahatyma (Lalitaa's greatness), that is correct. If you read that Brahmanda Purana has sections on Lalitaa Upakhyana (Lalitaa's Account), that is also correct. But if you read that Brahmanda Purana has Lalitaa Sahasranama (the text with Lalitaa's one thousand names), that is not quite correct. It does have a mantra with one thousand aksharas that has several additional names for Lalitaa/Devi. While the mantra has not been reproduced in the book, Lalitaa's names from it have been listed below. The names mentioned here do not add up to one thousand aksharas, since there are other expressions as part of the mantra. Naturally, the numbering doesn't exist in the original text. Although I have provided meanings of each of these names, it is necessary to note that more than one meaning is possible for some of the names. And sometimes, it is difficult to distinguish an adjective from a proper name.

Table 5: Devi's names from the Lalitaa Sahasranama, and their meanings

Name of Devi	*Name in Devanagari*	*Meaning of the name*
Tripurasundari	त्रिपुरसुन्दरी	
Hridayedevi	हृदयेदेवी	Devi in the heart
Shirodevi	शिरोदेवी	Devi in the head
Shikhadevi	शिखादेवी	Devi in the a tuft of hair
Kavachadevi	कवचदेवी	Devi in the kavacha
Netradevi	नेत्रदेवी	Devi in the eyes
Asyadevi	आस्यदेवी	Devi in the face
Kameshvari	कामेश्वरी	Ishvari of desire or Ishvari of the god of love
Bhagamalini	भगमालिनी	The one with a garland of suns
Nityaklinnaa	नित्यक्लिन्ना	The one who is always moist
Bherundaa	भेरुण्डा	The the terrible one
Vahnivasini	वह्निवासिनी	The one who resides in the fire
Mahavajreshvari	महावज्रेश्वरी	Ishvari who is like the great Vajra
Vidyeshvari	विद्येश्वरी	Ishvari of learning
Parashivaduti	परशिवदूती	The supreme Shiva's messenger
Tvaritaa	त्वरिता	The swift one
Kulasundari	कुलसुन्दरी	The beautiful one from of lineage

Nityaa	नित्या	The eternal one
Nilapatakaa	नीलपताका	The one with a blue banner
Vijayaa	विजया	The victorious one
Sarvamangalaa	सर्वमङ्गला	The one who is everything auspicious
Jvalamalini	ज्वालामालिनी	The one with a garland of flames
Chitraa	चित्रा	The colourful one
Mahanityaa	महानित्या	The great and eternal one
Parameshvari	परमेश्वरी	The Supreme Ishvari
Mantreshamayi	मन्त्रेशमयी	The one who is full of the lord of mantras
Shashtishamayi	षष्ठीशमयी	The one who is full of the lord of shashthi
Udyanamayi	उद्यानमयी	The one full of gardens
Lopamudramayi	लोपामुद्रामयी	The one who fills Lopamudraa (Agastya's wife)
Agastyamayi	अगस्त्यमयी	The one who fills Agastya
Kalatapanamayi	कालतापनमयी	The one who is full of the one who scorched the Destroyer, that is, Shiva, who destroyed Kala

Dharmacharamayi	धर्माचारमयी	The one who fills the good conduct of dharma
Muktakeshishvaramayi	मुक्तकेशीश्वरमयी	The one who is full of the lord of the one with loose hair (Devi herself)
Dipa-kalanathamayi	दीपकलानाथमयी	The one who fills lamps and the lord of kalaas (the moon)
Vishnudevamayi	विष्णुदेवमयी	The one who fills the divinity Vishnu
Prabhakara-devamayi	प्रभाकरदेवमयी	The one who fills the divinity that is the sun
Tejodevamayi	तेजोदेवमयी	The one who fills the divinity that is energy
Manojadevamayi	मनोजदेवमयी	The one who fills the divinity that is the god of love
Animasiddhaa	अणिमासिद्धा	The one who possesses the siddhi of anima
Mahimasiddhaa	महिमासिद्धा	The one who possesses the siddhi of mahima
Garimasiddhaa	गरिमासिद्धा	The one who possesses the siddhi of garima
Laghimasiddhaa	लघिमासिद्धा	The one who possesses the siddhi of laghima

Ishitvasiddhaa	ईशित्वसिद्धा	The one who possesses the siddhi of ishitva
Vashitvasiddhaa	वशित्वसिद्धा	The one who possesses the siddhi of vashitva
Praptisiddhaa	प्राप्तिसिद्धा	The one who possesses the siddhi of prapti
Prakamyasiddhaa	प्रकाम्यसिद्धा	The one who possesses the siddhi of prakamya
Rasasiddhaa	रससिद्धा	The one who possesses siddhi in rasa; the word rasa can be interpreted in multiple ways
Mokshasiddhaa	मोक्षसिद्धा	The one who possesses siddhi in the bestowing of moksha
Brahmi	ब्राह्मी	
Maheshvari	माहेश्वरी	
Koumari	कौमारी	
Vaishnavi	वैष्णवी	
Varahi	वाराही	
Indrani	इन्द्रानी	
Chamundaa	चामुण्डा	
Mahalakshmi	महालक्ष्मी	
Sarvasamkshobhini	सर्वसंक्षोभिणी	The one who agitates everything

Sarvavidravini	सर्वविद्राविणी	The one who drives away everything
Sarvakarshini	सर्वाकर्षिणी	The one who attracts everything
Sarvavashankari	सर्ववशङ्करी	The one who subjugates everything
Sarvonmadini	सर्वन्मादिनी	The one who maddens everyone
Sarvamahamkushaa	सर्वमहांकुशा	The great goad for everyone
Sarvakhechari	सर्वखेचरी	The one who travels everywhere in the sky
Sarvabijaa	सर्वबीजा	The seed for everything
Sarvayoni	सर्वयोनी	The womb of everything
Sarvastrakhandini	सर्वास्त्रखंण्डिनी	The one who shatters all weapons
Trailokyamohini	त्रैलोक्यमोहिनी	The one who deludes the three worlds
Chakrasvamini	चक्रस्वामिनी	The owner of the chakra
Prakatayogini	प्रकटयोगिनी	The one who manifests as a yogini
Bouddhadarshanangi	बौद्धदर्शनांगी	The one whose limbs have Bouddha darshana
Kamakarshini	कामाकर्षिणी	The one who attracts desire

[25]Ahamkara means ego, with the nuance, 'I am the doer.'

Buddhyakarshini	बुद्ध्याकर्षिणी	The one who attracts intelligence
Ahamkarakarshini	अहंकारकर्षिणी	The one who attracts ahamkara[25]
Shabdakarshini	शब्दाकर्षिणी	The one who attracts sound
Sparshakarshini	स्पर्शाकर्षिणी	The one who attracts touch
Rupakarshini	रुपाकर्षिणी	The one who attracts form
Rasakarshini	रसाकर्षिणी	The one who attracts rasa
Gandhakarshini	गन्धाकर्षिणी	The one who attracts smell
Chittakarshini	चित्ताकर्षिणी	The one who attracts the mind
Dhairyakarshini	धैर्याकर्षिणी	The one who attracts patience
Smrityakarshini	स्मृत्याकर्षिणी	The one who attracts memory
Namakarshini	नामाकर्षिणी	The one who attracts names
Bijakarshini	बीजाकर्षिणी	The one who attracts seeds
Atmakarshini	आत्माकर्षिणी	The one who attracts atmans
Amritakarshini	अमृताकर्षिणी	The one who attracts amrita
Sharirakarshini	शरीराकर्षिणी	The one who attracts bodies
Guptayogini	गुप्तयोगिनी	The secret yogini

Sarvasha-paripuraka-chakra-svamini	सर्वाशापरिपूरकचक्रस्वामिनी	The owner of the chakra that fulfils all wishes
Anangakusumaa	अनंगकुसुमा	The one with flowers of the god of love
Anangamekhalaa	अनंगमेखला	The one with the god of love as a girdle
Anangamadini	अनंगमादिनी	The one who maddens the god of love
Ananga-madanaturaa	अनंगमदनातुरा	The one who is full of desire for the god of love
Anangarekhaa	अनंगरेखा	The one with lines of the god of love
Anangavegini	अनंगवेगिनी	The one with the speed of the god of love
Anangankushaa	अनंगांकुशा	The one with the goad of the god of love
Anangamalini	अनंगमालिनी	The one with the garland of the god of love
Guptatarayogini	गुप्ततरयोगिनी	The most secret yogini
Vaidikadarshanangi	वैदिकदर्शनांगी	The one with *darshana*[26] of Vedas as limbs
Sarva-samkshobha-karaka-chakra-svamini	सर्वसंक्षोभकारकचक्रस्वामिनी	The owner of the chakra that causes agitation to everyone

[26]This means insight.

Purvamnayadhidevataa	पूर्वाम्नायाधिदेवता	The presiding divinity of the previous tradition
Shrishtirupaa	सृष्टिरुपा	The one with a form as creation
Sarvahladini	सर्वाह्लादिनी	The one who delights everyone
Sarvasammohini	सर्वसंमोहिनी	The one who enchants everyone
Sarvstambhini	सर्वस्तंभिणी	The one who stupefies everyone
Sarvajrimbhini	सर्वजृंभिणी	The one who makes everyone yawn
Sarvaranjini	सर्वरंजिनी	The one who delights everyone
Sarvarthasadhikaa	सर्वार्थसाधिका	The one who accomplishes every objective
Sarva-sampatprapurini	सर्वसंपत्प्रपूरिणी	The one who fills everything up with every kind of prosperity
Sarvamantramayi	सर्वमन्त्रमयी	The one who is full of every kind of mantra
Sarvadvandakshayakari	सर्वदंद्वक्षयकारी	The one who destroys every kind of duality
Sampradayayogini	सम्प्रदाययोगिनी	The yogini who follows tradition
Souradarshanangi	सौरदर्शनाङ्गी	The one whose limbs represent Surya's darshana

Sarva-soubhagya-dayaka-chakraa	सर्वसौभाग्यदायकचक्रा	The chakra that bestows every kind of good fortune
Sarvasiddhipradaa	सर्वसिद्धिप्रदा	The one who bestows every kind of siddhi
Sarvasampatpradaa	सर्वसम्पत्प्रदा	The one who bestows every kind of prosperity
Sarvapriyankari	सर्वप्रियङ्करी	The one who does what is agreeable for everyone
Sarvamangalakarini	सर्वमङ्गलकारिणी	The one who does everything that is auspicious
Sarvakamapradaa	सर्वकामप्रदा	The one who bestows everything desired
Sarva-duhkha-vimochini	सर्वदु:खविमोचिनी	The one who frees from every kind of misery
Sarvamrityu-prashamini	सर्वमृत्युप्रशमिनी	The one who pacifies death for everyone
Sarvavighnanivarini	सर्वविघ्ननिवारिणी	The one who counters every kind of impediment
Sarvangasundari	सर्वांगसुन्दरी	The one who is beautiful in every limb

[27]It is impossible to render this idea satisfactorily in English. *Kula* means the lineage or family, and rituals and practices have been progressively passed down from one generation to another, particularly in tantra. In general, this is called *kulachara* (the practice of the kula) or *kulamarga* (the path of the kula). Within this strand, there are further subdivisions.

Sarvasoubhagyadayini	सर्वसौभाग्यदायिनी	The one who bestows every kind of good fortune
Kulottirnayogini	कुलोत्तीर्णयोगिनी	The yogini who has gone beyond the kula mode[27]
Sarvarthasadhakachakreshi	सर्वार्थसाधकचक्रेशी	The owner of the chakra that accomplishes all objectives
Sarvajnaa	सर्वज्ञा	The omniscient one
Sarvashakti	सर्वशक्ति	The one possessing every kind of Shakti
Sarvaishvarya-phalapradaa	सर्वैश्वर्यफलप्रदा	The one who bestows every kind of prosperity as fruits
Sarvajnanamayi	सर्वज्ञानमयी	The one possessing every kind of jnana
Sarva-vyadhi-nivarini	सर्वव्याधिनिवारिणी	The one who counters every kind of ailment
Sarvadhara-svarupaa	सर्वाधारस्वरुपा	The one whose form is every kind of support
Sarvapapaharaa	सर्वपापहरा	The one who dispels every kind of sin
Sarvanandamayi	सर्वानन्दमयी	The one who is full of every kind of bliss
Sarva-raksha-svarupini	सर्वरक्षास्वरुपिणी	The one whose form protects everyone
Sarvepsita-phalapradaa	सर्वेप्सितफलप्रदा	The one who bestows every desired fruit

Niyogini	नियोगिनी	The one who engages
Vaishnava-darshanangi	वैष्णवदर्शनाङ्गी	The one whose limbs represent Vaishnava darshana
Sarva-raksha-kara-chakrasthaa	सर्वरक्षाकरचक्रस्था	The one who is established in the chakra that protects everyone
Dakshinamnayeshi	दक्षिणाम्नायेशी	Ishvari of the right-hand tradition
Sthitirupaa	स्थितिरुपा	The one with a form as preservation
Vashini	वशिनी	The one who controls
Modini	मोदिनी	The one who rejoices
Vimalaa	विमला	The sparkling one
Arunaa	अरुणा	The red one
Sarveshvari	सर्वेश्वरी	Ishvari of everything
Koulini	कौलिनी	The one who follows the kula rituals
Rahasyayogini	रहस्ययोगिनी	The mysterious yogini
Rahasyabhogini	रहस्यभोगिनी	The one who is mysterious in enjoying pleasures
Rahasyagopini	रहस्यगोपिनी	The one who protects secrets
Shakta-darshanangi	शक्तदर्शनाङ्गी	The one whose limbs represent Shakta darshana

Sarva-rogahara-chakreshi	सर्वरोगहरचक्रेशी	The owner of the chakra that dispels every kind of ailment
Pashchimnayaa	पश्चिमाम्नया	The follower of the western path
Dhanurbana-pashankusha-devataa	धर्नुर्बाणपाशङ्कुशदेवता	Devi with a bow, arrows, noose and goad
Kameshi	कामेशी	Kama's Ishvari
Vajreshi	वज्रेशी	Vajra's Ishvari
Bhagamalini	भगमालिनी	The one with a garland of good fortune
Ati-rahasyayogini	अतिरहस्ययोगिनी	The extremely mysterious yogini
Shaiva-darshanangi	शैवदर्शनाङ्गी	The one whose limbs represent Shaiva darshana
Sarva-siddhiprada-chakragaa	सर्वसिद्धिप्रदचक्रगा	The one who is in the chakra that bestows every kind of siddhi
Uttaramnayeshi	उत्तराम्नायेशी	Ishvari of the northern path
Samhararupaa	संहाररुपा	The one with the a form of a destroyer
Shuddhaparaa	शुद्धपरा	The pure and supreme
Bindupithagataa	बिन्दुपीठगता	The one based on bindu and the pedestal
Maharatri	महारात्री	The great night

Paraparati	परापराति	The one who is known as greater than the greatest
Shambhava-darshanangi	शाम्भवदर्शनाङ्गी	The one with Shambhu's darshana as limbs
Sarvananda-maya-chakreshi	सर्वानन्दमयचक्रेशी	The owner of the chakra with every kind of bliss
Tripuravasini	त्रिपुरवासिनी	The resident of Tripura
Tripurashri	त्रिपुरश्री	The prosperity of Tripura
Tripuramalini	त्रिपुरमालिनी	The one with Tripura as a garland
Tripurasiddhaa	त्रिपुरसिद्धा	The one with siddhi in Tripura
Tripurambaa	त्रिपुराम्बा	The mother of Tripura
Sarvachakrasthaa	सर्वचक्रस्था	The one present in all the chakras
Anuttaramnayakhyasvarupaa	अनुत्तराम्नायाख्यस्वरुपा	The one whose form is said to be that of the anuttara (absolute) path
Mahatripurabhairavi	महात्रिपुरभैरवी	
Chaturvidha-gunarupaa	चतुर्विधगुणरुपा	The one with a form that has the four kinds of gunas
Kulaa	कुला	The one with a lineage
Akulaa	अकुला	The one without a lineage

Kulakulaa	कुलाकुला	The one with a lineage and without a lineage
Mahakoulini	महाकोलिनी	The one with a great lineage
Sarvottaraa	सर्वोत्तरा	The one beyond everything else
Sarvadarshanangi	सर्वदर्शनाङ्गी	The one whose limbs have every kind of darshana
Navasanastithaa	नवासनस्थिता	The one seated on nine seats
Navakshari	नवाक्षरी	The one with nine aksharas
Navamithunakritaa	नवमिथुनाकृता	The one in the form of a new couple
Mahesha-Madhava-Vidhatri-Manmatha-Skanda-Nandindra-Manu-Chandra-Kuberagastya-Durvasahkrodha-Bhattaraka-vidyatmikaa	महेशमाधवविधातृमन्मथस्कन्दनन्दीन्द्रमनुचन्द्रकुबेरागस्त्यदुर्वास:क्रोद्धभट्टारकविद्यात्मिका	The one whose atman has Mahesha, Madhava, Vidhatri, Manmatha, Skanda, Nandi, Indra, Manu, Chandra, Kubera, the rage of Agastya and Durvasaa and venerable learning
Kalyana-tattva-trayarupaa	कल्याणतत्त्वत्रयरुपा	The one with a form that has the three beneficial truths
Shivashivaatmikaa	शिवशिवात्मिका	The one with an atman that has Shiva and Shivaa

Purnabrahmashakti	पुर्णब्रह्मशक्ति	The one who is full of the Shakti of the Brahman
Maha-parameshvari	महापरमेश्वरी	
Mahatripurasundari	महात्रिपुरसुन्दरी	
Jayini	जयिनी	The victorious one

This section of the Brahmanda Purana is sometimes described as a eulogy with three hundred names. As you can see, I have given you only 193. From the way I have understood this prayer, it is not about the number of names but about the aggregate amounting to one thousand aksharas. Sometimes, it is difficult to separate an adjective from a proper name. Sometimes, the same name has been repeated more than once. It also has bija mantras that I have left out.

However, there is indeed a eulogy that has one thousand names. Such hymns, with one thousand names, occur for other divinities too, including Shiva and Vishnu. You will often hear the Lalitaa Sahasranama being recited and sung, with Shiva having assumed the form of Kameshvara and Devi having assumed the form of Kameshvari. It is not clear who composed Lalitaa Sahasranama. Perhaps several people added to it before it assumed its present form. I have already given you several names. Therefore, I will not give you the names from this text. However, you should read it, for it is a beautiful composition. The verse that is used to perform dhyana on Lalitaa has been reproduced below with a translation.

सिन्दूरारुणविग्रहां त्रिनयनां माणिक्यमौलिस्फुरत्
तारानायकशेखरां स्मितमुखीमापीनवक्षोरुहाम् ।
पाणिभ्यामलिपूर्णरत्नचषकं रक्तोत्पलं बिभ्रतीं
सौम्यां रत्नघटस्थरक्तचरणां ध्यायेत् परामम्बिकाम् ॥

> Her body is as red as vermilion. She has three eyes and a sparkling crown of rubies on her head. The lord of the stars is on her crest. Her face is smiling and her thick breasts rise up. In her two hands, she holds a bejewelled drinking vessel filled with liquor and a shining red lotus. She is amiable, and her red feet are placed on a bejewelled pot. Supreme Ambikaa must be meditated upon.

Soundaryalahari

Before I conclude this chapter, I must mention another beautiful text, known as Soundaryalahari (सौन्दर्यलहरी), which means waves of beauty. There are many beautiful stories about how this text came to be composed. The version I like the best has been narrated below.

Adi Shankaracharya went to Kailasa to worship Shiva and Parvati. Shiva gave him this text, consisting of 100 verses, all describing Devi's beauty. Nandi didn't like the idea of Shankaracharya being given Soundaryalahari. As Adi Shankara was returning from Kailasa, Nandi seized the manuscript, and it got torn into two. Shankaracharya was crestfallen. He was only left with 41 verses, as Nandi had run off with the remaining 59. When Shankaracharya complained to Shiva, he asked Shankaracharya to compose the other 59 on the basis of what he remembered.

In another version of the story, when Shankaracharya visited Kailasa, he saw that Shiva had written about Devi's beauty on the walls. Shiva didn't want Shankaracharya to read what he had written about his wife's beauty. Therefore, he erased parts of it off of the walls. However, based on what he saw, Shankaracharya composed the rest of the verses.

In the third version of the story, Ganesha wrote these verses and gave them to Pushpadanta, one of Shiva's great devotees. Pushpadanta passed them on to the Sage Goudapada and following the guru to shishya succession, Shankaracharya received it.

In any event, the contemporary version of the text, with 103 verses, has two clear parts. The three additional verses are often regarded as later interpolations. The first part is about Devi's internal worship, and the second part is more about Devi's beauty. The form of Devi here is Tripurasundari, and the text is full of tantra, mantra and yantra. It is sometimes classified as a tantra text. Sometimes, the first 41 verses are known as Anandalahari, and the remaining verses are known as Soundaryalahari.[28] To illustrate the beauty of the poetry, here is just one verse:

> विधात्री धर्माणां त्वमसि सकलाम्नायजननी
> त्वमर्थानां मूलं धनदनमनीयांघ्रिकमले ।
> त्वमादिः कामानां जननि कृतकन्दर्पविजये
> सतां मुक्तेर्बीजं त्वमसि परमब्रह्ममहिषी ।।

> You are the origin of all dharma and the mother of all the traditional texts. You are the foundation of artha and all others. Kubera prostrates himself at your lotus feet. You are the primordial mother of all desire, and you have vanquished the god of love. You are the seed of emancipation for the virtuous. You are the supreme Brahman's queen.

[28]'Saundarya Lahari,' https://bit.ly/3onGSh4. Accessed on 22 July 2022.

six

DEVI GITA

The Devi Gita[1] features in the the seventh skandha of the Devi Bhagavata Purana, when the devas are suffering at the hands of Tarakasura and have prayed to Devi, who manifests and promises them that she will be born as Himalaya's daughter. In the Devi Bhagavata Purana, this story is being narrated by Vedavyasa to King Janamejaya. However, the Devi Gita is being narrated by Devi to Himalaya, which Vedavyasa then relays to Janamejaya. Once the conversation between Himalaya and Devi begins, which parts constitute Devi Gita? It is not as if there is a clear and unanimous identification. Most people say that there are 10 chapters in the Devi Gita. I have translated nine of them to English in this chapter. I believe that these nine chapters represent the core of the Devi Gita. The tenth doesn't add much to what has been said and will only burden the text.

Most people know of and have read the Bhagavad Gita. But there is an entire corpus of Gita literature with around 60 texts. Some are part of the Mahabharata. For example, the Mahabharata has Dharma Vyadha Gita, which is perhaps more relevant for householders than the Bhagavad Gita. The Mahabharata also has Anu Gita, where Krishna repeats the core teachings of the Bhagavad Gita for Arjuna. There are Gita

[1]'Devi Gita,' Sanskrit Documents, https://bit.ly/3oet9cm. Accessed on 19 July 2022.

texts that are part of the Purana corpus, just as Devi Gita is part of the Devi Bhagavata Purana. There are stand-alone Gita texts, like Ashtavakra Gita, where the Sage Ashtavakra teaches King Janaka. The Bhagavad Gita is the most read, translated and interpreted text, and rightly so. But these other Gita texts are also important.

Before writing this chapter, I thought a bit about whether I should. But in a book on Devi, how can I not include the Devi Gita? Most Gita texts are infused with the jnana of Vedanta and bhakti, and so is the Devi Gita. But, in addition, the Devi Gita brings in tantra. That's the reason I find it to be a remarkable text, and why I decided to include it.

As with the previous mantras, I have translated this one too. However, many layers of interpretation are possible, going beyond mechanical translation. This chapter isn't a primer on the Devi Gita with interpretations. There are other books for that. It is no more than an introduction to the Devi Gita, and I have tried to translate in a way that is as comprehensible as possible, without getting into the complexities of interpretation. Since I haven't quite followed the chapter ordering of the Devi Bhagavata Purana, I have not included any separate headings for the chapters. The first number within brackets at the end of each stanza is the number of the chapter, while the second is the number of the sloka within that chapter. If you are familiar with the Bhagavad Gita, you will recognize some of the slokas featured below.

हिमालय उवाच
योगं च भक्तिसहितं ज्ञानं च श्रुतिसम्मतम् ।
वदस्व परमेशानि त्वमेवाहं यतो भवे: ॥

Himalaya said, 'O Parameshi![2] Please tell me about yoga,

---

[2]The same as Parameshvari, the Supreme Ishvari.

along with the bhakti and jnana that is in conformity with the Shruti texts so that I can comprehend your existence.'

व्यास उवाच
इति तस्य वचः श्रुत्वा प्रसन्नमुखपङ्कजा ।
वक्तुमारभताम्बा सा रहस्यं श्रुतिगूहितम् ॥

Vyasa said, 'Hearing his words, her lotus face was pleased. Ambaa started to speak about the hidden mystery of the Shruti texts.'

देवी उवाच
शृण्वन्तु निर्जराः सर्वे व्याहरन्त्या वचो मम ।
यस्य श्रवणमात्रेण मद्रूपत्वं प्रपद्यते ॥ (1.1)

Devi said, 'O all of you who do not suffer from aging! Listen to the words I speak. As soon as you hear this, you will realize my form.'

अहमेवास पूर्वं मे नान्यत्किञ्चिन्नगाधिप ।
तदात्मरूपं चित्संवित्परब्रह्मैकनामकम् ॥ (1.2)

'O lord of mountains! In the beginning, I existed and there was nothing else. My form is one and I am known under the names of *chit, samvit* and the Supreme Brahman.'[3]

अप्रतर्क्यमनिर्देश्यमनौपम्यमनामयम् ।
तस्य काचित्स्वतः सिद्धा शक्तिर्मायेति विश्रुता ॥ (1.3)

'My Shakti is famous as mayaa, and it is self-evident that it is beyond conjecture, beyond determination, unparalleled and free from disease.'

न सती सा नासती सा नोभयात्मा विरोधतः ।
एतद्विलक्षणा काचिद्वस्तुभूतास्ति सर्वदा ॥ (1.4)

'It is neither existent nor non-existent. My atman does

[3]Chit is consciousness and samvit is understanding.

not manifest itself as either. Such are its attributes. In a substantive form, it always exists.'

पावकस्योष्णतेवेयमुष्णांशोरिव दीधितिः ।
चन्द्रस्य चन्द्रिकेवेयं ममेयं सहजा ध्रुवा ।। (1.5)

'There is heat in fire. There is splendour in the sun's hot rays. The moon has moonbeams. Just like that, my form certainly exists innately.'

तस्यां कर्माणि जीवानां जीवाः कालाश्च सञ्चरे ।
अभेदेन विलीनाः स्युः सुषुप्तौ व्यवहारवत् ।। (1.6)

'In the course of progress and movement, the karma of living beings, living beings and time all dissolve, without any differences, into a state of *sushupti*[4].'

स्वशक्तेश्च समायोगादहं बीजात्मतां गता ।
स्वाधारावरणात्तस्या दोषत्वं च समागतम् ।। (1.7)

'This multitude enters into my Shakti, into the seed that is my atman. What everything enters into, has a taint, since it shrouds its own foundation.'

चौतन्यस्य समायोगान्निमित्तत्वं च कथ्यते ।
प्रपञ्चपरिणामाच्च समवायित्वमुच्यते ।। (1.8)

'I am described as the consciousness that brings everything together, and as the cause. I am spoken of as the one who brings together this visible universe as an effect.'

केचित्तां तप इत्याहुस्तमः केचिज्जडं परे ।
ज्ञानं माया प्रधानं च प्रकृतिं शक्तिमप्यजाम् ।। (1.9)

'Some say *tapas*. Others speak of her as tamas and inert.

[4]Sushupti is deep sleep. Everything dissolves (at the time of dissolution) into Devi's mayaa, like sushupti.

Still others call her jnana, mayaa, Pradhana, Prakriti, Shakti and Ajaa.'[5]

विमर्श इति तां प्राहुः शैवशास्त्रविशारदाः ।
अविद्यामितरे प्राहुर्वेदतत्त्वार्थचिन्तकाः ।। (1.10)

'Those who are accomplished in texts about Shiva call her Vimarsha. Others, who have thought about the meanings of the Vedas, speak of her as Avidya.'[6]

एवं नानाविधानि स्युर्नामानि निगमादिषु ।
तस्या जडत्वं दृश्यत्वाज्ज्ञाननाशात्ततोऽसती ।। (1.11)

'In this way, Nigama[7] and other texts use many kinds of names. Inertness is seen in her. But such jnana is false and is destroyed.'

चौतन्यस्य न दृश्यत्वं दृश्यत्वे जडमेव तत् ।
स्वप्रकाशं च चौतन्यं न परेण प्रकाशितम् ।। (1.12)

'Consciousness cannot be seen. Were it to be seen, it would seem to be inert. Consciousness illuminates itself. It cannot be illuminated by anything else.'

अनवस्थादोषसत्त्वान्न स्वेनापि प्रकाशितम् ।
कर्मकर्तृविरोधः स्यात्तस्मात्तद्दीपवत्स्वयम् ।। (1.13)

'Any such entity itself has to be illuminated and suffers

---

[5]This is a translation, not an interpretation. Yet, each of these terms requires detailed explanation, which we will skip and stick to a brief overview of their meanings. Tapas refers to austerities, though there is also a sense of purification through scorching. Tamas means the guna of darkness/ ignorance. Jnana is knowledge, and mayaa is illusion. Pradhana (the creative principle) and Prakriti (primordial matter) are *tattvas* (principles) of *samkhya*. Ajaa means 'one without birth.'

[6]Vimarsha is reflective awareness. Avidya is ignorance, the opposite of vidya (knowledge).

[7]Here, Nigama refers to the Vedas.

from the taint of *anavastha*. There is conflict between the actor and the act. Any such entity cannot illuminate itself.'[8]

प्रकाशमानमन्येषां भासकं विद्धि पर्वत ।
अत एव च नित्यत्वं सिद्धसंवित्तनोर्मम ॥ (1.14)

'O mountain! Therefore, know that it illuminates itself and is not illuminated by another entity. Hence, it has been established that my intelligence is eternal.'

जाग्रत्स्वप्नसुषुप्त्यादौ दृश्यस्य व्यभिचारतः ।
संविदो व्यभिचारश्च नानुभूतोऽस्ति कर्हिचित् ॥ (1.15)

'There are changes in the states of being awake, sleep and deep sleep. However, one never experiences changes in one's intelligence.'

यदि तस्याप्यनुभवतर्ह्ययं येन साक्षिणा ।
अनुभूतः स एवात्र शिष्टः संविद्वपुः पुरा ॥ (1.16)

'If she is experienced by a witness, intelligence must have earlier assumed the form of the wisdom that experiences.'

अतएव च नित्यत्वं प्रोक्तं सच्छास्त्रकोविदः ।
आनन्दरूपता चास्याः परप्रेमास्पदत्वतः ॥ (1.17)

'This is the reason those well-versed in the sacred texts speak of her eternal nature. Her form is that of bliss. Supreme love flows from her.'

मा न भूवं हि भूयासमिति प्रेमात्मनि स्थितम् ।
सर्वस्यान्यस्य मिथ्यात्वादसङ्गत्वं स्फुटं मम ॥ (1.18)

---

[8]If some other entity illuminates consciousness, that entity cannot illuminate itself and has to be illuminated by another entity. Anavastha refers to the non-finality of a proposition and the endless chain of cause and effect.

'"I am not, but I am." In the form of love, this sense is established in the atman. Everything else is false. Thus, it is evident that I am not attached to anything else.'

अपरिच्छिन्नताप्येवमत एव मता मम ।
तच्च ज्ञानं नात्मधर्मो धर्मत्वे जडतात्मनः ॥ (1.19)

'It is my view that I exist continuously. In addition, jnana is not the natural dharma of the atman. Had it been the dharma, there would have been no senselessness.'

ज्ञानस्य जडशेषत्वं न दृष्टं न च सम्भवि ।
चिद्धर्मत्वं तथा नास्ति चितश्चिन्न हि भिद्यते ॥ (1.20)

'Senselessness cannot be seen in jnana. It is not possible. There are no attributes of dharma in consciousness. There is no difference between consciousness and its attribute.'

तस्मादात्मा ज्ञानरूपः सुखरूपश्च सर्वदा ।
सत्यः पूर्णोऽप्यसङ्गश्च द्वैतजालविवर्जितः ॥ (1.21)

'Therefore, the form of the atman is that of jnana. It always takes the form of happiness. It is truth and is complete. It is not attached and is devoid of any duality.'

स पुनः कामकर्मादियुक्तया स्वीयमायया ।
पूर्वानुभूतसंस्कारात् कालकर्मविपाकतः ॥ (1.22)

'Then again, because of my own mayaa, it is united with desire, karma and other things, thereby suffering from the misfortunes of earlier experiences, *samskaras*, destiny and karma.'

अविवेकाच्च तत्त्वस्य सिसृक्षावान्प्रजायते ।
अबुद्धिपूर्वः सर्गोऽयं कथितस्ते नगाधिप ॥ (1.23)

'O lord of mountains! Without any sense of discrimination about the truth, it desires to create. Hence, this creation is spoken of as one that occurs without the use of intelligence.'

एतद्धि यन्मया प्रोक्तं मम रूपमलौकिकम् ।
अव्याकृतं तदव्यक्तं मायाशबलमित्यपि ॥ (1.24)

'I have, thus, spoken about my supernormal form. My mayaa is spoken of as varied, without modification and without manifestation.'

प्रोच्यते सर्वशास्त्रेषु सर्वकारणकारणम् ।
तत्त्वानामादिभूतं च सच्चिदानन्दविग्रहम् ॥ (1.25)

'In all the sacred texts, it is spoken of as the cause behind all causes. Among all the principles, I am the primordial, and my form is that of truth, consciousness and bliss.'

सर्वकर्मघनीभूतमिच्छाज्ञानक्रियाश्रयम् ।
ह्रीङ्कारमन्त्रवाच्यं तदादितत्त्वं तदुच्यते ॥ (1.26)

'When all karma is solidified and resorts to desire, jnana and action, it is spoken of as the mantra "Hrim". This is spoken of as the first principle.'

तस्मादाकाश उत्पन्नः शब्दतन्मात्ररूपकः ।
भवेत्स्पर्शात्मको वायुस्तेजोरूपात्मकं पुनः ॥ (1.27)

'Space originates from this, and it possesses the attribute of this sound. From it emerges wind, possessing the attribute of touch. Fire emerges from it, possessing the attribute of form.'[9]

जलं रसात्मकं पश्चात्ततो गन्धात्मिका धरा ।
शब्दैकगुण आकाशो वायुः स्पर्शरवान्वितः ॥ (1.28)

---

[9]This is the way the five subtle elements (*tanmatras*) are progressively created. Each succeeding element possesses its attributes and that of the preceding one. Destruction/dissolution occurs in the reverse order.

'Water emerges from it, possessing the attribute of taste. Thereafter, earth originates, possessing the attribute of smell. Space possesses the single attribute of sound. Wind possesses the attributes of touch and sound.'

शब्दस्पर्शरूपगुणं तेज इत्युच्यते बुधैः ।
शब्दस्पर्शरूपरसैरापो वेदगुणाः स्मृताः ॥ (1.29)

'The learned say that fire possesses the attributes of sound, touch and form. Those who know about these attributes say that water possesses the attributes of sound, touch, form and taste.'

शब्दस्पर्शरूपरसगन्धैः पञ्चगुणा धरा ।
तेभ्योऽभवन्महत्सूत्रं यल्लिङ्गं परिचक्षते ॥ (1.30)

'Earth possesses the five attributes of sound, touch, form, taste and smell. Among these, there is a great thread, and that is described as lingam.'

सर्वात्मकं तत्सम्प्रोक्तं सूक्ष्मदेहोऽयमात्मनः ।
अव्यक्तं कारणो देहः स चोक्तः पूर्वमेव हि ॥ (1.31)

'This is spoken of as existing within all atmans. It is the subtle body of the atman. This body is the unmanifest cause. It is the one that has been spoken about earlier.'

यस्मिञ्जगद्बीजरूपं स्थितं लिङ्गोद्भवो यतः ।
ततः स्थूलानि भूतानि पञ्चीकरणमार्गतः ॥ (1.32)

'This lingam originates from what has been established as the seed of the universe. From this, the five gross elements follow the activity and course that has been set.'

पञ्चसङ्ख्यानि जायन्ते तत्प्रकारस्त्वथोच्यते ।
पूर्वोक्तानि च भूतानि प्रत्येकं विभजेद् द्विधा ॥ (1.33)

'When those enumerated five have been created, modification starts occuring there. Each of the elements mentioned earlier is divided into two parts.'[10]

एकैकं भागमेकस्य चतुर्धा विभजेद्गिरे ।
स्वस्वेतरद्वितीयांशे योजनात्पञ्च पञ्च ते ॥ (1.34)

'Each of those parts is divided into four parts. For all five, these halves combine with the halves of others to produce the five.'[11]

तत्कार्यं च विराड्देहः स्थूलदेहोऽयमात्मनः ।
पञ्चभूतस्थसत्त्वांशैः श्रोत्रादीनां समुद्भवः ॥ (1.35)

'This action leads to the body, Virat. This is the atman's gross body. From the sattva portions of these five elements, ears and the others[12] originate.'

ज्ञानेन्द्रियाणां राजेन्द्र प्रत्येकं मिलितैस्तु तैः ।
अन्तःकरणमेकं स्याद् वृत्तिभेदाच्चतुर्विधम् ॥ (1.36)

'O Indra, among kings! All these senses of jnana unite and form the single faculty of thought. Depending on its functioning, it is of four types.'

यदा तु सङ्कल्पविकल्पकृत्यं तदा भवेत्तन्मन इत्यभिख्यम् ।
स्याद्बुद्धिसंज्ञं च यदा प्रवेत्ति सुनिश्चितं संशयहीनरूपम् ॥ (1.37)

'When it forms resolutions and thinks of alternatives, it is known as the mind. When it is free from doubts and understands with certainty, it is known as intelligence.'

अनुसन्धानरूपं तच्चित्तं च परिकीर्तितम् ।
अहङ्कृत्यात्मवृत्या तु तदहङ्कारतां गतम् ॥ (1.38)

---

[10]Initially, the subtle elements, known as tanmatras, are created. The gross elements emerge from those.

[11]The parts of subtle elements mentioned here combine with parts of other subtle elements to produce the five gross elements.

[12]The senses of perception (jnana).

'When it assumes the form of investigation, it is described as consciousness. When the atman shrouds itself with "I have done", it assumes the form of ahamkara.'

तेषां रजोंशैर्जातानि क्रमात्कर्मेन्द्रियाणि च ।
प्रत्येकं मिलितैस्तैस्तु प्राणो भवति पञ्चधा ॥ (1.39)

'In the due order, from the portions of rajas, the organs of action arise. All of these unite to form the five types of prana.'[13]

हृदि प्राणो गुदेऽपानो नाभिस्थस्तु समानकः ।
कण्ठदेशेऽप्युदानः स्याद्व्यानः सर्वशरीरगः ॥ (1.40)

'Prana is in the heart, apana is in the anus. Samana is based in the navel. Udana is in the region of the throat, and vyana courses across the entire body.'

ज्ञानेन्द्रियाणि पञ्चौव पञ्चकर्मेन्द्रियाणि च ।
प्राणादि पञ्चकं चौव धिया च सहितं मनः ॥ (1.41)

'There are five organs of jnana, five organs of action, five types of prana and intelligence, along with the mind.'

एतत्सूक्ष्मं शरीरं स्यान्मम लिङ्गं यदुच्यते ।
तत्र या प्रकृतिः प्रोक्ता सा राजन्विविधा स्मृता ॥ (1.42)

'This is my subtle body, spoken of as lingam. O king! It is remembered in many kinds of ways and is known as Prakriti.'

सत्त्वात्मिका तु माया स्यादविद्या गुणमिश्रिता ।
स्वाश्रयं या तु संरक्षेत्सा मायेति निगद्यते ॥ (1.43)

[13]The five flows of the breath of life—prana, apana, samana, udana and vyana. Prana draws breath into the body, and apana exhales it. Vyana distributes it through the body, and samana assimilates it. Udana gives rise to sound.

'There is mayaa that possesses sattva in its atman. But there is also that which is mixed with gunas and is full of ignorance. Mayaa is known to be the one who protects all those who seek refuge with her.'

तस्यां यत्प्रतिबिम्बं स्याद्बिम्बभूतस्य चेशितुः ।
स ईश्वरः समाख्यातः स्वाश्रयज्ञानवान्परः ॥ (1.44)

'She has a reflection. That reflection assumes the form of Isha. He is known as Ishvara. He possesses Supreme Jnana and is his own refuge.'

सर्वज्ञः सर्वकर्ता च सर्वानुग्रहकारकः ।
अविद्यायां तु यत्किञ्चित्प्रतिबिम्बं नगाधिप ॥ (1.45)

'He is omniscient. He is the one who does everything. He is the one who bestows favours upon everyone. O lord of mountains! However, there is some part of the reflection that possesses ignorance.'

तदेव जीवसंज्ञं स्यात्सर्वदुःखाश्रयं पुनः ।
द्वयोरपीह सम्प्रोक्तं देहत्रयमविद्यया ॥ (1.46)

'That is known as the *jivatman*. It is also the source of all miseries. In this world, both are spoken about. As a result of ignorance, there are three kinds of bodies.'

देहत्रयाभिमानाच्चाप्यभून्नामत्रयं पुनः ।
प्राज्ञस्तु कारणात्मा स्यात्सूक्ष्मदेही तु तैजसः ॥ (1.47)

'Because of self-conceit, these three bodies and three names arise. In the form of a cause, the atman is Prajna. When the body is subtle, he is Taijasa.'

स्थूलदेही तु विश्वाख्यस्त्रिविधः परिकीर्तितः ।
एवमीशोऽपि सम्प्रोक्त ईशसूत्रविराट्पदैः ॥ (1.48)

'In the gross body, he is known as Vishva. These are described as the three forms. Thus, Isha is spoken of in these three forms of Isha, Sutra and Virat.'[14]

प्रथमो व्यष्टिरूपस्तु समष्ट्यात्मा परः स्मृतः ।
स हि सर्वेश्वरः साक्षाज्जीवानुग्रहकाम्यया ॥ (1.49)

'The first form is separated, and the other form is described as one that is the aggregate. He is himself Sarveshvara. He is the one who wishes to bestow favours upon living beings.'

करोति विविधं विश्वं नानाभोगाश्रयं पुनः ।
मच्छक्तिप्रेरितो नित्यं मयि राजन्प्रकल्पितः ॥ (1.50)

'He creates many entities in the universe with diverse objects for their pleasure. O king! He is always urged by my Shakti. That is how he conceives.'

देव्युवाच–
मन्मायाशक्तिसंक्लृप्तं जगत्सर्वं चराचरम् ।
सापि मत्तः पृथङ्माया नास्त्येव परमार्थतः ॥ (2.1)

Devi said, 'Everything in this universe, mobile and immobile, has been conceived by the Shakti of my mayaa. The supreme meaning is that my mayaa is not distinct from me.'

व्यवहारदृशा सेयं विद्या माया विश्रुता ।
तत्त्वदृष्ट्या तु नास्त्येव तत्त्वमेवास्ति केवलम् ॥ (2.2)

'Such is the conduct of this mayaa that it is known as learning. With the insight of the truth, there is no such thing. The truth alone exists.'

साहं सर्वं जगत्सृष्ट्वा तदन्तः प्रविशाम्यहम् ।
माया कर्मादिसहिता गिरे प्राणपुरःसरा ॥ (2.3)

[14]That is, Isha is the causal body, Sutra is the subtle body and Virat is the gross body.

'I am the creator of everything in the universe. O mountain! At the end, I enter mayaa, karma and everything else, with prana as the foremost.'

लोकान्तरगतिर्नो चेत्कथं स्यादिति हेतुना।
यथा यथा भवन्त्येव मायाभेदास्तथा तथा ।। (2.4)

'Without me as the cause, how can the progress of the worlds occur? Depending on circumstances, different kinds of mayaa occur.'

उपाधिभेदाद्भिन्नाऽहं घटाकाशादयो यथा ।
उच्चनीचादिवस्तूनि भासयन्भास्करः सदा ।। (2.5)

'Like space and other things inside a pot, I am addressed with different kinds of names. The sun always illuminates objects, whether they are superior or inferior.'

न दुष्यति तथैवाहं दोषैर्लिप्ता कदापि न ।
मयि बुद्ध्यादिकर्तृत्वमध्यस्यैवापरे जनाः ।। (2.6)

'It is not tainted by that. Similiarly, I am never tainted. Inferior and ignorant people attribute a sense of ownership over my intelligence.'

वदन्ति चात्मा कर्मेति विमूढा न सुबुद्धयः ।
अज्ञानभेदतस्तद्वन्मायाया भेदतस्तथा ।। (2.7)

'Those who are deluded enough speak about my karma, but not those who are excellent in their intelligence. There are differences in ignorance. Accordingly, there are differences in perceptions of mayaa.'

जीवेश्वरविभागश्च कल्पितो माययैव तु ।
घटाकाशमहाकाशविभागः कल्पितो यथा ।। (2.8)

'As a consequence of mayaa, among living beings, there are differences in the conception of Ishvara. This is like the great space being conceived in different ways, when space is enclosed in pots.'

तथैव कल्पितो भेदो जीवात्मपरमात्मनोः।
यथा जीवबहुत्वं च माययैव न च स्वतः।। (2.9)

'In that way, differences have been conceived between jivatmans and the *paramatman*. This is like mayaa leading to the status of many kinds of living beings. It is not the truth.'

तथेश्वरबहुत्वं च मायया न स्वभावतः ।
देहेन्द्रियादिसङ्घातवासनाभेदभेदिता ।। (2.10)

'Mayaa leads to the perception of many kinds of Ishvaras. This is not innate. These differences arise because of differences in bodies, senses, desires and their interactions.'

अविद्या जीवभेदस्य हेतुर्नान्यः प्रकीर्तितः ।
गुणानां वासनाभेदभेदिता या धराधर ।। (2.11)

'Differences in ignorance among living beings is the cause. Nothing else is described. O one who holds up the earth! These differences are caused by differences in gunas and desires.'

माया सा परभेदस्य हेतुर्नान्यः कदाचन ।
मयि सर्वमिदं प्रोतमोतं च धरणीधर ।। (2.12)

'It is mayaa that causes these great differences. There can be no other reason. O one who holds up the earth! The warp and weft of everything is woven into me.'

ईश्वरोऽहं च सूत्रात्मा विराडात्माऽहमस्मि च ।
ब्रह्माऽहं विष्णुरुद्रौ च गौरी ब्राह्मी च वैष्णवी ।। (2.13)

'I am Ishvara, who is in the atman as Sutra. I am Virat in the atman. I am Brahmaa, Vishnu and Rudra. I am Gouri, Brahmi and Vaishnavi.'

सूर्योऽहं तारकाश्चाहं तारकेशस्तथास्म्यहम् ।
पशुपक्षिस्वरूपाऽहं चाण्डालोऽहं च तस्करः ॥ (2.14)

'I am the sun. I am the stars. I am also the lord of the stars. My own form exists in animals and birds. I am a Chandala. I am also a thief.'

व्याधोऽहं क्रूरकर्माऽहं सत्कर्मोऽहं महाजनः ।
स्त्रीपुन्नपुंसकाकारोऽप्यहमेव न संशयः ॥ (2.15)

'I am a hunter. I am cruel through my deeds. I am the one who is virtuous through my deeds. I am the great person. There is no doubt that I exist in the forms of man, woman and eunuch.'

यच्च किञ्चित्क्वचिद्वस्तु दृश्यते श्रूयतेऽपि वा ।
अन्तर्बहिश्च तत्सर्वं व्याप्याहं सर्वदा स्थिता ॥ (2.16)

'In everything that is ever seen or heard—I am inside and outside it all. I am always established, pervading.'

न तदस्ति मया त्यक्तं वस्तु किञ्चिच्चराचरम् ।
यद्यस्ति चेत्तच्छून्यं स्याद्वन्ध्यापुत्रोपमं हि तत् ॥ (2.17)

'There is no object, mobile or immobile, that exists without me. If any such thing were to exist, it would be empty, like the son of a barren woman.'

रज्जुर्यथा सर्पमालाभेदैरेका विभाति हि ।
तथैवेशादिरूपेण भाम्यहं नात्र संशयः ॥ (2.18)

'A single rope appears as a snake or a garland. In that way, there is no doubt that I appear in the form of Isha and the others.'

अधिष्ठानातिरेकेण कल्पितं तन्न भासते ।
तस्मान्मत्सत्तयैवैतत्सत्तावन्नान्यथा भवेत् ॥ (2.19)

'Nothing can be conceived to exist, unless an entity

exists as its foundation. Hence, my excellence supports existence. It cannot but be otherwise.'

हिमालय उवाच-
यथा वदसि देवेशि समष्ट्यात्मवपुस्त्विदम् ।
तथैव द्रष्टुमिच्छामि यदि देवि कृपा मयि ।। (2.20)

Himalaya said, 'O Deveshi! You have spoken about it. O Devi! If you have compassion towards me, I wish to see your form in totality.'

व्यास उवाच-
इति तस्य वचः श्रुत्वा सर्वे देवाः सविष्णवः ।
ननन्दुर्मुदितात्मानः पूजयन्तश्च तद्वचः ।। (2.21)

Vyasa said, 'Hearing his words, all the devas, along with Vishnu, were delighted. Rejoicing in their minds, they honoured his words.'

अथ देवमतं ज्ञात्वा भक्तकामदुघा शिवा ।
अदर्शयन्निजं रूपं भक्तकामप्रपूरिणी ।। (2.22)

'Shivaa, who is like a Kamadhenu[15] for bhaktas, got to know the views of the devas. The one who satisfies the desires of bhaktas revealed her own form.'

अपश्यंस्ते महादेव्या विराडरूपं परात्परम् ।
द्यौर्मस्तकं भवेद्यस्य चन्द्रसूर्यौ च चक्षुषी ।। (2.23)

'They saw Mahadevi's Virat form, greater than the greatest. Her head extends up to the sky, and the sun and the moon are her eyes.'

दिशः श्रोत्रे वचो वेदाः प्राणो वायुः प्रकीर्तितः ।
विश्वं हृदयमित्याहुः पृथिवी जघनं स्मृतम् ।। (2.24)

'The directions are her ears. The Vedas are her speech.

---

[15]Kamadhenu is a cow that can be milked for anything desired.

The wind is described as her breath of life. The universe is said to be her heart. The earth is described as her hip.'

नभस्तलं नाभिसरो ज्योतिश्चक्रमुरस्थलम् ।
महर्लोकस्तु ग्रीवा स्याज्जनो लोको मुखं स्मृतम् ॥ (2.25)

'The firmament is the region around her navel. The circle of luminous bodies is the region around her thighs. Maharloka is her neck, and Janaloka is said to be her face.'

तपोलोको रराटिस्तु सत्यलोकादधः स्थितः ।
इन्द्रादयो बाहवः स्युः शब्दः श्रोत्रं महेशितुः ॥ (2.26)

'Tapoloka is her forehead, located below Satyaloka. Indra and the others are her arms. Maheshi's ears constitute sound.'

नासत्यदस्रौ नासे स्तौ गन्धो घ्राणं स्मृतो बुधैः ।
मुखमग्निः समाख्यातो दिवारात्री च पक्ष्मणी ॥ (2.27)

'Nasatya and Dasra[16] are her two nostrils. The learned say that her nose constitutes smell. Fire is described as her mouth. Night and day are her eyelashes.'

ब्रह्मस्थानं भ्रूविजृंभोऽप्यापस्तालुः प्रकीर्तिताः।
रसो जिह्वा समाख्याता यमो दंष्ट्राः प्रकीर्तिताः ॥ (2.28)

'Brahmaa's place is in the furrow of her brows. Water is described as her palate. Taste is said to be her tongue. Yama is described as her teeth.'

दन्ताः स्नेहकला यस्य हासो माया प्रकीर्तिता ।
सर्गस्त्वपाङ्गमोक्षः स्याद्व्रीडोर्ध्वोष्ठो महेशितुः ॥ (2.29)

'The smaller teeth are bits of her love. Mayaa is described as her smile. Her sidelong glances constitute creation. Maheshi's upper lip constitutes modesty.'

---

[16]Nasatya and Dasra are the names of the two Ashvins.

लोभः स्यादधरोष्ठोऽस्याधर्ममार्गस्तु पृष्ठभूः।
प्रजापतिश्च मेढ्रं स्याद्यः स्रष्टा जगतीतले ॥ (2.30)

'Greed is her lower lip. The path of dharma is her back. Prajapati is her genital organ. Her organ of creation is the surface of the earth.'

कुक्षिः समुद्रा गिरयोऽस्थीनि देव्या महेशितुः ।
नद्यो नाड्यः समाख्याता वृक्षाः केशाः प्रकीर्तिताः ॥ (2.31)

'The oceans are her belly. The mountains are Devi Maheshi's bones. The rivers are described as her veins. Trees are said to be her hair.'

कौमारयौवनजरावयोऽस्य गतिरुत्तमा ।
बलाहकास्तु केशाः स्युः सन्ध्ये ते वाससी विभोः ॥ (2.32)

'Childhood, youth, old age and lifespan are her excellent gait. Clouds are her hair. O lord! The two sandhyaas[17] are her garments.'

राजञ्छ्रीजगदम्बायाश्चन्द्रमास्तु मनः स्मृतः ।
विज्ञानशक्तिस्तु हरी रुद्रोन्तःकरणं स्मृतम् ॥ (2.33)

'O king! The beautiful moon is said to be the mind of the mother of the universe. Hari is her Shakti of *vijnana*. Rudra is said to be her Shakti of destruction.'

अश्वादिजातयः सर्वाः श्रोणिदेशे स्थिता विभोः ।
अतलादिमहालोकाः कट्यधोभागतां गताः ॥ (2.34)

'O lord! All horses, and others of the species, are located in her loins. The region that extends below her waist represents the great worlds, Atala and the others.'[18]

---

[17]Here, sandhyaas refer to dawn and dusk.

[18]Just as there are seven upper worlds, there are seven nether worlds (see p. 79)

एतादृशं महारूपं ददृशुः सुरपुङ्गवाः ।
ज्वालामालासहस्राढ्यं लेलिहानं च जिह्वया ।। (2.35)

'The bulls among gods beheld such a great form. There was an abundance of thousands of garlands of flames. Her tongue seemed to lick.'

दंष्ट्राकटकटारावं वमन्तं वह्निमक्षिभिः ।
नानायुधधरं वीरं ब्रह्मक्षत्रौदनं च यत् ।। (2.36)

'As she gnashed her teeth, there was a grating sound. Her eyes vomited blood. She held many kinds of weapons, and brave Brahmanas and Kshatriyas were her food.'

सहस्रशीर्षनयनं सहस्रचरणं तथा ।
कोटिसूर्यप्रतीकाशं विद्युत्कोटिसमप्रभम् ।। (2.37)

'She possessed thousands of heads and eyes. There were thousands of feet. She resembled one crore suns. She was as resplendent as crores of flashes of lightning.'

भयङ्करं महाघोरं हृदक्ष्णोस्त्रासकारकम् ।
ददृशुस्ते सुराः सर्वे हाहाकारं च चक्रिरे ।। (2.38)

'She was extremely horrible and caused terror. She struck fear in the eyes and the heart. All the gods saw her and lamented.'

विकम्पमानहृदया मूर्च्छामापुर्दुरत्ययाम्।
स्मरणं च गतं तेषां जगदम्बेयमित्यपि ।। (2.39)

'Their hearts trembled. They lost their senses and found it impossible to control themselves. In their memories, they forgot that this was the mother of the universe.'

अथ ते ये स्थिता वेदाश्चतुर्दिक्षु महाविभोः ।
बोधयामासुरत्युग्रं मूर्च्छातो मूर्च्छितान्सुरान् ।। (2.40)

'The gods had lost their senses. At this, the Vedas appeared on the four sides of this great manifestation. They removed the fierce senselessness from the gods and made them understand.'

अथ ते धैर्यमालम्ब्य लब्ध्वा च श्रुतिमुत्तमाम् ।
प्रेमाश्रुपूर्णनयना रुद्धकण्ठास्तु निर्जराः ।। (2.41)

'Having obtained the excellent Shruti texts, they resorted to their fortitude. Their eyes filled with tears of love. Words choked in the throats of the immortals.'

बाष्पगद्गददया वाचा स्तोतुं समुपचक्रिरे।
देवा ऊचुः-
अपराधं क्षमस्वाम्ब पाहि दीनांस्त्वदुद्भवान् ।। (2.42)

'They started to praise her in words that faltered because of their tears.
The devas said, "O mother! Please pardon our crimes. Please save the distressed ones who have originated from you."'

कोपं संहर देवेशि सभया रूपदर्शनात् ।
का ते स्तुतिः प्रकर्तव्या पामरैर्निजरैरिह ।। (2.43)

'"O Deveshi! Restrain your rage. Beholding this form, we are terrified. We are inferior immortals. What can we do to praise you?"'

स्वस्याप्यज्ञेय एवासौ यावान्यश्च स्वविक्रमः ।
तदर्वाग्जायमानानां कथं स विषयो भवेत् ।। (2.44)

'"Your own valour is unknown even to you. What need be said of others? We have been born after you. How can we know about this subject?"'

नमस्ते भुवनेशानि नमस्ते प्रणवात्मके ।
सर्व वेदान्तसंसिद्धे नमो ह्रीङ्कारमूर्तये ।। (2.45)

'"I prostrate myself before the Ishani of the universe. I prostrate myself before the one who has Pranava in her atman. You are the one who has been established in all Vedanta. I prostrate myself before the one whose form is hrim."'[19]

यस्मादग्निः समुत्पन्नो यस्मात्सूर्यश्च चन्द्रमाः ।
यस्मादोषधयः सर्वास्तस्मै सर्वात्मने नमः ॥ (2.46)

'"Fire originated from you. The sun and the moon originated from you. All the herbs originated from you. I prostrate myself before the one who is in all atmans."'

यस्माच्च देवाः संभूताः साध्याः पक्षिण एव च ।
पशवश्च मनुष्याश्च तस्मै सर्वात्मने नमः ॥ (2.47)

'"Devas, Sadhyaas, birds, animals and humans originated from you. I prostrate myself before the one who is in all atmans."'

प्राणापानौ व्रीहियवौ तपः श्रद्धा ऋतं तथा ।
ब्रह्मचर्यं विधिश्चैव यस्मात्तस्मै नमो नमः ॥ (2.48)

'"Prana, apana, *vrihi* rice, barley, austerities, faith, truth, brahmacharya and norms originated from you. I prostrate myself. I bow down."'

सप्त प्राणार्चिषो यस्मात्समिधः सप्त एव च ।
होमाः सप्त तथा लोकास्तस्मै सर्वात्मने नमः ॥ (2.49)

'"The force behind the seven flames of the fire, the seven kinds of kindling, the seven kinds of oblations and the seven worlds—they originated in you. I prostrate myself before the one who is in all atmans."'

---

[19]While this forms a part of the collective speech by the Devas, each Deva is praying individually, so the verse uses the first person singular.

यस्मात्समुद्रा गिरयः सिन्धवः प्रचरन्ति च ।
यस्मादोषधयः सर्वा रसास्तस्मै नमो नमः ॥ (2.50)

'"Oceans, mountains, rivers, herbs and all the tastes flow from you. I prostrate myself. I bow down."'

यस्माद्यज्ञः समुद्भूतो दीक्षा यूपश्च दक्षिणाः ।
ऋचो यजूंषि सामानि तस्मै सर्वात्मने नमः ॥ (2.51)

'"Sacrifices, their consecration, sacrificial posts, *dakshina*[20] and Rig, Yajur and Sama hymns originated from you. I prostrate myself before the one who is in all atmans."'

नमः पुरस्तात्पृष्ठे च नमस्ते पार्श्वयोर्द्वयोः ।
अध ऊर्ध्वं चतुर्दिक्षु मातर्भूयो नमो नमः ॥ (2.52)

'"I prostrate myself in front and at the back. I prostrate myself on the two sides. O mother! I prostrate myself above, below and on the four sides. I repeatedly prostrate myself."'

उपसंहर देवेशि रूपमेतदलौकिकम् ।
तदेव दर्शयास्माकं रूपं सुन्दरसुन्दरम् ॥ (2.53)

'"O Deveshi! Withdraw this supernormal form. Please show us your charming and beautiful form."'

व्यास उवाच–
इति भीतान्सुरान्दृष्ट्वा जगदम्बा कृपार्णवा ।
संहृत्य रूपं घोरं तद्दर्शयामास सुन्दरम् ॥ (2.54)

Vyasa said, 'In this way, the mother of the universe, an ocean of compassion, saw the frightened gods. She withdrew her terrible form and displayed her beautiful one.'

[20]Dakshina is the sacrificial fee paid to a priest.

पाशाङ्कुशवराभीतिधरं सर्वाङ्गकोमलम् ।
करुणापूर्णनयनं मन्दस्मितमुखाम्बुजम् ॥ (2.55)

'She held a noose and a goad, and gestured the Varada and Abhaya mudraas. All her limbs were delicate. Her eyes were full of compassion. Her lotus face smiled gently.'[21]

दृष्ट्वा तत्सुन्दरं रूपं तदा भीतिविवर्जिताः ।
शान्तिचित्ता प्रणेमुस्ते हर्षगद्गदनिःस्वनाः ॥ (2.56)

'On seeing that beautiful form, they cast aside their fear. Their minds were pacified, and they prostrated themselves, speaking in voices that faltered with delight.'

देव्युवाच–
क्व यूयं मन्दभाग्या वै क्वेदं रूपं महाद्भुतम् ।
तथापि भक्तवात्सल्यादीदृशं दर्शितं मया ॥ (3.1)

Devi said, 'O extremely unfortunate ones! Where are you and where is this great and wonderful form? Nevertheless, out of affection towards devotees, I have displayed it.'[22]

न वेदाध्ययनैर्योगैर्न दानैस्तपसेज्यया ।
रूपं द्रष्टुमिदं शक्यं केवलं मत्कृपां विना ॥ (3.2)

'Through studying the Vedas, yoga, donations, austerities and oblations, one is incapable of seeing this form. It becomes possible through my compassion alone.'

प्रकृतं शृणु राजेन्द्र परमात्मात्र जीवताम् ।
उपाधियोगात्सम्प्राप्तः कर्तृत्वादिकमप्युत ॥ (3.3)

'O Indra among kings! Listen to the truth. Among those who are alive, there is the paramatman alone. Because

---

[21]In this form, Devi was four-armed and two of them were in the mudraas of Abhaya (granting freedom from fear) and Varada (granting boons).
[22]Otherwise, you are not worthy of seeing it.

various appellations are applied, it is said that a sense of ownership comes into being.'

क्रियाः करोति विविधा धर्माधर्मैकहेतवः ।
नानायोनीस्ततः प्राप्य सुखदुःखैश्च युज्यते ॥ (3.4)

'Driven by dharma and adharma, he undertakes many kinds of action. Thereby, he is born as many species and experiences, happiness and unhappiness.'

पुनस्तत्संस्कृतिवशान्नानाकर्मरतः सदा ।
नानादेहान्समाप्नोति सुखदुःखैश्च युज्यते ॥ (3.5)

'Under the subjugation of his samskaras, he constantly engages in many kinds of karma again. He obtains many bodies and experiences, happiness and unhappiness.'

घटीयन्त्रवदेतस्य न विरामः कदापि हि ।
अज्ञानमेव मूलं स्यात्ततः कामः क्रियास्ततः ॥ (3.6)

'Like a mechanical clock, there is no end to this. With ignorance as the foundation, desire makes him engage in these acts.'

तस्मादज्ञाननाशाय यतेत नियतं नरः ।
एतद्धि जन्मसाफल्यं यदज्ञानस्य नाशनम् ॥ (3.7)

'Therefore, a man must always strive to destroy ignorance. The destruction of ignorance is the means to make birth successful.'

पुरुषार्थसमाप्तिश्च जीवन्मुक्तिदशापि च ।
अज्ञाननाशने शक्ता विद्यैव तु पटीयसी ॥ (3.8)

'One obtains the status of being a *jivanmukta* when the *purushartha*s end. Accomplishment in learning is capable of destroying ignorance.'[23]

[23]The three purusharthas, objectives of human existence, are dharma, artha

न कर्म तज्जं नोपास्तिर्विरोधाभावतो गिरे ।
प्रत्युताशाज्ञाननाशे कर्मणा नैव भाव्यताम् ॥ (3.9)

'O mountain! Since karma results from it, that contrary sentiment ensures it does not end. It is a futile hope to expect that karma will destroy ignorance.'[24]

अनर्थदानि कर्माणि पुनः पुनरुशन्ति हि ।
ततो रागस्ततो दोषस्ततोऽनर्थो महान्भवेत् ॥ (3.10)

'Repeatedly, they hope for the undesirable effects of karma. This results in attachment. Taints result from attachment and the consequence is greatly undesirable.'

तस्मात्सर्वप्रयत्नेन ज्ञानं सम्पादयेन्नरः ।
कुर्वन्नेवेह कर्माणीत्यतः कर्माप्यवश्यकम् ॥ (3.11)

'Therefore, a man must make every kind of effort to bring about jnana. However, when karma is necessary, one must also undertake karma.'

ज्ञानादेव हि कैवल्यमतः स्यात्तत्समुच्चयः ।
सहायतां व्रजेत्कर्म ज्ञानस्य हितकारि च ॥ (3.12)

'It is held that liberation is a consequence of jnana. Hence, if one engages in the aggregate of karma on the basis of jnana, it becomes beneficial.'

इति केचिद्वदन्त्यत्र तद्विरोधान्न संभवेत् ।
ज्ञानाधृद्ग्रन्थिभेदः स्याधृद्ग्रन्थौ कर्मसंभवः ॥ (3.13)

'There are some who say this is impossible because of their contrary natures. Jnana is used to sever the different bonds, but those bonds result from karma.'

---

and kama. A jivanmukta is a person who obtains liberation (*mukti*) while they are still alive.

[24]If karma results from ignorance, how can karma destroy ignorance?

यौगपद्यं न संभाव्यं विरोधात्तु ततस्तयोः ।
तमःप्रकाशयोर्यद्वद्यौगपद्यं न संभवि ॥ (3.14)

'Because of the conflict between the two, it is impossible to pursue both together. This is akin to the impossibility of darkness and illumination being brought together.'

तस्मात्सर्वाणि कर्माणि वैदिकानि महामते ।
चित्तशुद्ध्यन्तमेव स्युस्तानि कुर्यात्प्रयत्नतः ॥ (3.15)

'O immensely intelligent one! Therefore, until the consciousness has been purified, one must make efforts to undertake all the karma mentioned in the Vedas.'

शमो दमस्तितिक्षा च वैराग्यं सत्त्वसंभवः ।
तावत्पर्यन्तमेव स्युः कर्माणि न ततः परम् ॥ (3.16)

'Until inner control, external control, fortitude, non-attachment and generation of sattva occur, karma must be undertaken, but not after that.'

तदन्ते चौव संन्यस्य सश्रयेद् गुरुमात्मवान् ।
श्रोत्रियं ब्रह्मनिष्ठं च भक्त्या निर्व्याजया पुनः ॥ (3.17)

'After that, one must seek refuge with a guru, who is in control of his atman, and take *sannyasa*. He must be learned and be devoted to the Brahman. One must do this faithfully, without deceit.'

वेदान्तश्रवणं कुर्यान्नित्यमेवमतन्द्रितः ।
तत्त्वमस्यादिवाक्यस्य नित्यमर्थं विचारयेत् ॥ (3.18)

'Constantly, one must attentively listen to Vedanta. One must constantly reflect on the true meanings of those words.'

तत्त्वमस्यादिवाक्यं तु जीवब्रह्मैक्यबोधकम् ।
ऐक्ये ज्ञाते निर्भयस्तु मद्रूपो हि प्रजायते ॥ (3.19)

'"Tat tvam asi"[25]—these words make one understand the unity between the jivatman and Brahman. When this unity is understood, no fear originates as a result of my form.'

पदार्थावगतिः पूर्वं वाक्यार्थावगतिस्ततः ।
तत्पदस्य च वाच्यार्थो गिरेऽहं परिकीर्तितः ॥ (3.20)

'One must first understand the meaning of the sentence and the meaning of the word. O mountain! When the word "tat" is spoken, the meaning is that I am being described.'

त्वंपदस्य च वाच्यार्थो जीव एव न संशयः ।
उभयोरैक्यमसिना पदेन प्रोच्यते बुधैः ॥ (3.21)

'There is no doubt that when the word "tvam" is spoken, the jivatman is being referred to. The learned say that "asi" indicates unity between the two.'

वाच्यार्थयोर्विरुद्धत्वादैक्यं नैव घटेत ह ।
लक्षणाऽतः प्रकर्तव्या तत्त्वमोः श्रुतिसंस्थयोः ॥ (3.22)

'The meanings of these two spoken words seem to be contradictory, so that unity is not possible. Therefore, to establish the truth, one must consider the signs and depend on the Shruti texts.'

चिन्मात्रं तु तयोर्लक्ष्यं तयोरैक्यस्य सम्भवः ।
तयोरैक्यं तथा ज्ञात्वा स्वाभेदेनाद्वयो भवेत् ॥ (3.23)

'When consciousness is the sign in both of them, unity between the two is possible. When one understands unity between the two, there is no longer any natural difference between the two.'

---

[25]These words translate to: 'You are that.'

देवदत्तः स एवायमितिवल्लक्षणा स्मृता ।
स्थूलादिदेहरहितो ब्रह्म सम्पद्यते नरः ॥ (3.24)

'"This is Devadatta." When this is said, the signs are a function of age.[26] When a man is separated from the gross body, he obtains the Brahman.'

पञ्चीकृतमहाभूतसंभूतः स्थूलदेहकः ।
भोगालयो जराव्याधिसंयुतः सर्वकर्मणाम् ॥ (3.25)

'The gross body is a result of the five great elements being brought together. It suffers from old age and disease and is an abode for enjoying every kind of karma.'

मिथ्याभूतोऽयमाभाति स्फुटं मायामयत्वतः ।
सोऽयं स्थूल उपाधिः स्यादात्मनो मे नगेश्वर ॥ (3.26)

'This is a false existence. It is clearly evident that, in truth, this is nothing but mayaa. O lord of mountains! This is nothing but a gross appellation being given to my atman.'

ज्ञानकर्मेन्द्रिययुतं प्राणपञ्चकसंयुतम् ।
मनोबुद्धियुतं चौतत्सूक्ष्मं तत्कवयो विदुः ॥ (3.27)

'The wise know that the subtle body is formed by the senses of perception, the organs of action, the five types of prana, mind and intelligence.'

अपञ्चीकृतभूतोत्थं सूक्ष्मदेहोऽयमात्मनः ।
द्वितीयोऽयमुपाधिः स्यात्सुखादेरवबोधकः ॥ (3.28)

'The subtle body of the atman is formed when the five elements are not compounded together. This is the second appellation given, when one experiences pleasure and pain.'

[26]The Devadattas of yesterday, today and tomorrow are different.

अनाद्यनिर्वाच्यमिदमज्ञानं तु तृतीयकः ।
देहोऽयमात्मनो भाति कारणात्मा नगेश्वर ॥ (3.29)

'The third body of the atman results from an ignorance that cannot be spoken about and is without a beginning. O lord of mountains! This appears as a cause.'

उपाधिविलये जाते केवलात्मावशिष्यते ।
देहत्रये पञ्चकोशा अन्तस्थाः सन्ति सर्वदा ॥ (3.30)

'When these appellations dissolve away, only the true atman is left. Internally, the three bodies and the five sheaths always exist.'[27]

पञ्चकोशपरित्यागे ब्रह्मपुच्छं हि लभ्यते ।
नेतिनेतीत्यादिवाक्यैर्मम रूपं यदुच्यते ॥ (3.31)

'When one abandons the five sheaths, one understands the Brahman. Through the words, "Not this, not this," it is my form that is being spoken about.'

न जायते म्रियते तत्कदाचिन्नायं भूत्वा न बभूव कश्चित् ।
अजो नित्यः शाश्वतोऽयं पुराणो न हन्यते हन्यमाने शरीरे ॥ (3.32)

'It is never born. Nor does it ever die. It did not come into being. Nor will it ever come into being. It is without birth and is constant. It is eternal and ancient. When the body is killed, it is not killed.'

हन्ता चेन्मन्यते हन्तुं हतश्चेन्मन्यते हतम् ।
उभौ तौ न विजानीतो नायं हन्ति न हन्यते ॥ (3.33)

'A person may think of it as a killer and himself as the one killed. Another, wanting to kill it, may think that it has been killed. Both of them do not know. It does not

---

[27]The five sheaths (*koshas*) are *annamaya, pranamaya, manomaya, vijnanamaya* and *anandamaya*. The three bodies are *sthuladeha, lingadeha* and *karanadeha*.

kill and cannot be killed.'

अणोरणीयान्महतो महीयानात्मास्य जन्तोर्निहितो गुहायाम् ।
तमक्रतुः पश्यति वीतशोको धातुप्रसादान्महिमानमस्य ॥ (3.34)

'Residing in the cavity of the heart of a being, the atman is smaller than the smallest and greater than the greatest. If a person transcends the darkness, he perceives the greatness and, through its favours, is freed from grief.'

आत्मानं रथिनं विद्धि शरीरं रथमेव तु ।
बुद्धिं तु सारथिं विद्धि मनः प्रग्रहमेव च ॥ (3.35)

'Know that the atman is the chariot rider, and the body is the chariot. Know that intelligence is the charioteer, and that the mind represents the reins.'

इन्द्रियाणि हयानाहुर्विषयांस्तेषु गोचरान् ।
आत्मेन्द्रियमनोयुक्तं भोक्तेत्याहुर्मनीषिणः ॥ (3.36)

'The senses are described as horses, and material objects as objectives. The learned say that the atman, along with the senses and the mind, is the one who enjoys.'

यस्त्वविद्वान्भवति चामनस्कश्च सदाशुचिः ।
स तु तत्पदमवाप्नोति संसारं चाधिगच्छति ॥ (3.37)

'If a learned person is attentive and always pure, he crosses samsara and reaches that destination.'

यस्तु विज्ञानवान्भवति समनस्कः सदा शुचिः ।
स तु तत्पदमाप्नोति यस्माद्भूयो न जायते ॥ (3.38)

'If a person possesses vijnana, is attentive and is always pure, he obtains the destination, from which one does not have to be born again.'

विज्ञानसारथिर्यस्तु मनः प्रग्रहवान्नरः ।
सोऽध्वनः पारमाप्नोति मदीयं यत्परं पदम् ॥ (3.39)

'With vijnana as a charioteer, such a man reins in the mind. He crosses the path to the other side and obtains me as a supreme destination.'

इत्थं श्रुत्या च मत्या च निश्चित्यात्मानमात्मना ।
भावयेन्मामात्मरूपां निदिध्यासनतोऽपि च ॥ (3.40)

'Having heard this and having certainly made up his mind to fix himself on his atman, he should think of my form in his atman and fix himself in meditation on me.'

योगवृत्तेः पुरा स्वामिन्भावयेदक्षरत्रयम् ।
देवीप्रणवसंज्ञस्य ध्यानार्थं मन्त्रवाच्ययोः ॥ (3.41)

'Having first mastered the practice of yoga, he should think of the three aksharas that are spoken of in Devi's Pranava Mantra and use it for dhyana.'

हकारः स्थूलदेहः स्याद्रकारः सूक्ष्मदेहकः ।
ईकारः काराणात्माऽसौ ह्रीङ्कारोऽहं तुरीयकम् ॥ (3.42)

'ह stands for the gross body, while र indicates the subtle body. ई stands for the causal body. My *turiya* state is in the bindu of ह्री.'[28]

एवं समष्टिदेहेऽपि ज्ञात्वा बीजत्रयं क्रमात् ।
समष्टिव्यष्ट्योरेकत्वं भावयेन्मतिमान्नरः ॥ (3.43)

'In this way, in the due order, an intelligent man will know the aggregate of the three bijas in the body and meditate on them, separately and in the aggregate, and on their union.'

समाधिकालात्पूर्वं तु भावयित्वैवमादृतः ।
ततो ध्यायेन्निलीनाक्षो देवीं मां जगदीश्वरीम् ॥ (3.44)

---

[28]A living being has four states—waking, dreaming, sleeping and turiya, which is the fourth state, when one perceives union between the human atman and the Brahman. In addition to ha, ra and i, there is the bindu in hrim.

'Before embarking on samadhi, he should meditate in this way. Thus, he should close his eyes and perform dhyana on me, Devi, the Ishvari of the universe.'

प्राणापानौ समौ कृत्वा नासाभ्यन्तरचारिणौ ।
निवृत्तविषयाकाङ्क्षो वीतदोषो विमत्सरः ॥ (3.45)

'He must ensure equilibrium between prana and apana, moving around inside the nose. He must withdraw from material objects and desires and be devoid of taints and envy.'

भक्त्या निर्व्याजया युक्तो गुहायां निःस्वने स्थले ।
हकारं विश्वमात्मानं रकारे प्रविलापयेत् ॥ (3.46)

'With devotion that lacks deceit, he must engage in yoga. "Ha", with the universe in its atman, will be dissolved in "ra", in the silent cavity of his heart.'[29]

रकारं तैजसं देवमीकारे प्रविलापयेत् ।
ईकारं प्राज्ञयात्मानं ह्रीङ्कारे प्रविलापयेत् ॥ (3.47)

'In this way, the "ra" of *taijasa* dissolves into the "i" of wisdom, and that, in turn, dissolves into "hrim".'[30]

वाच्यवाचकताहीनं द्वैतभावविवर्जितम् ।
अखण्डं सच्चिदानन्दं भावयेत्तच्छिखान्तरे ॥ (3.48)

'That state is devoid of speech or a speaker. It is devoid of duality. It is complete truth, consciousness and bliss, and he should meditate on this, inside the flames.'

इति ध्यानेन मां राजन्साक्षात्कृत्य नरोत्तमः ।
मद्रूप एव भवति द्वयोरप्येकता यतः ॥ (3.49)

---

[29]The gross body dissolves into the subtle body.

[30]Taijasa is the radiant third state. The first state of wakefulness is *vishva* (universe). The second state of sleep/dreaming is taijasa. The third state of deep sleep (sushupti) is *praja* (wisdom). Beyond that is the fourth state of turiya.

'O king! If an excellent man performs dhyana in this way, he directly realizes my form, with unity in the duality.'

योगयुक्त्याऽनया द्रष्टा मामात्मानं परात्परम् ।
अज्ञानस्य सकार्यस्य तत्क्षणे नाशको भवेत् ॥ (3.50)

'Engaged in yoga this way, he sees my atman, beyond the greatest. At that instant, all ignorance and tasks are destroyed.'

हिमालय उवाच–
योगं वद महेशानि साङ्गं संवित्प्रदायकम् ।
कृतेन येन योग्योऽहं भवेयं तत्त्वदर्शने ॥ (4.1)

Himalaya said, 'O Maheshani! Please tell me about yoga and its limbs, which bestow consciousness. So that, if I practise that yoga, I can behold the truth.'

देव्युवाच–
न योगो नभसः पृष्ठे न भूमौ न रसातले ।
ऐक्यं जीवात्मनोराहुर्योगं योगविशारदाः ॥ (4.2)

Devi replied, 'Yoga does not exist in the vault of heaven, on earth or in the nether regions. Those who are accomplished in yoga say that unity between the jivatman and the paramatman is yoga.'

तत्प्रत्यूहाः षडाख्याता योगविघ्नकरानघ ।
कामक्रोधौ लोभमोहौ मदमात्सर्यसंज्ञकौ ॥ (4.3)

'O one without blemish! There are said to be six impediments to yoga, known as desire, anger, greed, delusion, insolence and envy.'

योगाङ्गैरेव भित्त्वा तान्योगिनो योगमाप्नुयुः ।
यमं नियममासनप्राणायामौ ततःपरम् ॥ (4.4)

'Yogis attain yoga when they destroy these, using the limbs of yama, niyama and asana, and after that, pranayama...'[31]

प्रत्याहारं धारणाख्यं ध्यानं सार्धं समाधिना ।
अष्टाङ्गान्याहुरेतानि योगिनां योगसाधने ॥ (4.5)

'...And those known as pratyahara, dharanaa and dhyana, along with samadhi. Yogis who pursue sadhana through yoga speak of these as the eight limbs.'

अहिंसा सत्यमस्तेयं ब्रह्मचर्यं दयार्जवम् ।
क्षमा धृतिर्मिताहारः शौचं चेति यमा दश ॥ (4.6)

'The ten types of yama are non-violence, truthfulness, lack of theft, brahmacharya, compassion, uprightness, forgiveness, fortitude, restraint in diet and purity.'

तपः सन्तोष आस्तिक्यं दानं देवस्य पूजनम् ।
सिद्धान्तश्रवणं चौव ह्रीर्मतिश्च जपो हुतम् ॥ (4.7)

'Austerities, contentment, belief, donations, worship of the divinity, firmness in conviction, hearing, modesty, japa and oblations.'

दशैते नियमाः प्रोक्ता मया पर्वतनायक ।
पद्मासनं स्वस्तिकं च भद्रं वज्रासनं तथा ॥ (4.8)

वीरासनमिति प्रोक्तं क्रमादासनपञ्चकम् ।
ऊर्वोरुपरि विन्यस्य सम्यक्पादतले शुभे ॥ (4.9)

'O leader of mountains! I have, thus, spoken about the ten aspects of niyama. *Padmasana, svastikasana, bhadrasana, vajrasana, virasana*. In the due order,

---

[31]Yoga has eight elements—yama (restraint), niyama (rituals), asana (posture), pranayama (breathing), pratyahara (withdrawal), dharanaa (retention), dhyana (meditation) and samadhi (liberation). That's the reason the expression Ashtanga (eight-formed) Yoga is used.

these are spoken of as the five kinds of asanas. It is auspicious to properly place the soles of the feet on top of the thighs.'

अङ्गिष्ठौ च निबध्नीयाद्धस्ताभ्यां व्युत्क्रमात्ततः ।
पद्मासनमिति प्रोक्तं योगिनां हृदयंगमम् ॥ (4.10)

'Starting from below, the body must be fixed, straight. Yogis say that this posture, which pleases the heart, is padmasana.'

जानूर्वोरन्तरे सम्यक्कृत्वा पादतले शुभे ।
ऋजुकायो विशेद्योगी स्वस्तिकं तत्प्रचक्षते ॥ (4.11)

'It is auspicious to properly place the soles of the feet inserted inside the thighs, with the body straight. When a yogi does this, it is said to be svastikasana.'

सीवन्याः पार्श्वयोर्न्यस्य गुल्फयुग्मं सुनिश्चितम् ।
वृषणाधः पादपार्ष्णी पाणिभ्यां परिबन्धयेत् ॥ (4.12)

'The two heels must be firmly placed near the anus and, using the two hands, the two heels must be placed towards the bottom of the testicles.'

भद्रासनमिति प्रोक्तं योगिभिः परिपूजितम् ।
ऊर्वोः पादौ क्रमान्न्यस्य जान्वोः प्रत्यङ्मुखाङ्गुली ॥ (4.13)

'This is spoken of as bhadrasana and is revered by yogis. In the due order, the feet are placed on the thighs and the fingers are inserted under the thighs.'

करौ विदध्यादाख्यातं वज्रासनमनुत्तमम् ।
एकं पादमधः कृत्वा विन्यस्योरुं तथोत्तरे ॥ (4.14)

'When the hands are placed in this way, it is known as the excellent vajrasana. One foot is placed under one thigh, and this is also done with the other one.'

ऋजुकायो विशेद्योगी वीरासनमितीरितम् ।
इडयाकर्षयेद्वायुं बाह्यं षोडशमात्रया ॥ (4.15)

'When a yogi holds his body straight in this way, it is known as virasana. The breath is drawn in from outside through *ida* and held for 16 matraas.'[32]

धारयेत्पूरितं योगी चतुःषष्ट्या तु मात्रया ।
सुषुम्नामध्यगं सम्यग्द्वात्रिंशन्मात्रया शनैः ॥ (4.16)

'Having filled it up in this way, the yogi holds it for 64 matraas, maintaining equilibrium with the central sushumna and, gradually, extending it to over 32 matraas.'

नाड्या पिङ्गलया चैव रेचयेद्योगवित्तमः ।
प्राणायाममिमं प्राहुर्योगशास्त्रविशारदाः ॥ (4.17)

'An excellent yogi then uses *pingala nadi* to perform *rechaka*. Those who are accomplished in the texts of yoga speak of this as pranayama.'

भूयो भूयः क्रमात्तस्य बाह्यमेवं समाचरेत् ।
मात्रावृद्धिः क्रमेणैव सम्यग्द्वादश षोडश ॥ (4.18)

'As one repeatedly does this properly, inhaling from outside, the number of matraas can be gradually increased to 12 and 16.'

जपध्यानादिभिः सार्थं सगर्भं तं विदुर्बुधाः ।
तदपेतं विगर्भं च प्राणायामं परे विदुः ॥ (4.19)

'The learned speak of Sagarbha Pranayama as one where dhyana is performed along with japa. The learned know that Vigarbha[33] is superior.'

---

[32]Ida is the left channel, pingala is the right channel and sushumna is the one in the centre. Here, matraa means an instant. *Puraka, kumbhaka* and rechaka are respectively inhalation, retention and exhalation.

[33]When no japa is necessary.

क्रमादभ्यस्यतः पुंसो देहे स्वेदोद्गमोऽधमः ।
मध्यमः कंपसंयुक्तो भूमित्यागः परो मतः ॥ (4.20)

'When this is repeatedly practised, a man's body starts to sweat. This is inferior. When there is trembling, it is middling. When one rises up from the ground, it is considered superior.'

उत्तमस्य गुणावाप्तिर्यावच्छीलनमिष्यते ।
इन्द्रियाणां विचरतां विषयेषु निरर्गलम् ॥ (4.21)

'One should wish to practise until one attains those excellent qualities. Senses that roam among material objects will then be restrained.'

बलादाहरणं तेभ्यः प्रत्याहारोऽभिधीयते ।
अङ्गुष्ठगुल्फजानूरुमूलाधारलिङ्गनाभिषु ॥ (4.22)

हृद्ग्रीवाकण्ठदेशेषु लंबिकायां ततो नसि ।
भ्रूमध्ये मस्तके मूर्ध्नि द्वादशान्ते यथाविधि ॥ (4.23)

धारणं प्राणमरुतो धारणेति निगद्यते ।
समाहितेन मनसा चौतन्यान्तरवर्तिना ॥ (4.24)

'When these are forcibly restrained, it is known as pratyahara. Toes, heels, knees, thighs, *muladhara*, genital organs, navel, heart, neck, throat, tongue, nose, between the brows, forehead, head and *dvadashanta*[34], these in the due order holding the breath of life is said to be dharanaa. The mind must be controlled and fixed on the consciousness inside.'

आत्मन्यभीष्टदेवानां ध्यानं ध्यानमिहोच्यते ।
समत्वभावना नित्यं जीवात्मपरमात्मनोः ॥ (4.25)

---

[34]Dvadashanta, ending in 12, is another name for Brahmarandhra. However, dvadashanta is also interpreted as the width of 12 fingers, inside the skull, or outside the skull and above it, thus, external to the body.

'Meditating on one's *ishta devata* is said to be dhyana. One must always think of identity between the jivatman and the paramatman.'

समाधिर्माहुर्मुनयः प्रोक्तमष्टाङ्गलक्षणम् ।
इदानीं कथये तेऽहं मन्त्रयोगमनुत्तमम् ॥ (4.26)

'The sages say that this is samadhi. I have spoken about the nature of ashtanga. I will now speak to you about the excellent yoga of mantras.'

विश्वं शरीरमित्युक्तं पञ्चभूतात्मकं नग ।
चन्द्रसूर्याग्नितेजोभिर्जीवब्रह्मैक्यरूपकम् ॥ (4.27)

'O mountain! This body, known as Vishva, consists of the five elements. It possesses the energy of the moon and the sun and has the form of unity between the jivatman and the Brahman.'

तिस्रः कोट्यस्तदर्धेन शरीरे नाडयो मताः ।
तासु मुख्या दश प्रोक्तास्ताभ्यस्तिस्रो व्यवस्थिताः ॥ (4.28)

'It is believed that there are three and a half crore *nadi*s in the body. Of these, 10 are principal. Among them, there are three.'

प्रधाना मेरुदण्डेऽत्र चन्द्रसूर्याग्निरूपिणी ।
इडा वामे स्थिता नाडी शुभ्रा तु चन्द्ररूपिणी ॥ (4.29)

'The chief is in the centre of the spinal cord and takes the form of the moon, the sun and the fire. The auspicious ida is the nadi to the left and takes the form of the moon.'

शक्तिरूपा तु सा नाडी साक्षादमृतविग्रहा ।
दक्षिणे या पिङ्गलाख्या पुंरूपा सूर्यविग्रहा ॥ (4.30)

'This nadi is Shakti's form, and it directly takes the form of amrita. The one to the right is known as pingala. It is masculine and takes the form of the sun.'

सर्वतेजोमयी सा तु सुषुम्ना वह्निरूपिणी ।
तस्या मध्ये विचित्राख्ये इच्छाज्ञानक्रियात्मकम् ॥ (4.31)

'Sushumna possesses every kind of energy and takes the form of the fire. It is in the centre and is said to be colourful. Within it, it possesses the power of will, knowledge and action.'

मध्ये स्वयंभूलिङ्गं तु कोटिसूर्यसमप्रभम् ।
तदूर्ध्वं मायाबीजं तु हरात्माबिन्दुनादकम् ॥ (4.32)

'The self-manifested lingam is in the centre, with the resplendence of one crore suns. The bija of mayaa is above this. In its atman is Hara, with bindu and nada.'

तदूर्ध्वं तु शिखाकारा कुण्डली रक्तविग्रहा ।
देव्यात्मिका तु सा प्रोक्ता मदभिन्ना नगाधिप ॥ (4.33)

'The *kundali*, red in form, is above this, in the form of a flame. O lord of mountains! Its atman is said to be that of Devi, and it is no different from me.'

तद्बाह्ये हेमरूपाभं वादिसान्तचतुर्दलम् ।
द्रुतहेमसमप्रख्यं पद्मं तत्र विचिन्तयेत् ॥ (4.34)

'Outside this, there is a four-petalled lotus, golden in complexion. It is described as gold, and one should meditate on this, with the *pada* that starts with "va" and ends with "sa".'[35]

तदूर्ध्वं त्वनलप्रख्यं षड्दलं हीरकप्रभम् ।
बादिलान्तषड्वर्णेन स्वाधिष्ठानमनुत्तमम् ॥ (4.35)

[35]Chakras are centres of energy in the body, and the usual list, ascending upwards, is Muladhara, Svadhishthana, Manipura, Anahata, Vishuddhi (or Vishuddha) and Ajna. Beyond these is Sahasrara. This is a description of Muladhara, in the form of a lotus with four petals. The pada for meditation is व श ष स. The number of varnas in the pada depends on the number of petals in the lotus. For svadhishthana, with six petals, it is व भ म य र and ल.

'Above this, there is a six-petalled lotus, as resplendent as a diamond and known as fire. This is the excellent svadhishthana, and one meditates with six varnas, starting with "va" and ending with "la".'

मूलाधारषट्कोणं मूलाधारं ततो विदुः ।
स्वशब्देन परं लिङ्गं स्वाधिष्ठानं ततो विदुः ॥ (4.36)

'Muladhara is in the form of a six-pointed star[36] and is known to be the support and the foundation. The word "sva" stands for a supreme lingam and is, therefore, known as svadhishthana.'

तदूर्ध्वं नाभिदेशे तु मणिपूरं महाप्रभम् ।
मेघाभं विद्युदाभं च बहुतेजोमयं ततः ॥ (4.37)

'Above this, in the region of the navel, there is Manipura and it is immensely radiant. It has the complexion of clouds, the complexion of lightning. It is full of great energy.'

मणिवद्भिन्नं तत्पद्मं मणिपद्मं तथोच्यते ।
दशभिश्च दलैर्युक्तं डादिफान्ताक्षरान्वितम् ॥ (4.38)

'That lotus is like a jewel and is no different from it. Hence, it is spoken of as Manipadma. It has ten petals and the aksharas start with "da" and end with "pha".'[37]

विष्णुनाऽधिष्ठितं पत्रं विष्ण्वालोकनकारणम् ।
तदूर्ध्वेनाहतं पद्ममुद्यदादित्यसन्निभम् ॥ (4.39)

'Vishnu is established on the petals, and it enables one to see Vishnu. Above this, is the lotus, known as Anahata, which resembles the sun.'

---

[36]The triangle that points upwards is Shiva, and the triangle pointing downwards is Shakti.

[37]The ten aksharas include: ड, ढ, ण, त, थ, द, ड, न, प and फ.

कादिठान्तदलैरर्कपत्रैश्च समधिष्ठितम् ।
तन्मध्ये बाणलिङ्गं तु सूर्यायुतसमप्रभम् ।। (4.40)

'The petals of that sun are established such that they start with "ka" and end with "tha". In the centre, there is a Bana Lingam, and it is as resplendent as ten thousand suns.'[38]

शब्दब्रह्ममयं शब्दानाहतं तत्र दृश्यते ।
अनाहताख्यं तत्पद्मं मुनिभिः परिकीर्तितम् ।। (4.41)

'It is full of *shabda-brahma*, and the sound can be seen there, without being struck. That is the reason sages speak of that lotus as Anahata.'[39]

आनन्दसदनं तत्तु पुरुषाधिष्ठितं परम् ।
तदूर्ध्वं तु विशुद्धाख्यं दलषोडशपङ्कजम् ।। (4.42)

'This is the abode of bliss, and the Supreme Purusha presides over it. About that is the one known as Vishuddha, the lotus with 16 petals.'

स्वरैः षोडशभिर्युक्तं धूम्रवर्णं महाप्रभम् ।
विशुद्धं तनुते यस्माज्जीवस्य हंसलोकनात् ।। (4.43)

'It is associated with the 16 vowel sounds. It is smoky in complexion and is immensely radiant. Since the jivatman sees *hamsa* in his form, it is known as Vishuddha.'[40]

विशुद्धं पद्ममाख्यातमाकाशाख्यं महाद्भुतम् ।
आज्ञाचक्रं तदूर्ध्वे तु आत्मनाऽधिष्ठितं परम् ।। (4.44)

---

[38]This lotus has 12 petals—क, ख, ग, घ, ङ, च, छ, ज, झ, ञ, त, थ. Bana Lingam is an immobile Shiva lingam.

[39]Shabda-brahma is the sound that is the Brahman. Anahata means something that has not been struck.

[40]These vowel sounds include: अ, आ, इ, ई, उ, ऊ, ऋ, ॠ, ऌ, ॡ ए, ऐ, ओ, औ, अः and अं. Vishuddha means purified, while hamsa (swan) is an image for the Brahman.

'The lotus known as Vishuddha is extremely wonderful and is known as space. Above that is the chakra known as Ajna, and the Supreme Atman is established there.'

आज्ञासङ्क्रमणं तत्र तेनाज्ञेति प्रकीर्तितम् ।
द्विदलं हक्षसंयुक्तं पद्मं तत्सुमनोहरम् ।। (4.45)

'Since the command comes from there, it is described as Ajna.[41] The lotus has two petals, and it is extremely beautiful, with the pada consisting of ह and क्ष.'

कैलासाख्यं तदूर्ध्वं तु रोधिनी तु तदूर्ध्वतः ।
एवं त्वाधारचक्राणि प्रोक्तानि तव सुव्रत ।। (4.46)

'The one known as Kailasa is above that, and atop that is the one known as Rodhini. O one excellent in vows! I have, thus, spoken to you about the chakras that are the foundation.'

सहस्रारयुतं बिन्दुस्थानं तदूर्ध्वमीरितम् ।
इत्येतत्कथितं सर्वं योगमार्गमनुत्तमम् ।। (4.47)

'Sahasrara, with one thousand petals, is said to be above that and is the place for bindu. I have, thus, told you everything about the excellent path of yoga.'

आदौ पूरकयोगेनाप्याधारे योजयेन्मनः ।
गुदमेढ्रान्तरे शक्तिस्तामाकुञ्च्य प्रबोधयेत् ।। (4.48)

'In the beginning, use the yoga of puraka to support and fix the mind between the genital organ and the anus. Then contract and awaken the Shakti there.'

लिङ्गभेदक्रमेणैव बिन्दुचक्रं च प्रापयेत् ।
शम्भुना तां पराशक्तिमेकीभूतां विचिन्तयेत् ।। (4.49)

'In the appropriate order, ascend up the lingams, until

[41]The word ajna means command.

you reach the chakra of bindu. Then, meditate on Shambhu and Supreme Shakti as one.'

तत्रोत्थितामृतं यत्तु द्रुतलाक्षारसोपमम् ।
पाययित्वा तु तां शक्तिं मायख्यां योगसिद्धिदाम् ॥ (4.50)

'Resembling the juice of lac, amrita swiftly begins to flow from there. Having drunk what is known as my mayaa shakti, one obtains siddhi in yoga.'

षट्चक्रदेवतास्तत्र सन्तर्प्यामृतधारया ।
आनयेत्तेन मार्गेण मूलाधारं ततः सुधीः ॥ (4.51)

'The flow of amrita there satisfies the divinities of the six chakras. Following the same path, an intelligent person then brings it down to Muladhara.'

एवमभ्यस्यमानस्याप्यहन्यहनि निश्चितम् ।
पूर्वोक्तदूषिता मन्त्राः सर्वे सिध्यन्ति नान्यथा ॥ (4.52)

'In this way, one must practise from one day to another. Those pure mantras, stated earlier, will bring about every kind of siddhi. There will be no violation of this.'

जरामरणदुःखाद्यैर्मुच्यते भवबन्धनात् ।
ये गुणाः सन्ति देव्या मे जगन्मातुर्यथा तथा ॥ (4.53)

'They will be freed from old age, death, miseries and other bonds of this world. I am Devi, the mother of the universe, and they will obtain my qualities.'

ते गुणाः साधकवरे भवन्त्येव न चान्यथा ।
इत्येवं कथितं तात वायुधारणमुत्तमम् ॥ (4.54)

'Those excellent sadhakas will obtain these qualities. There will be no violation of this. O child! I have spoken to you about the excellent means of holding breath.'

इदानीं धारणाख्यं तु शृणुष्वावहितो मम ।
दिक्कालाद्यनवच्छिन्नदेव्यां चेतो विधाय च ॥ (4.55)

'Now, listen, as I tell you about what is known as dharanaa. I constantly pervade the directions, time and space. Fix the consciousness on me, Devi.'

तन्मयो भवति क्षिप्रं जीवब्रह्मैक्ययोजनात् ।
अथवा समलं चेतो यदि क्षिप्रं न सिध्यति ॥ (4.56)

'If a person is immersed in me, he swiftly realizes unity between the jivatman and the Brahman. However, if the consciousness has impurities, success may not come swiftly.'

तदावयवयोगेन योगी योगान्समभ्यसेत् ।
मदीयहस्तपादादावङ्गे तु मधुरे नग ॥ (4.57)

'Then a yogi must practise Avayava Yoga[42]. O mountain! He must fix himself on my gentle hands, feet and other limbs.'

चित्तं संस्थापयेन्मन्त्री स्थानस्थानजयात्पुनः ।
विशुद्धचित्तः सर्वस्मिन्रूपे संस्थापयेन्मनः ॥ (4.58)

'Fixing his consciousness with the use of mantras, he must seek to conquer these places, one by one. When his consciousness has been purified, he should fix his mind on the entire form.'

यावन्मनो लयं याति देव्यां संविदि पर्वत ।
तावदिष्टमिनुं मन्त्री जपहोमैः समभ्यसेत् ॥ (4.59)

'O mountain! Until the mind is dissolved into Devi's consciousness, he must use mantras and practise japa and oblations in the way instructed.'

[42]Avayava means parts of the body, or the entire body.

मन्त्राभ्यासेन योगेन ज्ञेयज्ञानाय कल्पते ।
न योगेन विना मन्त्रो न मन्त्रेण विना हि सः ॥ (4.60)

'By practising mantra and yoga, what should be known is thought to become jnana. There is no yoga without mantras and no mantras without yoga.'

द्वयोरभ्यासयोगो हि ब्रह्मसंसिद्धिकारणम् ।
तमःपरिवृते गेहे घटो दीपेन दृश्यते ॥ (4.61)

'The practice of both together leads to realization of the Brahman. This is like a pot in a room enveloped in darkness becoming visible through a lamp.'

एवं मायावृतो ह्यात्मा मनुना गोचरीकृतः ।
इति योगविधिः कृत्स्नः साङ्गः प्रोक्तो मयाऽधुना ॥ (4.62)

'The atmans of humans are enveloped in mayaa. In this way, things are perceived. I have now described to you the method of yoga, along with all its limbs.'

देव्युवाच-
इत्यादि योगयुक्तात्मा ध्यायेन्मां ब्रह्मरूपिणीम् ।
भक्त्या निर्व्याजया राजन्नासने समुपस्थितः ॥ (5.1)

Devi said, 'O king! In this way, seated in an asana, one must fix one's atman in yoga and perform dhyana on me, the form of the Brahman. The devotion must be without deceit.'

आविः सन्निहितं गुहाचरं नाम महत्परम् ।
अत्रैतत्सर्वमर्पितमेजत्प्राणन्निमिषच्च यत् ॥ (5.2)

'The one named the Great and the Supreme is near, secreted in the cavity of the heart. Everything is dedicated to him—movement, breath of life, the blinking of an eye.'

एतज्जानथ सदसद्वरेण्यं परं विज्ञानाद्यद्वरिष्ठं प्रजानाम् ।
यदर्चिमद्यदणुभ्योऽणु च यस्मिंल्लोका निहिता लोकिनश्च ॥ (5.3)

'It should be known that the one to be worshipped is greater than existence and non-existence. For beings, he is the best kind of vijnana. The radiant one is smaller than the smallest. The worlds, and those presiding over them, are established in him.'

तदेतदक्षरं ब्रह्म स प्राणस्तदु वाङ् मनः ।
तदेतत्सत्यममृतं तद्वेद्धव्यं सौम्य विद्धि ॥ (5.4)

'He is the imperishable Brahman. He is the breath of life, speech and the mind. He is truth. He is amrita. O amiable one! Know that he is the one to be known.'

धनुर्गृहीत्वौपनिषदं महास्त्रं शरं ह्युपासानिशितं सन्धयीत ।
आयम्य तद्भावगतेन चेतसा लक्ष्यं तदेवाक्षरं सौम्य विद्धि ॥ (5.5)

'Accept the bow of the Upanishads. Using the great weapon of *upasanaa*,[43] with that sharp arrow, fix your aim. Restrain your consciousness with that sentiment. O amiable one! Know that the imperishable one is the objective.'

प्रणवो धनुः शरो ह्यात्मा ब्रह्मतल्लक्ष्यमुच्यते ।
अप्रमत्तेन वेद्धव्यं शरवत्तन्मयो भवेत् ॥ (5.6)

'Pranava is the bow. The atman is the arrow. The Brahman is spoken of as the target. If one is not distracted, one becomes like the arrow and strikes the target.'

यस्मिन्द्यौश्च पृथिवी चान्तरिक्षमोतं मनः सह प्राणैश्च सर्वैः ।
तमेवैकं जानथात्मानमन्या वाचो विमुञ्चथामृतस्यैष सेतुः ॥ (5.7)

'The firmament, the earth, the sky, the mind, the breath of life and everything else are woven into him. Know that the atman is alone the one who is the support. Let go of speech. He is the bridge to immortality.'

---

[43]Upasanaa means worship. But the word is also used in archery to fix one's aim.

अरा इव रथनाभौ संहता यत्र नाड्यः ।
स एषोऽन्तश्चरते बहुधा जायमानः ॥ (5.8)

'Like spokes fixed to the nave of a chariot, the nadis are affixed to him. He roams around inside and manifests himself in many ways.'

ओमित्येवं ध्यायथात्मानं स्वस्ति वः पाराय तमसः परस्तात् ।
दिव्ये ब्रह्मपुरे व्योम्नि आत्मा सम्प्रतिष्ठितः ॥ (5.9)

'In the form of "OUM", one should perform dhyana on the atman. He enables one to cross over to what is beneficial. He is beyond darkness. The atman is established in the divine space that is the city of the Brahman.'

मनोमयः प्राणशरीरनेता प्रतिष्ठितोऽन्ने हृदयं सन्निधाय ।
तद्विज्ञानेन परिपश्यन्ति धीरा आनन्दरूपममृतं यद्विभाति ॥ (5.10)

'He is in the mind. He leads the breath of life and the body. He is established in the heart and controls it. Using vijnana, the persevering see him manifested in the form of bliss and amrita.'

भिद्यते हृदयग्रन्थिश्छिद्यन्ते सर्वसंशयाः ।
क्षीयन्ते चास्य कर्माणि तस्मिन्दृष्टे परावरे ॥ (5.11)

'The bonds of the heart are severed. All doubts are sliced away. When the greatest of the great is seen, all karma withers away.'

हिरण्मये परे कोशे विराजं ब्रह्म निष्कलम् ।
तच्छुभ्रं ज्योतिषां ज्योतिस्तद्यदात्मविदो विदुः ॥ (5.12)

'Without separate parts, the Brahman, bereft of passion, is in a supreme and golden sheath. He is auspicious and most luminous among everything luminous. Those who know the atman know him.'

न तत्र सूर्यो भाति न चन्द्रतारकं नेमा विद्युतो भान्ति कुतोऽयमग्निः।
तमेव भान्तमनुभाति सर्वं तस्य भासा सर्वमिदं विभाति ॥ (5.13)

'The sun does not shine there. Nor do the moon and the stars. Lightning does not shine there, not to speak of fire. When he shines, everything else shines because of it. His radiance illuminates everything else.'

ब्रह्मैवेदममृतं पुरस्ताद्ब्रह्म पश्चाद्ब्रह्म दक्षिणश्चोत्तरेण ।
अधश्चोर्ध्वं च प्रसृतंब्रह्मैवेदं विश्वं वरिष्ठम् ॥ (5.14)

'The immortal Brahman is in front. The Brahman is at the rear. The Brahman is to the south and the north. The Brahman extends upwards and downwards. He is the greatest in the universe.'

एतादृगनुभवो यस्य स कृतार्थो नरोत्तमः ।
ब्रह्मभूतः प्रसन्नात्मा न शोचति न काङ्क्षति ॥ (5.15)

'An excellent man who comprehends this is successful in his objective. He becomes the Brahman and is pleased in his atman. He does not grieve. Nor does he desire.'

द्वितीयाद्वै भयं राजंस्तदभावाद्बिभेति न ।
न तद्वियोगो मेऽप्यस्ति मद्वियोगोऽपि तस्य न ॥ (5.16)

'There is fear when there is a second. In the absence of rajas, there is no fear. He is not separated from me, and I am not separated from him either.'

अहमेव स सोऽहं वै निश्चितं विद्धि पर्वत ।
मद्दर्शनं तु तत्र स्याद्यत्र ज्ञानी स्थितो मम ॥ (5.17)

'O mountain! Know certainly that I am him, and he is me. My sight can be beheld there. The jnana about me is established there.'

नाहं तीर्थे न कैलासे वैकुण्ठे वा न कर्हिचित् ।
वसामि किं तु मज्ज्ञानिहृदयांभोजमध्यमे ॥ (5.18)

'I am not present in tirthas, Kailasa or Vaikuntha. However, I reside at the centre of the lotus heart of someone who possesses jnana about me.'

मत्पूजाकोटिफलदं सकृन्मज्ज्ञानिनोऽर्चनम् ।
कुलं पवित्रं तस्यास्ति जननी कृतकृत्यका ॥ (5.19)

'If one worships a person who possesses jnana about me only once, the fruits are one crore times the fruits obtained from worshipping me. His lineage is sanctified and his mother becomes successful in her objective.'

विश्वम्भरा पुण्यवती चिल्लयो यस्य चेतसः ।
ब्रह्मज्ञानं तु यत्पृष्टं त्वया पर्वतसत्तम ॥ (5.20)

'This is about the most sacred one, the one who holds up the universe. This is the consciousness into which consciousness dissolves. O excellent mountain! This is jnana about the Brahman. You asked me about it.'

कथितं तन्मया सर्वं नातो वक्तव्यमस्ति हि ।
इदं ज्येष्ठाय पुत्राय भक्तियुक्ताय शीलिने ॥ (5.21)

'I have told you everything. Nothing more remains to be said. This should be told to the eldest son, who possesses devotion and good conduct.'

शिष्याय च यथोक्ताय वक्तव्यं नान्यथा क्वचित् ।
यस्य देवे परा भक्तिर्यथा देवे तथा गुरौ ॥ (5.22)

'What has been told should be revealed to a shishya and never to anyone else. He should be devoted to the Supreme Divinity and the guru, just as he is to the devas.'

तस्यैते कथिता ह्यर्थाः प्रकाशन्ते महात्मनः ।
येनोपदिष्टा विद्येयं स एव परमेश्वरः ॥ (5.23)

'A great-souled person who reveals the meaning of what has been said and instructs this learning is like Parameshvara himself.'

यस्यायं सुकृतं कर्तुमसमर्थस्ततो ऋणी ।
पित्रोरप्यधिकः प्रोक्तो ब्रह्मजन्मप्रदायकः ।। (5.24)

'No one is capable of repaying the debt of someone who does this a good turn. He is said to be greater than a father, since he gives birth to the Brahman.'

पितृजातं जन्म नष्टं नेत्थं जातं कदाचन ।
तस्मै न द्रुह्येदित्यादि निगमोऽप्यवदन्नग ।। (5.25)

'A birth from a father is destroyed, but never this kind of birth. O mountain! Therefore, the Nigama texts say that one should never harm such a person.'

तस्माच्छास्त्रस्य सिद्धान्तो ब्रह्मदाता गुरुः परः ।
शिवे रुष्टे गुरुस्त्राता गुरौ रुष्टे न शङ्करः ।। (5.26)

'Hence, it is the determination of the sacred texts that a person who bestows the Brahman is a Supreme Guru. When Shiva is enraged, the guru is a saviour. But when the guru is enraged, not even Shankara can be the saviour.'

तस्मात्सर्वप्रयत्नेन श्रीगुरुं तोषयेन्नग ।
कायेन मनसा वाचा सर्वदा तत्परो भवेत् ।। (5.27)

'O mountain! Therefore, one must make every kind of effort to satisfy the illustrious guru, in deeds, thoughts and words. One must always be attentive.'

अन्यथा तु कृतघ्नः स्यात्कृतघ्ने नास्ति निष्कृतिः ।
इन्द्रेणाथर्वणायोक्ता शिरश्छेदप्रतिज्ञया ।। (5.28)

'Otherwise, one is ungrateful, and there is no salvation for an ingrate. Indra told a sage from the Atharvan lineage that he should take a pledge about his head being severed.'[44]

अश्विभ्यां कथने तस्य शिरश्छिन्नं च वज्रिणा ।
अश्वीयं तच्छिरो नष्टं दृष्ट्वा वैद्यो सुरोत्तमौ ॥ (5.29)

'When he told the two Ashvins about this, the wielder of the Vajra severed his head. The two excellent gods, the Ashvins, the physicians, saw that his head had been destroyed.'

पुनः संयोजितं स्वीयं ताभ्यां मुनिशिरस्तदा ।
इति सङ्कटसम्पाद्या ब्रह्मविद्या नगाधिप ।
लब्धा येन स धन्यः स्यात्कृतकृत्यश्च भूधर ॥ (5.30)

'At this, they fixed the sage's head back. O lord of mountains! Such a calamity can arise. O one who holds up the earth! A person who obtains this is blessed and successful in his objective.'

हिमालय उवाच–
स्वीयां भक्तिं वदस्वाम्ब येन ज्ञातं सुखेन हि ।
जायते मनुजस्यास्य मध्यमस्यविरागिणः ॥ (6.1)

Himalaya said, 'O mother! Please tell me about bhakti towards you. Knowing this, happiness is generated among men who are middling in non-attachment.'

देव्युवाच–
मार्गास्त्रयो मे विख्याता मोक्षप्राप्तौ नगाधिप ।
कर्मयोगो ज्ञानयोगो भक्तियोगश्च सत्तम ॥ (6.2)

---

[44]This sage, named Dadhyam, obtained the knowledge from Indra (wielder of the Vajra) on the condition that he would not reveal it to the unworthy. If he did so, his head would be severed. When he revealed it to the two Ashvins, his head was severed. The Ashvins fixed a horse's head on Dadhyam.

Devi said, 'O lord of mountains! To obtain moksha, three paths are famous. O excellent one! These are Karma Yoga, Jnana Yoga and Bhakti Yoga.'

त्रयाणामप्ययं योग्यः कर्तुं शक्योऽस्ति सर्वथा ।
सुलभत्वान्मानसत्वात्कायचित्ताद्यपीडनात् ॥ (6.3)

'Among these three, one should always pursue what one is worthy of—the one that is easily done and does not cause hardships to the being's mind, body or consciousness.'

गुणभेदान्मनुष्याणां सा भक्तिस्त्रिविधा मता ।
परपीडां समुद्दिश्य दंभं कृत्वा पुरःसरम् ॥ (6.4)

'Depending on differences in qualities among humans, bhakti is said to be of three types. There is one that oppresses others and is driven by insolence as the primary motive.'

मात्सर्यक्रोधयुक्तो यस्तस्य भक्तिस्तु तामसी ।
परपीडादिरहितः स्वकल्याणार्थमेव च ॥ (6.5)

'Bhakti based on jealousy and rage is tamas in nature. There is one that does not oppress others but is done with the motive of one's own welfare.'

नित्यं सकामो हृदयं यशोऽर्थी भोगलोलुपः ।
तत्तत्फलसमावाप्त्यै मामुपास्तेऽतिभक्तितः ॥ (6.6)

'This is always with a desire in the heart, greedy for fame or objects of pleasure. He worships me with great devotion so that some fruits can be obtained.'

भेदबुद्ध्या तु मां स्वस्मादन्यां जानाति पामरः ।
तस्य भक्तिः समाख्याता नगाधिप तु राजसी ॥ (6.7)

'Because his intelligence has a sense of differences, that idiot knows me as different from him. O lord of mountain! That bhakti is said to be rajas in nature.'

परमेशार्पणं कर्म पापसंक्षालनाय च ।
वेदोक्तत्वादवश्यं तत्कर्तव्यं तु मयानिशम् ॥ (6.8)

'For the sake of cleansing sins, karma should be offered up to Paramesha. While constantly thinking of me, the rites spoken about in the Vedas must be undertaken.'

इति निश्चितबुद्धिस्तु भेदबुद्धिमुपाश्रितः ।
करोति प्रीतये कर्म भक्तिः सा नग सात्त्विकी ॥ (6.9)

'When a person makes up his mind in this way, he still retains a sense of difference. O mountain! When he undertakes these with pleasure, that bhakti is sattva in nature.'

परभक्तेः प्रापिकेयं भेदबुद्ध्यवलम्बनात् ।
पूर्वप्रोक्ते ह्युभे भक्ती न परप्रापिके मते ॥ (6.10)

'To achieve para bhakti, the intelligence should not depend on differences. It is held that both the kinds of bhakti[45] mentioned earlier do not lead to para bhakti.'

अधुना परभक्तिं तु प्रोच्यमानां निबोध मे ।
मद्गुणश्रवणं नित्यं मम नामानुकीर्तनम् ॥ (6.11)

'I will now speak about para bhakti. Listen to me. One must constansly hear about my qualities and chant my name.'

कल्याणगुणरत्नानामाकरायां मयि स्थिरम् ।
चेतसो वर्तनं चौव तैलधारासमं सदा ॥ (6.12)

'He is fixed in the reservoir of my auspicious qualities and names. Like a constant flow of oil, his consciousness is a vessel that holds these jewels.'

---

[45]The two kinds of bhakti being referred to here are of the rajas and sattva kind.

हेतुस्तु तत्र को वापि न कदाचिद्भवेदपि ।
सामीप्यसार्ष्टिसायुज्यसलोक्यानां न चएषणा ॥ (6.13)

'There is no cause and never any motive behind this. He does not desire *samipya, sarshti, sayujya* or *salokya*.'[46]

मत्सेवातोऽधिकं किञ्चिन्नैव जानाति कर्हिचित् ।
सेव्यसेवकताभावातत्र मोक्षं न वाञ्छति ॥ (6.14)

'Beyond the desire to serve me, he never knows anything else. Since there is no difference between the server and the served, he does not seek moksha.'

परानुरक्त्या मामेव चिन्तयेद्यो ह्यतन्द्रितः ।
स्वाभेदेनैव मां नित्यं जानाति न विभेदतः ॥ (6.15)

'He is supremely devoted to me and constantly thinks of me. He never knows any difference between me and himself.'

मद्रूपत्वेन जीवानां चिन्तनं कुरुते तु यः ।
यथा स्वस्यात्मनि प्रीतिस्तथैव च परात्मनि ॥ (6.16)

'He thinks of all living beings as my form and acts accordingly. Therefore, he displays the same affection towards others as he does towards his own self.'

चौतन्यस्य समानत्वान्न भेदं कुरुते तु यः ।
सर्वत्र वर्तमानानां मां सर्वरूपां च सर्वदा ॥ (6.17)

'Since it is the same consciousness everywhere, he does not act according to differences. The same presence is everywhere. I am always present in every form.'

---

[46]These are different grades of emancipation. Salokya is the ability to reside with the divinity, samipya is proximity to the divinity, sarupya is to be like the divinity in form, sarshti is to be like the divinity in prosperity and sayujya is identification with the divinity.

नमते यजते चौवाप्याचाण्डालान्तमीश्वरम् ।
न कुत्रापि द्रोहबुद्धिं कुरुते भेदवर्जनात् ।। (6.18)

'Starting with a Chandala and ending with Ishvara, he bows down before everyone and worships them. Since he has given up all differences, his mind never displays any enmity.'

मत्स्थानदर्शने श्रद्धा मद्भक्तदर्शने तथा ।
मच्छास्त्रश्रवणे श्रद्धा मन्त्रतन्त्रादिषु प्रभो ।। (6.19)

'When he sees my place, he is filled with devotion. It is just the same when he sees my devotees. O lord! When he hears about my sacred texts, mantras, tantras and other things, he is filled with devotion.'

मयि प्रेमाकुलमती रोमाञ्चिततनुः सदा ।
प्रेमाश्रुजलपूर्णाक्षः कण्ठगद्गदनिस्वनः ।। (6.20)

'His mind is overwhelmed with love for me, and his body hair always stands up. His eyes fill with tears of love. His throat chokes, and his voice falters.'

अनन्येनैव भावेन पूजयेद्यो नगाधिप ।
मामीश्वरीं जगद्योनिं सर्वकारणकारणम् ।। (6.21)

'O lord of mountains! I am Ishvari, the womb of the universe, the cause behind all causes. He worships me with such single-minded sentiments.'

व्रतानि मम दिव्यानि नित्यनैमित्तिकान्यपि ।
नित्यं यः कुरुते भक्त्या वित्तशाठ्यविवर्जितः ।। (6.22)

'He observes my divine vows, nitya, naimittika and the others. Without any deceit about wealth, he devoutly performs the nitya rites.'

मदुत्स्वदिदृक्षा च मदुत्स्वकृतिस्तथा ।
जायते यस्य नियतं स्वभावादेव भूधर ।। (6.23)

'He looks forward to my festivities and performs my festivities. O one who holds up the earth! This innate nature is constantly generated within him.'

उच्चैर्गायंश्च नामानि ममैव खलु नृत्यति ।
अहङ्कारादिरहितो देहतादात्म्यवर्जितः ॥ (6.24)

'Indeed, he sings my name loudly and dances. He has no sense of ego and is devoid of any sense about his body.'

प्रारब्धेन यथा यच्च क्रियते तत्तथा भवेत् ।
न मे चिन्तास्ति तत्रापि देहसंरक्षणादिषु ॥ (6.25)

'He thinks that everything will happen according to *prarabdha*[47]. Therefore, I do not have to think about anything, including preservation of the body.'

इति भक्तिस्तु या प्रोक्ता परभक्तिस्तु सा स्मृता ।
यस्यां देव्यतिरिक्तं तु न किञ्चिदपि भाव्यते ॥ (6.26)

'When this kind of bhakti is spoken about, it is described as para bhakti. Beyond Devi, the person does not think about anything else.'

इत्थं जाता परा भक्तिर्यस्य भूधर तत्त्वतः ।
तदैव तस्य चिन्मात्रे मद्रूपे विलयो भवेत् ॥ (6.27)

'O one who holds up the earth! When this kind of para bhakti is generated, the truth is that he dissolves into my form, which is only consciousness.'

भक्तेस्तु या पराकाष्ठा सैव ज्ञानं प्रकीर्तितम् ।
वैराग्यस्य च सीमा सा ज्ञाने तदुभयं यतः ॥ (6.28)

'This measure of para bhakti is described as the highest state of jnana. It represents the ultimate non-attachment and jnana.'

---

[47]Prarabdha karma is karma that has ripened.

भक्तौ कृतायां यस्यापि प्रारब्धवशतो नग ।
न जायते मम ज्ञानं मणिद्वीपं स गच्छति ।। (6.29)

'Under the control of his prarabdha, when he accomplishes bhakti but does not obtain jnana about me, he goes to Manidvipa.'

तत्र गत्वाखिलान्भोगाननिच्छन्नपि चर्च्छति ।
तदन्ते मम चिद्रूपज्ञानं सम्यग्भवेन्नग ।। (6.30)

'Having gone there, he incessantly enjoys all the objects of pleasure he desires. O mountain! In the end, he obtains proper jnana about my consciousness.'

तेन मुक्तः सदैव स्याज्ज्ञानान्मुक्तिर्न चान्यथा ।
इहैव यस्य ज्ञानं स्याधृद्गतप्रत्यगात्मनः ।। (6.31)

'Emancipation is possible when one is united with that jnana, not otherwise. If a person obtains this jnana, he does not return to this world again.'

मम संवित्परतनोस्तस्य प्राणा व्रजन्ति न ।
ब्रह्मैव संस्तदाप्नोति ब्रह्मैव ब्रह्म वेद यः ।। (6.32)

'When his breath of life leaves his body, he realizes my Supreme Consciousness and obtains the status of the Brahman. A person who knows the Brahman is like the Brahman.'

कण्ठचामीकरसममज्ञानात्तु तिरोहितम् ।
ज्ञानादज्ञाननाशेन लब्धमेव हि लभ्यते ।। (6.33)

'This is like a golden necklace, and ignorance vanishes. When jnana destroys ignorance, he obtains what is worthy of being obtained.'

विदिताविदितादन्यन्नगोत्तम वपुर्मम ।
यथादर्शे तथात्मनि यथा जले तथा पितृलोके ।। (6.34)

'O excellent mountain! He knows about my form, which is not known to others. The atman is seen in the world of the ancestors, like a reflection in a mirror or in the water.'

छायातपौ तथा स्वच्छौ विविक्तौ तद्वदेव हि ।
मम लोके भवेज्ज्ञानं द्वैतभावविवर्जितम् ॥ (6.35)

'When the sun exists, the shadow is clear. It is as clear as that. Jnana exists in my world, and it is devoid of any notion of duality.'

यस्तु वैराग्यवानेव ज्ञानहीनो म्रियेत चेत् ।
ब्रह्मलोके वसेन्नित्यं यावत्कल्पं ततःपरम् ॥ (6.36)

'If a person possesses non-attachment but dies devoid of jnana, he resides constantly in Brahmaa's world, until the next kalpa arrives.'

शुचीनां श्रीमतां गेहे भवेत्तस्या जनिः पुनः ।
करोति साधनं पश्चात्ततो ज्ञानं हि जायते ॥ (6.37)

'He is then born in a home that is prosperous and pure. He strives, and, thereafter, jnana is generated.'

अनेकजन्मभी राजन् ज्ञानं स्यान्नैकजन्मना ।
ततः सर्वप्रयत्नेन ज्ञानार्थं यत्नमाश्रयेत् ॥ (6.38)

'O king! Jnana arises after many births, not in a single birth. Therefore, one should make every kind of effort to obtain jnana and strive accordingly.'

नोचेन्महान् विनाशः स्याज्जन्मैतद्दुर्लभं पुनः ।
तत्रापि प्रथमे वर्णे वेदप्राप्तिश्च दुर्लभा ॥ (6.39)

'Otherwise, having obtained a birth that is extremely rare, there is a great calamity. It should be known that birth as the first varna is rarer still.'[48]

---

[48]Birth as a human is rare and that as a Brahmana, rarer.

शमादिषट्कसम्पत्तिर्योगसिद्धिस्तथैव च ।
तथोत्तमगुरुप्राप्तिः सर्वमेवात्र दुर्लभम् ।। (6.40)

'The six treasures[49], self-control and the others, success in yoga and obtaining an excellent guru—these are always extremely rare.'

तथेन्द्रियाणां पटुता संस्कृतत्वं तनोस्तथा ।
अनेकजन्मपुण्यैस्तु मोक्षेच्छा जायते ततः ।। (6.41)

'This is also true of control over the senses and cleansing of the body. The desire for emancipation arises after many births full of good merits.'

साधने सफलेऽप्येवं जायमानेऽपि यो नरः ।
ज्ञानार्थं नैव यतते तस्य जन्म निरर्थकम् ।। (6.42)

'If a man who has been born does not strive for success in sadhana and jnana, his birth is futile.'

तस्माद्राजन् यथाशक्त्या ज्ञानार्थं यत्नमाश्रयेत् ।
पदे पदेऽश्वमेधस्य फलमाप्नोति निश्चितम् ।। (6.43)

'O king! Therefore, according to capacity, one should resort to effort so that one can acquire jnana. It is then certain that, at every step, he obtains the fruits of a horse sacrifice.'

घृतमिव पयसि निगूढं भूते च वसति विज्ञानम् ।
सततं मन्थयितव्यं मनसा मन्थानभूतेन ।। (6.44)

'Vijnana resides in beings, just as ghee is hidden inside milk. Using the mind as a churning rod, it must be constantly churned.'

ज्ञानं लब्ध्वा कृतार्थः स्यादिति वेदान्तडिण्डिमः ।
सर्वमुक्तं समासेन किं भूयः श्रोतुमिच्छसि ।। (6.45)

---

[49]The six treasures include internal self-control, external self-control, devotion, patience, non-attachment and focus.

'When one obtains jnana, one is successful and becomes like a drum that proclaims Vedanta. In brief, he is freed in every possible way. What else do you desire to hear?'

हिमालय उवाच-
कति स्थानानि देवेशि द्रष्टव्यानि महीतले ।
मुख्यानि च पवित्राणि देवीप्रियतमानि च ॥ (7.1)

Himalaya asked, 'O Deveshi! On the surface of the earth, how many places exist that are foremost and sacred, those that are loved most by Devi?'

व्रतान्यपि तथा यानि तुष्टिदान्युत्सवा अपि ।
तत्सर्वं वद मे मातः कृतकृत्यो यतो नरः ॥ (7.2)

'What are the vratas and other festivals that bring satisfaction? O mother! Please describe all that so that a man can strive to be successful.'

देव्युवाच-
सर्वं दृश्यं मम स्थानं सर्वे काला व्रतात्मकाः ।
उत्सवाः सर्वकालेषु यतोऽहं सर्वरूपिणी ॥ (7.3)

Devi replied, 'I am present in all the places and all of them should be seen. My vratas take place all the time. Since I assume every form, my festivals also occur all the time.'

तथापि भक्तवात्सल्यात्किञ्चित्किञ्चिदथोच्यते ।
शृणुष्वावहितो भूत्वा नगराज वचो मम ॥ (7.4)

'Nevertheless, out of affection towards my devotee, I will say a few things. O king of mountains! Listen attentively to my words.'

कोलापुरं महास्थानं यत्र लक्ष्मीः सदा स्थिता ।
मातुःपुरं द्वितीयं च रेणुकाधिष्ठितं परम् ॥ (7.5)

'Kolapura is a great place, and Lakshmi is always

established there. Matuhpura[50] is the second spot, and the supreme Renukaa is established there.'

तुलजापुरं तृतीयं स्यात्सप्तशृङ्गं तथैव च ।
हिङ्गुलायां महास्थानं ज्वालामुख्यास्तथैव च ।। (7.6)

'Tuljapura[51] is the third, and there is also Saptashringa[52]. Hingula is a great place and so is Jvalamukhi.'

शाकंभर्याः परं स्थानं भ्रामर्याः स्थानमुत्तमम् ।
श्रीरक्तदन्तिकास्थानं दुर्गास्थानं तथैव च ।। (7.7)

'There is the supreme place of Shakambhari and the excellent place of Bhramari.[53] There is the place for Shriraktadantikaa and the place for Durgaa.'

विन्ध्याचलनिवासिन्याः स्थानं सर्वोत्तमोत्तमम् ।
अन्नपूर्णामहास्थानं काञ्चीपुरमनुत्तमम् ।। (7.8)

'The place where she resides in the Vindhya mountains is the best among all the spots. There is the great place of Annapurnaa and the excellent Kanchipura.'

भीमादेव्याः परं स्थानं विमलास्थानमेव च ।
श्रीचन्द्रलामहास्थानं कौशिकीस्थानमेव च ।। (7.9)

'There is the supreme place of Bhimaa Devi and Vimalaa's place. There is the great place of Shrichandralaa[54] and Koushiki's spot.'

नीलांबायाः परं स्थानं नीलपर्वतमस्तके ।
जांबूनदेश्वरीस्थानं तथा श्रीनगरं शुभम् ।। (7.10)

---

[50]Matuhpura refers to Mahur or Mahurgad in Nanded district.
[51]Tuljapura refers to a place in Maharashtra.
[52]Saptashringa is a place near Nashik in Maharashtra.
[53]There are alternative claimants for Shakambhari, and Bhramari is probably the one in Shrishaila.
[54]This refers to Chandralamba in Gulbarga, Karnataka.

'On the summit of Mount Nila, there is the supreme place of Nilambaa. There is Jambunadeshvari's place and the auspicious Shrinagara.'

गुह्यकाल्या महास्थानं नेपाले यत्प्रतिष्ठितम् ।
मीनाक्ष्याः परमं स्थानं यच्च प्रोक्तं चिदंबरे ॥ (7.11)

'The great place of Guhyakali has been established in Nepal. It is said that Minakshi's supreme place is in Chidambara.'[55]

वेदारण्यं महास्थानं सुन्दर्या समधिष्ठितम् ।
एकांबरं महास्थानं परशक्त्या प्रतिष्ठितम् ॥ (7.12)

'There is the great place of Vedaranya[56], where Sundari is established. There is the great place of Ekambaram[57], where Para-Shakti is established.'

महालसा परं स्थानं योगेश्वर्यास्तथैव च ।
तथा नीलसरस्वत्याः स्थानं चीनेषु विश्रुतम् ॥ (7.13)

'There is the supreme place of Mahalasaa[58] and Yogeshvari. In China,[59] the place of Nila Sarasvati is famous.'

वैद्यनाथे तु बगलास्थानं सर्वोत्तमं मतम् ।
श्रीमच्छ्रीभुवनेश्वर्या मणिद्वीपं मम स्मृतम् ॥ (7.14)

'It is believed that Bagalaa's place in Vaidyanatha is the best. My place of Manidvipa is described as the one where Shri Bhuvaneshvari resides.'

---

[55]Though there is some distance between Madurai and Chidambaram, this ought to be the one in Madurai.
[56]This refers to Nagapattinam.
[57]Ekambaram is a place in Kanchipuram, Tamil Nadu.
[58]This probably refers to a place in Goa.
[59]This refers to Tibet.

श्रीमत्त्रिपुरभैरव्याः कामाख्यायोनिमण्डलम् ।
भूमण्डले क्षेत्ररत्नं महामायाधिवासितम् ॥ (7.15)

'There is the circle of the yoni in Kamakhya, Shri Tripura Bhairavi's place. This is a jewel among *kshetras* on earth, and Mahamayaa resides there.'

नातः परतरं स्थानं क्वचिदस्ति धरातले ।
प्रतिमासं भवेद्देवी यत्र साक्षाद्रजस्वला ॥ (7.16)

'There is no other superior spot on the surface of the earth. Every month, Devi herself goes through her season there.'

तत्रत्या देवताः सर्वाः पर्वतात्मकतां गताः ।
पर्वतेषु वसन्त्येव महत्यो देवता अपि ॥ (7.17)

'All the devas go there and remain there in the form of mountains. All those great devas reside atop the mountains.'

तत्रत्या पृथिवी सर्वा देवीरूपा स्मृता बुधैः ।
नातः परतरं स्थानं कामाख्यायोनिमण्डलात् ॥ (7.18)

'The learned say that among all the places on earth that are Devi's form, there is none that is superior to Kamakhya, the circle of the yoni.'

गायत्र्याश्च परं स्थानं श्रीमत्पुष्करमीरितम् ।
अमरेशे चण्डिका स्यात्प्रभासे पुष्करेक्षिणी ॥ (7.19)

'The illustrious Pushkara is described as Gayatri's supreme place. Chandikaa is in Amaresha and Pushkarekshini is in Prabhasa.'

नैमिषे तु महास्थाने देवी सा लिङ्गधारिणी ।
पुरुहूता पुष्कराक्षे आषाढौ च रतिस्तथा ॥ (7.20)

'Devi Lingadharini's great place is in Naimisha, Puruhutaa is in Pushkareksha and Rati is in Ashadhi.'

चण्डमुण्डी महास्थाने दण्डिनी परमेश्वरी ।
भारभूतौ भवेद्भूतिर्नाकुले नकुलेश्वरी ॥ (7.21)

'Dandini Parameshvari's great place is in Chandamundi. Bhuti is in Bharabhuti, and Nakuleshvari is in Nakula.'

चन्द्रिका तु हरिश्चन्द्रे श्रीगिरौ शाङ्करी स्मृता ।
जप्येश्वरे त्रिशूला स्यात्सूक्ष्मा चाम्रातकेश्वरे ॥ (7.22)

'Chandrikaa is in Harishchandra, and Shankari is said to be in Shrigiri. Trishulaa is in Japyeshvara and Sukshmaa in Amratakeshvara.'

शाङ्करी तु महाकाले शर्वाणी मध्यमाभिधे ।
केदाराख्ये महाक्षेत्रे देवी सा मार्गदायिनी ॥ (7.23)

'Shankari is in Mahakala[60], and Sharvani resides in Madhyama. In the great kshetra known as Kedara, Devi is Margadayini.'

भैरवाख्ये भैरवी सा गयायां मङ्गला स्मृता ।
स्थाणुप्रिया कुरुक्षेत्रे स्वायंभुव्यपि नाकुले ॥ (7.24)

'She is Bhairavi in Bhairava. In Gaya, she is described as Mangalaa. She is Sthanupriyaa in Kurukshetra, and Svayambhuvi in Nakula.'

कनखले भवेदुग्रा विश्वेशा विमलेश्वरे ।
अट्टहासे महानन्दा महेन्द्रे तु महान्तका ॥ (7.25)

'She is Ugraa in Kankhala, and Vishveshaa in Vimaleshvara. She is Mahanandaa in Attahasa, and Mahantakaa in Mahendra.'

भीमे भीमेश्वरी प्रोक्ता स्थाने वस्त्रापथे पुनः।
भवानी शाङ्करी प्रोक्ता रूद्राणी त्वर्धकोटिके ॥ (7.26)

---

[60]This refers to Ujjain.

'She is Bhimaa in Bhimeshvari. In the place known as Vastrapatha, she is said to be Bhavani Shankari. She is Rudrani in Arddhakotika.'

अविमुक्ते विशालाक्षी महाभागा महालये ।
गोकर्णे भद्रकर्णी स्याद्भद्रा स्याद्भद्रकर्णके ॥ (7.27)

'She is Vishalakshi in Avimukta[61], and Mahabhagaa in Mahalaya. In Gokarana, she is Bhadrakarni. In Bhadrakarnaka, she is Bhadraa.'

उत्पलाक्षी सुवर्णाक्षे स्थाण्वीशा स्थाणुसंज्ञके ।
कमलालये तु कमला प्रचण्डा छगलण्डके ॥ (7.28)

'She is Utpalakshi in Suvarnaksha and is known as Sthanvishaa in Sthanu. She is Kamalaa in Kamalalaya, and Prachandaa in Chhagalandaka.'

कुरण्डले त्रिसन्ध्या स्यान्माकोटे मुकुटेश्वरी ।
मण्डलेशे शाण्डकी स्यात्काली कालञ्जरे पुनः ॥ (7.29)

'In Kurandala, she is Trisandhyaa. In Makota, she is Mukuteshvari. She is Shandaki in Mandalesha, and Kali in Kalanjara.'

शङ्कुकर्णे ध्वनिः प्रोक्ता स्थूला स्यात्स्थूलकेश्वरे ।
ज्ञानिनां हृदयांभोजे हृल्लेखा परमेश्वरी ॥ (7.30)

'She is described as Dhvani in Shankukarna, and Sthulaa in Sthulakeshvara. Parameshvari Hrillekhaa resides in the lotus hearts of those who possess jnana.'

प्रोक्तानीमानि स्थानानि देव्याः प्रियतमानि च ।
तत्तत्क्षेत्रस्य माहात्म्यं श्रुत्वा पूर्वं नगोत्तम ॥ (7.31)

'The names that have been mentioned are of places loved by Devi. O excellent mountain! The greatness of these

[61]This refers to Kashi.

kshetras must be heard first.'

तदुक्तेन विधानेन पश्चाद्देवीं प्रपूजयेत् ।
अथवा सर्वक्षेत्राणि काश्यां सन्ति नगोत्तम ॥ (7.32)

'After that, Devi must be worshipped in accordance with the rules mentioned. O excellent mountain! Alternatively, all the kshetras exist in Kashi.'

अतस्तत्र वसेन्नित्यं देवीभक्तिपरायणः ।
तानि स्थानानि सम्पश्यञ्जपन्देवीं निरन्तरम् ॥ (7.33)

'Thus, she resides there always. Those who are full of bhakti towards Devi must see those places and constantly perform japa on Devi.'

ध्यायंस्तच्चरणांभोजं मुक्तो भवति बन्धनात् ।
इमानि देवीनामानि प्रातरुत्थाय यः पठेत् ॥ (7.34)

भस्मीभवन्ति पापानि तत्क्षणान्नग सत्वरम् ।
श्राद्धकाले पठेदेतान्यमलानि द्विजाग्रतः ॥ (7.35)

'If a person performs dhyana on her lotus feet, one is freed of bonds. O mountain! If a man gets up in the morning and reads Devi's names, all his sins are instantly and swiftly burnt to ashes. At the time of a *shraddhaa,* in front of *dvijas*, these unblemished names must be read.'

मुक्तास्तत्पितरः सर्वे प्रयान्ति परमां गतिम् ।
अधुना कथयिष्यामि व्रतानि तव सुव्रत ॥ (7.36)

'All his ancestors are, then, liberated and proceed to the Supreme Destination. O one excellent in vows! I will now describe my vratas.'

नारीभिश्च नरैश्चौव कर्तव्यानि प्रयत्नतः ।
व्रतमनन्ततृतीयाख्यं रसकल्याणिनीव्रतम् ॥ (7.37)

'Men and women must make efforts to observe the vrata known as Ananta Tritiya and Rasa-Kalyani vrata.'[62]

आर्द्रानन्दकरं नाम्ना तृतीयायां व्रतं च यत् ।
शुक्रवारव्रतं चौव तथा कृष्णचतुर्दशी ॥ (7.38)

'There is another vrata named Ardranandakara for tritiya. This is a vrata for Friday and Krishna Chaturdashi.'

भौमवारव्रतं चौव प्रदोषव्रतमेव च ।
यत्र देवो महादेवो देवीं संस्थाप्य विष्टरे ॥ (7.39)

'There is the vrata for Tuesday and the vrata for the evening. During these times, along with Devi, Mahadeva is at the seat.'

नृत्यं करोति पुरतः सार्धं देवैर्निशामुखे ।
तत्रोपोष्य रजन्यादौ प्रदोषे पूजयाच्छिवाम् ॥ (7.40)

'When it is the onset of the night, along with devas, he dances in front of her. Therefore, having fasted, in the evening, before it is night, Shivaa should be worshipped.'

प्रतिपक्षं विशेषेण तद्देवीप्रीतिकारकम् ।
सोमवारव्रतं चौव ममातिप्रियकृन्नग ॥ (7.41)

'O mountain! In particular, in every paksha, the Monday vrata brings Devi pleasure. It is greatly loved by me.'

तत्रापि देवीं सम्पूज्य रात्रौ भोजनमाचरेत् ।
नवरात्रद्वयं चौव व्रतं प्रीतिकरं मम ॥ (7.42)

---

[62]Vrata simply means a vow, and ananta means the fruits obtained are infinite. Tritiya means the third lunar tithi in shukla paksha. Usually, Ananta Tritiya Vrata is observed on a tritiya starting in the months of Bhadra, Margashirsha or Vaishakha, once a month for an entire year. Rasa-kalyani vrata is a synonym, performed on the same days, though Ananta Tritiya can be for other deities, while 'Rasa-Kalyani' is specifically for Parvati. The expression Rasa-Kalyani means that the vrata bestows good fortune and prosperity.

'Then, having worshipped Devi, one must eat at night. The vratas at the time of the two Navaratris bring me pleasure.'

एवमन्यान्यपि विभो नित्यनैमित्तिकानि च ।
व्रतानि कुरुते यो वै मत्प्रीत्यर्थं विमत्सरः ॥ (7.43)

'O lord! In this way, there are other nitya and naimittika vratas. To bring me pleasure, these should be observed, without any jealousy.'

प्राप्नोति मम सायुज्यं स मे भक्तः स मे प्रियः ।
उत्सवानपि कुर्वीत दोलोत्सवमुखान्विभो ॥ (7.44)

'Such a devotee is loved by me and obtains sayujya with me. O lord! The festivals must be observed, Dolotsava[63] being the most important.'

शयनोत्सवं तथा कुर्यात्तथा जागरणोत्सवम् ।
रथोत्सवं च मे कुर्याद्दमनोत्सवमेव च ॥ (7.45)

'Shayanotsava and Jagaranotsava must be observed.[64] Rathotsava and Damanotsava must be observed.'[65]

पवित्रोत्सवमेवापि श्रावणे प्रीतिकारकम् ।
मम भक्तः सदा कुर्यादेवमन्यान्महोत्सवान् ॥ (7.46)

'The sacred festivals in the month of Shravana bring pleasure. My devotees should always observe the other great festivals.'

मद्भक्तान्भोजयेत्प्रीत्या तथा चौव सुवासिनीः ।
कुमारीबटुकांश्चापि मद्बुद्ध्या तद्गतान्तरः ॥ (7.47)

---

[63]This refers to the swing festival held on the full-moon day in Phalguna.
[64]Shayanotsava and Jagaranotsava refer to times when the deity is put to bed and woken up, respectively.
[65]Rathotsava is the chariot festival, and Damanotsava is performed on chaturdashi in shukla paksha, during the month of Chaitra.

'My devotees should be happily fed. The young girls and boys should be dressed well. One should tend attentively to them, considering them to be my own self.'

वित्तशाठ्येन रहितो यजेदेतान्सुमादिभिः ।
य एवं कुरुते भक्त्या प्रतिवर्षमतन्द्रितः ॥ (7.48)

स धन्यः कृतकृत्योऽसौ मत्प्रीतेः पात्रमञ्जसा ।
सर्वमुक्तं समासेन मम प्रीतिप्रदायकम् ।
नाशिष्याय प्रदातव्यं नाभक्ताय कदाचन ॥ (7.49)

'Without any deception about wealth, the worship should be performed with flowers. If a person does this attentively and devoutly every year, he is blessed and becomes successful in his objective. He easily becomes someone loved by me. Everything mentioned here briefly brings me pleasure. This should never be revealed to a person who is not a shishya or is not my devotee.'

हिमालय उवाच–
देवदेवि महेशानि करुणासागरेऽम्बिके ।
ब्रूहि पूजाविधिं सम्यग्यथावदधुना निजम् ॥ (8.1)

Himalaya said, 'O Devi of devas! O Maheshvari! O Ambikaa! You are an ocean of compassion. Please tell me now about the proper norms for performing your pujaa.'

श्रीदेव्युवाच–
वक्ष्ये पूजाविधिं राजन्नम्बिकाया यथाप्रियम् ।
अत्यन्तश्रद्धया सार्धं शृणु पर्वतपुङ्गव ॥ (8.2)

Shri Devi said, 'O king! I will now tell you about the norms for pujaa, which are loved by Ambikaa. O bull among mountains! Listen to this with a great deal of devotion.'

द्विविधा मम पूजा स्याद्बाह्या चाभ्यान्तरापि च ।
बाह्यापि द्विविधा प्रोक्ता वैदिकी तान्त्रिकी तथा ॥ (8.3)

'My pujaa is of two types—external and internal. The external is said to be of two types—following the Vedas and following tantra.'

वैदिक्यर्चापि द्विविधा मूर्तिभेदेन भूधर ।
वैदिकी वैदिकैः कार्या वेददीक्षासमन्वितैः ।। (8.4)

'O one who holds up the earth! Depending on the differences in the image used, worship according to the Vedas is of two types. Those who have taken diksha in the Vedas perform worship according to the Vedas, following the rites of the Vedas.'

तन्त्रोक्तदीक्षावद्भिस्तु तान्त्रिकी संश्रिता भवेत् ।
इत्थं पूजारहस्यं च न ज्ञात्वा विपरीतकम् ।। (8.5)

करोति यो नरो मूढः स पतत्येव सर्वथा ।
तत्र या वैदिकी प्रोक्ता प्रथमा तां वदाम्यहम् ।। (8.6)

'Those who have taken diksha in tantra follow the rites of tantra. If a person does not know about the secret of pujaa and acts in a contrary way, that foolish man always falls down. I will first tell you about the one that follows the Vedas.'

यन्मे साक्षात्परं रूपं दृष्टवानसि भूधर ।
अनन्तशीर्षनयनमनन्तचरणं महत् ।। (8.7)

'O one who holds up the earth! You directly saw my supreme and great form earlier, with an infinite number of heads and eyes and an infinite number of feet.'

सर्वशक्तिसमायुक्तं प्रेरकं यत्परात्परम् ।
तदेव पूजयेन्नित्यं नमेद्ध्यायेत्स्मरेदपि ।। (8.8)

'I am the one who possesses every kind of Shakti. I am the one who urges. I am greater than the greatest. This is the form that one must prostrate oneself before. This is the form that one must always perform pujaa for, perform dhyana on it and remember it.'

इत्येतत्प्रथमाचार्याः स्वरूपं कथितं नग ।
शान्तः समाहितमना दंभाहङ्कारवर्जितः ॥ (8.9)

'O mountain! I have spoken about my form, and this is the first kind of worship to be performed—tranquil, controlled in one's mind, devoid of insolence and ego.'

तत्परो भव तद्याजी तदेव शरणं व्रज ।
तदेव चेतसा पश्य जप ध्यायस्व सर्वदा ॥ (8.10)

'Worship that supreme form and seek refuge in it. Behold it in your consciousness and always perform japa and dhyana.'

अनन्यया प्रेमयुक्तभक्त्या मद्भावमाश्रितः ।
यज्ञैर्यज तपोदानैर्मामेव परितोषय ॥ (8.11)

'Be full of love and devotion for it alone. Be full of sentiments about me. Worship, perform sacrifices and austerities, and practise donations to satisfy me.'

इत्थं ममानुग्रहतो मोक्ष्यसे भवबन्धनात् ।
मत्परा ये मदासक्तचित्ता भक्तपरा मताः ॥ (8.12)

'In this way, through my favours, you will be freed from the bonds of the world. If a person is devoted to me, with his consciousness attached to me, he is held to be my supreme devotee.'

प्रतिजाने भवादस्मादुद्धाराम्यचिरेण तु ।
ध्यानेन कर्मयुक्तेन भक्तिज्ञानेन वा पुनः ॥ (8.13)

'It should be known that I will shortly save from the world. This is the result of dhyana united with karma and bhakti united with jnana.'

प्राप्याहं सर्वथा राजन्न तु केवलकर्मभिः ।
धर्मात्सञ्जायते भक्तिर्भक्तया सञ्जायते परम् ॥ (8.14)

'O king! I can be reached in all these ways, not only through karma. Bhakti results from dharma, and from bhakti, the Supreme is obtained.'

श्रुतिस्मृतिभ्यामुदितं यत्स धर्मः प्रकीर्तितः ।
अन्यशास्त्रेण यः प्रोक्तो धर्माभासः स उच्यते ॥ (8.15)

'What is stated in the Shruti and Smriti texts is described as dharma. Anything stated in other sacred texts are said to be suggestions of dharma.'

सर्वज्ञात्सर्वशक्तेश्च मत्तो वेदः समुत्थितः ।
अज्ञानस्य ममाभावादप्रमाणा न च श्रुतिः ॥ (8.16)

'I am omniscient. I possess all the Shaktis. The Vedas have arisen from me. Those who are ignorant about my nature say this. The Shruti texts are not the only proof.'

स्मृतयश्च श्रुतेरर्थं गृहीत्वैव च निर्गताः ।
मन्वादीनां स्मृतीनां च ततः प्रामाण्यमिष्यते ॥ (8.17)

'The Smriti texts emerged after accepting the meanings of the Shruti texts. Manu and the others desired to accept thc proof of the Smriti texts.'

क्वचित्कदाचित्तन्त्रार्थकटाक्षेण परोदितम् ।
धर्मं वदन्ति सोंऽशस्तु नैव ग्राह्योऽस्ति वैदिकैः॥ (8.18)

'Sometimes, there are some who look askance at the meanings of the tantra texts, saying they were enunciated later. Despite these texts speaking about dharma, those who follow the Vedas do not accept them.'

अन्येषां शास्त्रकर्तॄणामज्ञानं प्रभवत्वतः ।
अज्ञानदोषदुष्टत्वात्तदुक्तेर्न प्रमाणता ॥ (8.19)

'There are other composers of sacred texts who are under the influence of ignorance. Since they are tainted by ignorance, their wicked words cannot be stated as proof.'

तस्मान्मुमुक्षुर्धर्मार्थं सर्वथा वेदमाश्रयेत् ।
राजाज्ञा च यथा लोके हन्यते न कदाचन ॥ (8.20)

'Hence, anyone wishing to follow the dharma of moksha must always seek refuge in the Vedas. This is just like people never transgressing a king's command.'

सर्वेशाया ममाज्ञा सा श्रुतिस्त्याज्या कथं नृभिः ।
मदाज्ञारक्षणार्थं तु ब्रह्मक्षत्रियजातयः ॥ (8.21)

'In every possible way, the Shruti texts represent my command. How can men abandon them? Brahmanas and Kshatriyas were born to protect my commands.'

मया सृष्टास्ततो ज्ञेयं रहस्यं मे श्रुतेर्वचः ।
यदा यदा हि धर्मस्य ग्लानिर्भवति भूधर ॥ (8.22)

अभ्युत्थानमधर्मस्य तदा वेषान्बिभर्म्यहम् ।
देवदैत्यविभागश्चाप्यत एवाभवन्नृप ॥ (8.23)

'Since I created the Shruti texts, it should be known that my mysteries exist in their words. O one who holds up the earth! Whenever dharma suffers, and there is a rise in adharma, I assume a form. O king! The divisions between devas and *daityas* happen accordingly.'

ये न कुर्वन्ति तद्धर्मं तच्छिक्षार्थं मया सदा ।
सम्पादितास्तु नरकास्त्रासो यच्छ्रवणाद्भवेत् ॥ (8.24)

'For those who do not act in accordance with that dharma, I always create hells. Hearing about those, they are terrified.'

यो वेदधर्ममुज्झित्य धर्ममन्यं समाश्रयेत् ।
राजा प्रवासयेद्देशान्निजादेतानधर्मिणः ॥ (8.25)

'If a person gives up the dharma of the Vedas and follows some other dharma, the king must exile such followers of adharma from his own dominion.'

ब्राह्मणैर्न च सम्भाष्याः पङ्क्तिग्राह्या न च द्विजैः ।
अन्यानि यानि शास्त्राणि लोकेऽस्मिन्विविधानि च ।। (8.26)

'A Brahmana should not converse with such a person. A dvija should not eat in the same row with him. This is for those who resort to many other sacred texts in this world.'

श्रुतिस्मृतिविरुद्धानि तामसान्येव सर्वशः ।
वामं कापालकं चौव कौलकं भैरवागमः ।। (8.27)

शिवेन मोहनार्थाय प्रणीतो नान्यहेतुकः ।
दक्षशापाद् भृगोः शापाद्दधीचस्य च शापतः ।। (8.28)

दग्धा ये ब्राह्मणवरा वेदमार्गबहिष्कृताः ।
तेषामुद्धरणार्थाय सोपानक्रमतः सदा ।। (8.29)

'Everything against the shruti and smriti texts is tamas in nature. Vama, Kapalaka, Koulaka and Bhairava Agama texts[66]—to cause delusion, Shiva created these. There is no other reason. As a result of Daksha's curse, Bhrigu's curse and Dadhicha's curse, the best of Brahmanas were scorched and expelled from the path of the Vedas. It is to always save them that he progressively framed these steps.'

शैवाश्च वैष्णवाश्चौव सौराः शाक्तास्तथैव च ।
गाणपत्या आगमाश्च प्रणीताः शङ्करेण तु ।। (8.30)

'Shankara framed Shaiva, Vaishnava, Soura, Shakta and Ganapatya Agama texts.'

तत्र वेदाविरुद्धोंऽशोऽप्युक्त एव क्वचित्क्वचित् ।
वैदिकस्तद्ग्रहे दोषो न भवत्येव कर्हिचित् ।। (8.31)

[66]These are different schools of tantra.

'In these, there are some parts that are against the Vedas. There is never any taint in accepting parts that are in conformity with the Vedas.'

सर्वथा वेदभिन्नार्थे नाधिकारी द्विजो भवेत् ।
वेदाधिकारहीनस्तु भवेत्तत्राधिकारवान् ।। (8.32)

'Dvijas never have a right to something that has a different meaning from the Vedas. Only those who do not have a right to the Vedas can possess rights to these.'

तस्मात्सर्वप्रयत्नेन वैदिको वेदमाश्रयेत् ।
धर्मेण सहितं ज्ञानं परं ब्रह्म प्रकाशयेत् ।। (8.33)

'Therefore, those who follow the Vedas must make every effort to seek refuge in the Vedas. The Supreme Brahman is illuminated when dharma is united with jnana.'

सर्वैषणाः परित्यज्य मामेव शरणं गताः ।
सर्वभूतदयावन्तो मानाहङ्कारवर्जिताः ।। (8.34)

'Abandoning everything else, one should seek refuge with me, full of compassion towards all beings and devoid of pride and ego.'

मच्चित्ता मद्गतप्राणा मत्स्थानकथने रताः ।
संन्यासिनो वनस्थाश्च गृहस्था ब्रह्मचारिणः ।। (8.35)

'Whether one is in sannyasa, *vanaprastha, garhasthya* or brahmacharya, consciousness and hearts must be immersed in me, devoted to speaking about my places.'

उपासन्ते सदा भक्त्या योगमैश्वरसंज्ञितम् ।
तेषां नित्याभियुक्तानामहमज्ञानजं तमः ।। (8.36)

'I must always be devoutly worshipped, in my glory, described as that of yoga. For those who are constantly engaged in this way, I dispel the darkness of ignorance.'

ज्ञानसूर्यप्रकाशेन नाशयामि न संशयः ।
इत्थं वैदिकपूजायाः प्रथमाया नगाधिप ॥ (8.37)

'There is no doubt that I destroy, with the illumination of the sun of jnana. O lord of mountains! I have, thus, initially described pujaa according to the Vedas.'

स्वरूपमुक्तं सङ्क्षेपाद् द्वितीयाया अथो ब्रुवे ।
मूर्तौ वा स्थण्डिले वापि तथा सूर्येन्दुमण्डले ॥ (8.38)

'I will briefly speak about the second type. My own form is said to exist in an image, in the ground or in the solar or lunar disc.'

जलेऽथवा बाणलिङ्गे यन्त्रे वापि महापटे ।
तथा श्रीहृदयांम्भोजे ध्यात्वा देवीं परात्पराम् ॥ (8.39)

'In water, in a Bana Lingam, in a yantra, a large piece of cloth or in the beautiful lotus of the heart, one should perform dhyana on Devi, greater than the greatest.'

सगुणां करुणापूर्णां तरुणीमरुणारुणाम् ।
सौन्दर्यसारसीमां तां सर्वावयवसुन्दरीम् ॥ (8.40)

'She is with gunas and full of compassion. She is young and as red as the rising sun. Her beauty brims over, and all her limbs are exceedingly charming.'

शृङ्गाररससम्पूर्णां सदा भक्तार्तिकातराम् ।
प्रसादसुमुखीमम्बां चन्द्रखण्डाशिखण्डिनीम् ॥ (8.41)

'She is complete with the rasa of *shringara*. She is always pained by the afflictions of devotees. With a pleasant face, wearing the crescent of the moon on her crest, Ambaa shows her favours.'

पाशाङ्कुशवराभीतिधरामानन्दरूपिणीम् ।
पूजयेदुपचारैश्च यथावित्तानुसारतः ॥ (8.42)

'Her hands hold a noose and a goad and are in the Varada and Abhaya mudraas. In accordance with wealth, one should use upachara to worship her.'

यावदान्तरपूजायामधिकारो भवेन्न हि ।
तावद् बाह्यामिमां पूजां श्रयेज्जाते तु तां त्यजेत् ।। (8.43)

'Until a person obtains the right to internal pujaa, he must always seek refuge in the external pujaa and never abandon it.'

आभ्यन्तरा तु या पूजा सा तु संविल्लयः स्मृतः ।
संविदेव परं रूपमुपाधिरहितं मम ।। (8.44)

'Internal pujaa is said to happen when one dissolves into the Supreme Consciousness. This form of mine has no name.'

अतः संविदि मद्रूपे चेतः स्थाप्यं निराश्रयम् ।
संविद्रूपातिरिक्तं तु मिथ्या मायामयं जगत् ।। (8.45)

'Thus, this form of mine is just consciousness. Without any other support, establish your mind in this. Everything beyond this form of consciousness is false. The universe is full of mayaa.'

अतः संसारनाशाय साक्षिणीमात्मरूपिणीम् ।
भावयन्निर्मनस्केन योगयुक्तेन चेतसा ।। (8.46)

'My atman takes the form of a witness. Hence, to destroy samsara[67], think of me single-mindedly, with your mind immersed in yoga.'

अतःपरं बाह्यपूजाविस्तारः कथ्यते मया ।
सावधानेन मनसा शृणु पर्वतसत्तम ।। (8.47)

'After this, I will speak about the external pujaa in detail.

[67]This refers to the worldly cycle of death and rebirth.

O excellent mountain! Listen with an attentive mind.'

देव्युवाच-
प्रातरुत्थाय शिरसि संस्मरेत्पद्ममुज्ज्वलम् ।
कर्पूराभं स्मरेत्तत्र श्रीगुरुं निजरूपिणम् ॥ (9.1)

Devi said, 'Getting up in the morning, one must remember the blazing lotus on top of one's head, with the complexion of camphor. After that, one should remember the illustrious guru, who is one's own form.'

सुप्रसन्नं लसद्भूषाभूषितं शक्तिसंयुतम् ।
नमस्कृत्य ततो देवीं कुण्डलीं संस्मरेद् बुधः ॥ (9.2)

'A learned person will, then, remember Devi in the *kundalini* and prostrate himself before her. She is extremely pleasing, decorated in blazing ornaments and is with her Shakti.'

प्रकाशमानां प्रथमे प्रयाणे प्रतिप्रयाणेऽप्यमृतायमानाम् ।
अन्तः पदव्यामनुसञ्चरन्तीमानन्दरूपामबलां प्रपद्ये ॥ (9.3)

'"She will be illuminated in the first *prayana* and assume the form of Amrita in the last prayana.[68] In the end, she will be seen moving in the form of a woman who is full of bliss. I seek refuge in her."'

ध्यात्वैवं तच्छिखामध्ये सच्चिदानन्दरूपिणीम् ।
मां ध्यायेदथ शौचादिक्रियाः सर्वाः समापयेत् ॥ (9.4)

'In the midst of the flame, he must perform dhyana on me, in the form of truth, consciousness and bliss. After having performed dhyana on me, he must complete all his ablution and other rites.'

---

[68]The first prayana means brahmarandhra and the last prayana means muladhara. There is a movement up sushumna and a subsequent movement down sushumna. The second round of quotes means that the devotee is saying this.

अग्निहोत्रं ततो हुत्वा मत्प्रीत्यर्थं द्विजोत्तमः ।
होमान्ते स्वासने स्थित्वा पूजासङ्कल्पमाचरेत् ॥ (9.5)

'To bring pleasure to me, an excellent dvija will next offer oblations into the *agnihotra* fire. Once the oblations are over, he must take his seat and resolve to perform the pujaa.'

भूतशुद्धिं पुरा कृत्वा मातृकान्यासमेव च ।
हृल्लेखामातृकान्यासं नित्यमेव समाचरेत् ॥ (9.6)

'He must first purify the elements and perform nyasa of the matrikaas. He must always use Hrillekha to perform Matrikaa Nyasa.'[69]

मूलाधारे हकारं च हृदये च रकारकम् ।
भ्रूमध्ये तद्वदीकारं ह्रीङ्कारं मस्तके न्यसेत् ॥ (9.7)

'ह will be placed in muladhara, र in the heart, ई between the eyebrows and the nyasa of ह्री will be done on the head.'

तत्तन्मन्त्रोदितानन्यान्न्यासान्सर्वान्समाचरेत् ।
कल्पयेत्स्वात्मनो देहे पीठं धर्मादिभिः पुनः ॥ (9.8)

'After that, using the respective mantra, all the other kinds of nyasa must be performed. He will next think of his own body as a seat of dharma and the others.'[70]

ततो ध्यायेन्महादेवीं प्राणायामैर्विजृम्भिते ।
हृदम्भोजे मम स्थाने पञ्चप्रेतासने बुधः ॥ (9.9)

'Extended by the pranayama, a learned person will then perform dhyana on Mahadevi in the lotus of his heart. My seat is atop the seats of the five *preta*s.'

---

[69]Starting with hrim, Hrillekha consists of 12 aksharas. Stating the mantra, nyasa of the 12 aksharas is performed on different parts of the body.
[70]These others include dharma, jnana, non-attachment and prosperity.

ब्रह्मा विष्णुश्च रुद्रश्च ईश्वरश्च सदाशिवः ।
एते पञ्च महाप्रेताः पादमूले मम स्थिताः ॥ (9.10)

'Brahmaa, Vishnu, Rudra, Ishvara and Sadashiva—these are the five great pretas, stationed at my feet.'

पञ्चभूतात्मका ह्येते पञ्चावस्थात्मका अपि ।
अहं त्वव्यक्तचिद्रूपा तदतीतास्मि सर्वदा ॥ (9.11)

'They represent the five elements and also the five states.[71] I am unmanifest in the form of consciousness, and I am always beyond these.'

ततो विष्टरतां याताः शक्तितन्त्रेषु सर्वदा ।
ध्यात्वैवं मानसैर्भोगैः पूजयेन्मां जपेदपि ॥ (9.12)

'This is always explained further in the tantra texts on Shakti. Using objects of pleasure and thinking of this in his mind, he should perform dhyana, pujaa and japa on me.'

जपं समर्प्य श्रीदेव्यै ततोऽर्घ्यस्थापनं चरेत् ।
पात्रासादनकं कृत्वा पूजाद्रव्याणि शोधयेत् ॥ (9.13)

'He must offer the japa to Shri Devi and next act so as to offer *arghya*. The water in the vessel must be sanctified, and the objects used for pujaa purified with this.'

जलेन तेन मनुना चास्त्रमन्त्रेण देशिकः ।
दिग्बन्धं च पुरा कृत्वा गुरून्नत्वा ततः परम् ॥ (9.14)

'Using the *astra* mantra for the locality, he must first close the directions and then bow down before the guru.'[72]

---

[71]The five states include being awake, asleep, in deep sleep, in turiya and the fifth state that is beyond these four.

[72]An astra mantra is like armour (kavacha) used to guard against evil influences from all the directions.

तदनुज्ञां समादाय बाह्यपीठे ततः परम् ।
हृदिस्थां भावितां मूर्तिं मम दिव्यां मनोहराम् ॥ (9.15)

'My divine and beautiful form has been thought of in the heart. Having obtained his permission, this must next be placed on the external pedestal.'

आवाहयेत्ततः पीठे प्राणस्थापनविद्यया ।
आसनावाहने चार्घ्यं पाद्याद्याचमनं तथा ॥ (9.16)

'Having invoked her on the pedestal and using the learning to instate prana, asana, *vahana*, arghya, *padya* and *achamana* must be offered.'[73]

स्नानं वासोद्वयं चौव भूषणानि च सर्वशः ।
गन्धपुष्पं यथायोग्यं दत्त्वा देव्यै स्वभक्तितः ॥ (9.17)

'She must be bathed and offered two pieces of cloth, all the ornaments and worthy fragrances. Flowers must be offered to Devi according to one's own devotion.'

यन्त्रस्थानामावृतीनां पूजनं सम्यगाचरेत् ।
प्रतिवारमशक्तानां शुक्रवारो नियम्यते ॥ (9.18)

'Divinities presiding over the yantra must be worshipped in the proper way. If one is incapable of doing this every day, it must be a rule to do it every Friday.'

मूलदेवीप्रभारूपाः स्मर्तव्या अङ्गदेवताः ।
तत्प्रभापटलव्याप्तं त्रैलोक्यं च विचिन्तयेत् ॥ (9.19)

'One must remember Devi as the main, in the form of radiance, and the other side devas. One must think of her circle of radiance pervading the three worlds.'

---

[73]Avahana means invocation. Asana, vahana, arghya, padya and achamana are a seat, a mount, a gift, water for washing the feet and water for rinsing the mouth, respectively.

पुनरावृत्तिसहितां मूलदेवीं च पूजयेत् ।
गन्धादिभिः सुगन्धैस्तु तथा पुष्पैः सुवासितैः ॥ (9.20)

'Repeating everything, the main Devi must again be worshipped with incense, excellent fragrances and extremely fragrant flowers.'

नैवेद्यैस्तर्पणैश्चैव तांबूलैर्दक्षिणादिभिः ।
तोषयेन्मां त्वत्कृतेन नाम्नां साहस्रकेण च ॥ (9.21)

'She must be offered *naivedya*[74], betel leaves and dakshina. Once this is done, I should be satisfied by reciting my one thousand names.'

कवचेन च सूक्तेनाहं रुद्रेभिरिति प्रभो ।
देव्यथर्वशिरोमन्त्रैर्हृल्लेखोपनिषद्भवैः ॥ (9.22)

'O lord! After that kavacha mantra, suktam, "Aham Rudrebhih", the Atharvashiras Mantra, Hrillekha Mantra and mantras from the Upanishads must be used.'[75]

महाविद्यामहामन्त्रैस्तोषयेन्मां मुहुर्मुहुः ।
क्षमापयेज्जगद्धात्रीं प्रेमार्द्रहृदयो नरः ॥ (9.23)

'I must repeatedly be satisified with this great learning and mantras. His heart overflowing with love, a man must seek forgiveness from the mother of the universe.'

पुलकाङ्कितसर्वाङ्गैर्बाल्यरुद्धाक्षिनिःस्वनः ।
नृत्यगीतादिघोषेण तोषयेन्मां मुहुर्मुहुः ॥ (9.24)

'All his limbs will be thrilled. His voice will falter and

---

[74]This is the food offered to a deity.

[75]A kavacha mantra essentially says that may this form of Devi protect me in the east, may that form of Devi protect me in the west, and so on. Suktam, here, refers to one of the Devi suktams—we don't quite know which one. Aham Rudrebhih is section 10.125 of Rig Veda. Atharvashiras Mantra is a mantra from the Atharvashiras Upanishad.

his voice will choke. He will repeatedly satisfy me with dancing, singing and loud music.'

वेदपारायणैश्चौव पुराणैः सकलैरपि ।
प्रतिपाद्या यतोऽहं वै तस्मात्तैस्तोषयेत्तु माम् ॥ (9.25)

'I am established in the Vedas and all the Puranas. Therefore, I should be satisfied with their oral recital and reading.'

निज सर्वस्वमपि मे सदेहं नित्यशोऽर्पयेत् ।
नित्यहोमं ततः कुर्याद्ब्राह्मणांश्च सुवासिनीः ॥ (9.26)

बटुकान्पामराननन्यान्देवीबुद्ध्या तु भोजयेत्।
नत्वा पुनः स्वहृदये व्युत्क्रमेण विसर्जयेत् ॥ (9.27)

'Without any doubt, everything that belongs to him must constantly be offered to me. After offering oblations every day, Brahmanas, well-dressed girls, young boys and all the other ordinary people must be fed, considering them to be forms of Devi. Having again prostrated himself in his heart, he must perform visarjana, following the reverse order.'[76]

सर्वं हृल्लेखया कुर्यात् पूजनं मम सुव्रत ।
हृल्लेखा सर्वमन्त्राणां नायिका परमा स्मृता ॥ (9.28)

'O one excellent in vows! Hrillekha Mantra must always be worshipped. Hrillekha is supreme and is described as the foremost of all mantras.'

हृल्लेखादर्पणे नित्यमहं तु प्रतिबिम्बिता ।
तस्माधृल्लेखया दत्तं सर्वमन्त्रैः समर्पितम् ॥ (9.29)

'I am always reflected in the mirror of Hrillekha. When anything is offered with Hrillekha, it is like offering it with all the mantras.'

---

[76]Visarjana is release of a deity. The order followed is the reverse of avahana.

गुरुं सम्पूज्य भूषाद्यैः कृतकृत्यत्वमावहेत् ।
य एवं पूजयेद्देवीं श्रीमद्भुवनसुन्दरीम् ॥ (9.30)

न तस्य दुर्लभं किञ्चित्कदाचित्क्वचिदस्ति हि ।
देहान्ते तु मणिद्वीपं मामं यात्येव सर्वथा ॥ (9.31)

'The guru must be worshipped with ornaments and other things. Everything will, then, be accomplished. If a person worships Shri Bhuvanasundari Devi in this way, there is nothing that is impossible for him to obtain, there is nothing that is left for him to obtain. When he dies, in every situation, he goes to me in Manidvipa.'

ज्ञेयो देवीस्वरूपोऽसौ देवा नित्यं नमन्ति तम् ।
इति ते कथितं राजन् महादेव्याः प्रपूजनम् ॥ (9.32)

'He gets to know Devi's form, and devas always bow down before him. O king! I have, thus, told you how Mahadevi should be worshipped.'

विमृश्यैतदशेषेणाप्यधिकारानुरूपतः ।
कुरु मे पूजनं तेन कृतार्थस्त्वं भविष्यसि ॥ (9.33)

'Do not forget any of this and worship me according to your entitlement. You will accomplish your objective.'

इदं तु गीताशास्त्रं मे नाशिष्याय वदेत् क्वचित् ।
नाभक्ताय प्रदातव्यं न धूर्ताय च दुर्हृदे ॥ (9.34)

'This sacred text of Gita must not be revealed to a person who is not a shishya. It must not be given to a person who is not devoted or is crooked and evil-hearted.'

एतत्प्रकाशनं मातुरुद्घाटनमुरोजयोः ।
तस्मादवश्यं यत्नेन गोपनीयमिदं सदा ॥ (9.35)

'Revealing this is like uncovering a mother's breasts. Therefore, one must always take efforts to keep it a secret.'

देयं भक्ताय शिष्याय ज्येष्ठपुत्राय चौव हि ।
सुशीलाय सुवेषाय देवीभक्तियुताय च ॥ (9.36)

'It must be given to a devotee, a shishya, the eldest son, a person who possesses good conduct, is well-dressed and is full of devotion towards Devi.'

श्राद्धकाले पठेदेतद् ब्राह्मणानां समीपतः ।
तृप्तास्तत्पितरः सर्वे प्रयान्ति परमं पदम् ॥ (9.37)

'If it is read at the time of a shraddhaa, in the presence of Brahmanas, all the ancestors are satisfied and proceed to the Supreme Destination.'

व्यास उवाच-
इत्युक्त्वा सा भगवती तत्रैवान्तरधीयत ।
देवाश्च मुदिताः सर्वे देवीदर्शनतोऽभवन् ॥ (9.38)

Vyasa said, 'Bhagavati said this and vanished from that place. Having been able to see Devi, all the devas were delighted.'

तता हिमालये जज्ञे देवी हैमवती तु सा ।
या गौरीति प्रसिद्धासीद्दत्ता सा शङ्कराय च ॥ (9.39)

'After this, Devi was born as Haimavati, Himalaya's daughter. She became famous as Gouri and was bestowed upon Shankara.'

ततः स्कन्दः समुद्भूतस्तारकस्तेन पातितः ।
समुद्रमन्थने पूर्वं रत्नान्यासुर्नराधिप ॥ (9.40)

'Skanda originated from this and brought down Taraka. O lord of men! In earlier times, many jewels resulted from the churning of the ocean.'

तत्र देवैः स्तुता देवी लक्ष्मीप्राप्त्यर्थमादरात् ।
तेषामनुग्रहार्थाय निर्गता तु रमा ततः ॥ (9.41)

'There, so as to obtain Lakshmi, devas lovingly praised Devi. To show them her favours, Ramaa emerged.'

वैकुण्ठाय सुरैर्दत्ता तेन तस्य शमोऽभवत् ।
इति ते कथितं राजन् देवीमाहात्म्यमुत्तमम् ॥ (9.42)

'The gods bestowed her on Vaikuntha[77] and obtained peace. O king! I have, thus, described to you Devi's excellent greatness.'

गौरीलक्ष्म्योः समुद्भूतिविषयं सर्वकामदम् ।
न वाच्यं त्वेतदन्यस्मै रहस्यं कथितं यतः ॥ (9.43)

'This is about the emergence of Gouri and Lakshmi, and bestows everything desired. I have told you a secret. You should not speak about it to others.'

गीता रहस्यभूतेयं गोपनीया प्रयत्नतः ।
सर्वमुक्तं समासेन यत्पृष्टं तत्वयानघ ।
पवित्रं पावनं दिव्यं किं भूयः श्रोतुमिच्छसि ॥ (9.44)

'This is the mystery of the Gita, and one must make efforts to keep it a secret. O unblemished one! I have briefly told you everything you asked me about. It is sacred, purifying and divine. What else do you wish to hear?'

[77]This refers to Vishnu.

seven

IN CONCLUSION

What else do you wish to hear? What else do you wish to read? What else remains to be said? As I come to the end of this book, everything has been said. I have spoken to you about Devi's stories and mantras, yantras and tantra. I have spoken to you about her forms and worship—external and internal. Devi is everywhere—outside us and inside us. Where this book ends, your own search for Devi begins. You will find your own form of pujaa, and it need not be complicated, esoteric and mysterious. There is a path for each one of us.

Bhavani Ashtakam

I can do no better than end this book with Adi Shankaracharya's Bhavani Ashtakam[1] (meaning eight verses). To worship Devi, there may be nothing more that you need.

> न तातो न माता न बन्धुर्न दाता न पुत्रो न पुत्री न भृत्यो न भर्ता ।
> न जाया न विद्या न वृत्तिर्ममैव गतिस्त्वं गतिस्त्वं त्वमेका भवानि ।। (1)
>
> You are not the father or the mother. You are not a relative[2] or a person who gives. You are not a son or a daughter. You are not a servant or a master. You are not

[1]'Eight stanzas to Goddess Bhavani,' Sanskrit Documents, https://bit.ly/3yklWMi. Accessed on 5 July 2022.

[2]The word *bandhu* can also be translated as friend.

a wife. You are not learning or my profession. You are the refuge. O Bhavani! You alone are the refuge.

भवाब्धावपारे महादुःखभीरु पपात प्रकामी प्रलोभी प्रमत्तः ।
कुसंसारपाशप्रबद्धः सदाहं गतिस्त्वं गतिस्त्वं त्वमेका भवानि ॥ (2)

This ocean of worldly existence is without a shore. I am extremely miserable and terrified. Full of desire, avarice and intoxication, I have fallen down. I am always bound in the nooses of this wicked sansara. You are the refuge. O Bhavani! You alone are the refuge.

न जानामि दानं न च ध्यानयोगं न जानामि तन्त्रं न च स्तोत्रमन्त्रम् ।
न जानामि पूजां न च न्यासयोगं गतिस्त्वं गतिस्त्वं त्वमेका भवानि ॥ (3)

I do not know *dana*, or dhyana or yoga. I do not know tantra, stotrams and mantras. I do not know pujaa, or the yoga of nyasa. You are the refuge. O Bhavani! You alone are the refuge.

न जानामि पुण्यं न जानामि तीर्थं न जानामि मुक्तिं लयं वा कदाचित् ।
न जानामि भक्तिं व्रतं वापि मातर्गतिस्त्वं गतिस्त्वं त्वमेका भवानि ॥ (4)

I do not know good deeds. I do not know tirthas. I do not know about emancipation or even about dissolution. I do not know bhakti or vratas. O mother! You are the refuge. O Bhavani! You alone are the refuge.

कुकर्मी कुसङ्गी कुबुद्धिः कुदासः कुलाचारहीनः कदाचारलीनः ।
कुदृष्टिः कुवाक्यप्रबन्धः सदाहं गतिस्त्वं गतिस्त्वं त्वमेका भवानि ॥ (5)

I have been wicked in deeds, wicked in association, wicked in intelligence and wicked in service. I have been devoid of the good conduct of the lineage and have immersed myself in bad conduct. I have always been wicked in sight and bound to using wicked words. You are the refuge. O Bhavani! You alone are the refuge.

प्रजेशं रमेशं महेशं सुरेशं दिनेशं निशीथेश्वरं वा कदाचित् ।
न जानामि चान्यत् सदाहं शरण्ये गतिस्त्वं गतिस्त्वं त्वमेका भवानि ॥ (6)

I do not know anyone else—Prajesha, Ramesha, Mahesha, Suresha, Dinesha or Nishitheshvara.[3] I always seek refuge in you. You are the refuge. O Bhavani! You alone are the refuge.

विवादे विषादे प्रमादे प्रवासे जले चानले पर्वते शत्रुमध्ये ।
अरण्ये शरण्ये सदा मां प्रपाहि गतिस्त्वं गतिस्त्वं त्वमेका भवानि ॥ (7)

O one who is the refuge! Please always save me in disputes, distress, intoxication and travels; in water, fire and mountains; in the midst of enemies and in forests. You are the refuge. O Bhavani! You alone are the refuge.

अनाथो दरिद्रो जरारोगयुक्तो महाक्षीणदीनः सदा जाड्यवक्त्रः ।
विपत्तौ प्रविष्टः प्रनष्टः सदाहं गतिस्त्वं गतिस्त्वं त्वमेका भवानि ॥ (8)

I am without a protector and poor. I suffer from old age and disease. I am extremely decayed and dejected. In speech, my mouth is always dumb. Having been destroyed, I always enter these hardships. You are the refuge. O Bhavani! You alone are the refuge.

While the worship of Devi can be complicated, it can also be this simple.

[3]Prajesha, Ramesha, Mahesha, Suresha, Dinesha or Nishitheshvara refer to Brahmaa, Vishnu, Shiva, Indra, Surya and Chandra, respectively.

INDEX

www.ingramcontent.com/pod-product-compliance
Lightning Source LLC
LaVergne TN
LVHW101636100826
845155LV00014B/29/J

* 9 7 8 9 3 5 5 2 0 7 8 5 2 *